"MURDER POINTS A FINGER

is fascinating, entertaining
. . . Your grasp of fingerprints and fingerprinting
is exceptionally fine."

STANLEY TRACY, Ass't.
Director to J. Edgar Hoover,
Head of F.B.I. Identification Bureau, Retired

Lieutenant Linton, New York Homicide, had convicted
seventeen murderers on fingerprint evidence alone.

One night the eighteenth murderer walked through
Linton's living room window and emptied a forty-five
into Linton's belly.

But even in his agony the dying detective managed
to lay out nine fingerprint cards in a pattern that
showed the way to his murderer.

An intensely exciting mystery
novel about real people
in strange circumstances.

MURDER POINTS A FINGER

DAVID ALEXANDER

WILDSIDE PRESS

Murder Points a Finger

Published by Wildside Press LLC
www.wildsidepress.com

THIS BOOK IS DEDICATED to Michael J. DeLuca, Lieutenant (Retired) of the New York Police Department, Director of the New York Institute of Criminology, who taught the author all he knows about the fascinating science of fingerprinting.

1

Murder walked softly down the cold, dark street where old trees reached out pleading arms like bony beggars.

Murder walked slowly.

There was no need for haste. The man who was about to die was just ahead.

Despite the frost-crisp air that sighed up from the black river, the man who was about to die moved leisurely, as if long, contented years were yet to be enjoyed. But there would be no years for him to savor, nor even hours. Now there were only minutes left.

Across the river, on the Jersey Palisades, an enormous, illuminated clock outshone the pale full moon of winter. The clock was a familiar sight to the man who was about to die. He had read widely in history and biography and the clock made him think of the *Grosse Horloge* which had given its name to a square in Rouen. He imagined that the clock across the Hudson, the clock the Mad Hatter had constructed, was far larger than the clock in the square where Joan of Arc had perished on a pile of faggots.

The man did not know it, of course, but the great bright clock was ticking away the final moments of his life. Behind him in the shadows, Murder was twenty feet away, walking softly.

The lights of the clock's dial danced and sparkled on the dark river, like diamond slivers on fluid velvet. The clock's huge hand would shiver, then jerk forward, and another minute of the night, of the man's life, of eternity would be gone. The great arrow was moving down from 12 to 6, from top to bottom. The sands were running out.

Each time the hand jerked, lights would flash a word:

    TIC

then:

    TOC

then:

    TIC TOC HATS

ALWAYS UP TO THE MINUTE IN STYLE

1

The street on which the man walked—and Murder followed—was one of the few in Manhattan bordered by trees. It was one of the few in the city where houses were built of wood and brick instead of steel and concrete. It wound up from Broadway to the top of a bluff that overlooked the river. At the very summit of the bluff there was a castle.

The end—or the top—of this quiet street, with its small houses built early in the century, was a strange place for a medieval castle with turrets and battlements and sentry towers. Frank Tocci, "The Mad Hatter of Manhattan," had built the castle as his home. It was deserted now. Tocci was the man who had constructed the clock across the river to advertise the merchandise that made his millions.

The little houses that sprawled at the foot of the castle were very much alike. In the darkness, beside the sky-shadowing bulk of the medieval pile, they might well have been mistaken for serf dwellings on a feudal lord's estate. But these were no peasant hovels. The houses were comfortable middle-class homes, their façades somewhat overdecorated in the naively ornate gingerbread style of the Teddy Roosevelt era. At this time of night, when the hand of the big clock jerked spasmodically toward the half hour before midnight, the windows of the little houses glowed warm and friendly, though the street itself was chill and dark.

The man who was about to die was small and wiry-tough. Though he walked slowly, his movements were decisive, purposeful. There was an air of suppressed energy, abundant vitality about him. He was Lieutenant (Retired) Philip Linton of the New York Police Department. He had retired from the force after thirty-five years of service, many of them spent in the Identification Bureau. He was regarded as one of the outstanding fingerprint experts of his time by those who studied the esoteric patterns of whorls and arches and loops that nature engraves upon the end joints of the human hand —and never duplicates.

Linton's expert testimony had helped send nineteen murderers to the electric chair.

Linton pushed open the iron gate of a little house at the top of the hill, directly across from the towering castle. He crossed the short walk and mounted the three steps of the porch. The man who was about to die turned the key of a familiar lock for the last time, and entered his home.

Murder drew back into the shadows and waited beneath the gaunt old trees.

2

The hand of the clock across the river jerked:
TIC
The hand of the clock quivered forward again:
TOC
The man inside the house now had few precious minutes left. Murder was pushing the iron gate open.

A night light was burning in the hall of the little house. In its dim radiance the hall tree sprawled a gallows shadow on the wall. In the parlor to the right only one shaded lamp was lighted. Pat isn't home yet, Linton thought. Well, his granddaughter was out with young Detective Allan Walters that evening and she had an important thing to say to him. Perhaps the most important thing a girl her age ever has to say. Young Walters was very much in love with Pat. It was only natural that this evening should be a long one for the two of them.

Linton hung his hat and coat upon the hall tree. Pat, he thought, had never liked the hall tree. She called it ugly, and said he should hang his clothes in the closet at the back of the hall. But that closet was filled to overflowing with his fingerprinting paraphernalia. Mostly, he pampered Pat. He'd let her give the old leather sofa to the Salvation Army, and paint the walls of the parlor French gray, and take down his pictures of Sir Francis Galton and Sir William Herschel and Dr. Henry Faulds and Sergeant William Faurot and other pioneers of fingerprinting and put up pretty colored etchings instead. But the hall tree remained. It had always been there. Pat was all he had left in the way of relatives. His wife had died years before and his only son, Pat's father, had received the Department's medal when he was killed in the line of duty.

Of course he still had good friends. Many of them were on the force. And there was old Dab, his best friend of all. J. Dabney Ashton, the Broadway and television actor who spent most of his spare time playing chess and working puzzles. Linton snapped his fingers with annoyance. He must be growing old. He'd forgotten to mail the note to Dab when he went out for his walk. Well, he could call him in the morning instead. You could nearly always catch old Dab in the morning. Dab didn't like getting up early.

Linton started to enter the parlor, changed his mind, turned back into the hall. He found the house uncomfortably warm. Women always wanted houses too warm, even Pat who was a healthy outdoors girl. Linton glanced at the thermostat and lowered the gauge. He took off his jacket and his vest and hung them on the hall tree beside his coat and hat. He thought he heard an iron gate close. Probably a neighbor's.

3

He entered the parlor and turned on more light. The four-by-five cards with fingerprinting symbols drawn on them were scattered over Pat's new coffee table. On top of them was the note to Dab, addressed and stamped. For a second he thought of going out again to mail the letter. Had he done so he might possibly have saved his life. But the mail had probably already been picked up from the corner box and a call tomorrow would do as well. He rather relished the idea of waking old Dab before his accustomed hour.

I'll have to clean up this litter before Pat gets home, Linton thought. She'd give me what for if she found it on her brand-new table. He'd sorted out the cards for use in his projection machine the next evening when he was to make a talk before the Women's Civic Club. Slides were a great help in explaining the elementary aspects of fingerprinting. People were fascinated by fingerprinting symbols, just as old Dab was fascinated by puzzles. Making the public conscious of the science of fingerprinting had been the chief aim of Linton's life since his retirement from the force. He believed that every citizen of the country should be fingerprinted and that his prints should be classified and filed in a central agency. The advantages of such a scheme were so obvious that Linton had been appalled at the resistance to the idea. Aside from the fact that it might act as a great deterrent to crime, such a system would mean there would be no more unidentified dead, no more unidentified injured, no more unidentified amnesia victims. But liberal elements—"radicals," Linton called them—had opposed the suggestion on the grounds that it was the first step in a police state. And powerful labor unions, whose bosses had prison records, had got the bill killed in congressional committee.

Linton heard a noise. It was a very small noise, and not at all ominous. It was a rather pleasant, tinkling little noise. He turned toward the French window of the porch. A leaded pane near the window catch had been splintered. A gloved hand was lifting the latch.

Instinctively Linton's right hand groped toward the left armpit, reached for the gun he had not carried now for years.

The French window opened.

Philip Linton faced his murderer, and recognized him.

"You!" said Linton.

There was no fright in his voice. There was only amazement. He had never thought this man would kill him.

Linton's mind was very clear, as it had always been in emergencies. He saw that the gun was a .45. He knew that it would make a large hole. He knew the impact of the bullet would

4

knock him off his feet. The murderer was no more than ten feet away. It was virtually impossible that he could miss.

The murderer was quite businesslike. He wasted no time. He did not speak. He simply aimed the gun with a steady hand. He aimed it very carefully.

He's aiming for the belly, Linton thought. I wonder why? Does he hate me so much? I never knew he did. When the hole is through the belly, it takes a little while to die. You bleed a lot and dying hurts.

He watched the gloved finger squeeze the trigger.

The explosion filled the room. The tremendous noise was followed by an absurdly tiny tinkling sound. The reverberation had knocked one of Pat's small glass animals off the mantelpiece.

Linton was on the floor, a foot or two from where he had stood when the bullet hit him, before the echo of the shot died. He thought of a time, more than thirty years ago, when he had been a rookie cop walking a beat in Yorkville. There had been a moronic tough called Butter Billy who had delighted in ramming his hard head into the midriffs of policemen. In those days, many officers had bulging stomachs. Linton had been slim, but Butter Billy had given him the treatment just the same. One day he'd come leaping out at Linton from an alley. The impact of the heavy bullet and the jolt of Butter Billy's head were much the same. There was no real pain at first. Just an empty sense of breathlessness. But the pain would come, he knew, and it would be unbearable.

Before the fog of shock cleared from Linton's eyes, the murderer was gone. The French window with the broken pane had been closed.

Linton grasped his belly with his left hand. As he expected, there was already a thick flow of blood. He had, perhaps, ten minutes to live and suffer. If he tried to move about, to rise, that brief life expectancy would be cut considerably.

Linton rejoiced that his head seemed quite clear, although the awful pain already had begun. He was contemptuous of the pain. It can't last long, he thought.

He took stock of his chances. He knew he was going to die, of course. He knew that, and accepted it. But he was still a cop and he had a job to do. There was one more murderer he must convict. There was, of course, some hope that the shot had been heard. In that case the murderer might be seen by a person who would live to identify him. Or someone might rush to his side in time for him to breathe the killer's name. A neighbor might have heard. Old Groscz, the watchman at the castle, might possibly be making his rounds. Or Bellinger, the cop on the beat, might just be passing by. But he could depend upon none of these fortuitous circumstances. His own house was at the very top of the hill and there was no neighbor to his west. His other neighbors, the Ferrises, were skiing enthusiasts and were at Bear Mountain for the winter sports. Old Groscz was a poor excuse for a watchman at best, and he was usually drunk. And Linton had passed Bellinger, the cop, when he'd gone out for his bedtime walk. The officer would not be back for another hour or so.

Besides, a loud noise was likely to attract little notice on this street. Cars coughed their way up from Broadway to the Drive and the bridge approaches, and they often backfired.

Linton could not delude himself with false hopes. Time was too short. The obvious thing was to write down the murderer's name. But even as his right hand groped toward his breast, Linton knew that it was hopeless. His fountain pen and his mechanical pencil were in the pocket of his vest, and his vest was hanging on the hall tree. And he would never make the hall. There had been a writing desk in the parlor once, with pen and ink inside it, but when Pat had redecorated the room she had moved that into the hall. The telephone was on the desk. The only thing that he could reach was the coffee table, just above his head. He must use what was at hand. He lay on the floor, grasping his belly, thinking hard, as the pain increased to scalding intensity.

"Yes," he said. "Yes, I think it can be done." He thought he spoke aloud, but he could not be sure.

All he had to work with were the cards with the fingerprint symbols drawn on them and the unmailed letter addressed to J. Dabney Ashton. His right hand fumbled for them, pulled them from the table to the floor. As he sorted the cards, sought to examine them, his eyes glazed over and for the first time he knew stark fear. I mustn't go blind, he thought. I can't become unconscious until the thing is done.

The mist swam away and the cards came into focus. He shuffled through them, then, oddly, he chuckled. A thought had gone through his mind and it amused him: "The corpse was playing solitaire." Old Dab would have liked that.

At last he selected a card and laid it face up on the floor. "A plain arch," he said to himself, giving the symbol on the card a name. "It will do very nicely." Next he found a card with a simple loop pattern on it and placed it on the floor next to the other. Then he left a space. The space is most important, he thought. I mustn't forget the space. There were black spots in

6

front of his eyes and he had some trouble in deciding upon the third card. There must be no mistake, he thought. Old Dab has got to understand. He drew out a card on which the designation for a whorl was drawn and laid it down, making sure the space was there between the second and the third cards. "I've given him the major patterns now," he muttered to himself. "The arch, the loop, the whorl. The rest won't be so easy."

Now he had to go into the composite patterns. The first he found was the irregular, bastard pattern known as the accidental. It will serve, he thought, and placed it beside the others. He found another composite, a central pocket loop, and looked at it closely for a moment. He cast it aside in favor of a lateral pocket. "Five," he gasped. The pain had become excruciating beyond belief. Even such simple movements were sheer agony. He needed two more arch patterns. Luckily, he found them together in the pile. He placed an arch of the tented type on the floor, an arch of the exceptional type beside it. He was almost done. Sevèn cards were on the floor. He counted to make sure. Seven cards, with a space between the second and the third. Now for another loop, marked and tilted in such a manner that it would be distinguished as a radial loop that pointed toward the thumb, not an ulnar loop that pointed toward the little finger. At first he had a hard time making his eyes and his mind select between the two cards, the one with the ulnar loop and the one with the radial. At last he was sure and he chose the card with a hand that was trembling almost beyond control. One more card, the ninth and the most difficult. He had found eight cards that he could use among the set that showed fingerprint patterns. Now he must look elsewhere.

He riffled through the cards that demonstrated the five characteristics of fingerprints. Characteristics were unlike the patterns, in that they were used for identification rather than classification. He had explained that often in his lectures. The five cards showed the designs of each characteristic: the dot, the ridge ending, the bifurcation, the enclosure, and the ridge fragment. Old Dab knew a little about fingerprinting. Linton himself had taught him the elements of the science. But switching from the patterns to the characteristics on the very last card might confuse him. He had to take that chance. There was nothing else to do. He took the card with a curving, snaky design representing the ridge fragment and laid it beside the others. It was complete. Nine cards were on the floor, arranged in proper order. There was nothing left to do except direct old Dab's attention to the cards. Linton's last act was to set the

7

addressed letter against the leg of the coffee table beside the cards.

Just before his eyes finally clouded, Linton looked at the array of nine cards:

They were arranged correctly. Old Dab would puzzle it out.

Philip Linton, whose testimony had helped convict nineteen murderers, died in the belief that the mute testimony on the floor beside him would convict a twentieth.

He was a good cop to the very end.

2

IT WAS midnight.

Abner Ellison appeared nervous and distraught as he paced the floor of the small room he occupied in the Heights Hotel on upper Broadway. Ellison was a tall, heavy-shouldered young man. His clothes always seemed to be slightly rumpled and the knots of his ties were usually a bit askew. Despite the protests of barbers, he kept the dark ringlets of his curly hair closely clipped. The short, unruly curls still spilled down over his high forehead. Abner paused in his pacing and glanced in the mirror that hung above the washbowl. Through force of habit, he picked up a plastic comb and dug it through the massed curls. It was a useless gesture. The obstinate ringlets were like small springs that snapped back over his forehead immediately.

He put down the comb, rolled up his shirtsleeves. He picked up an inadequate cake of hotel soap and began to scrub his hands in the bowl. He washed his right hand with a ferocity that was almost savage. He seemed to be making a futile attempt to wash off a stain as ineradicable as Lady Macbeth's "damned spot." When he finally dried the hand he looked upon it with disgust. He wondered how a woman felt when a hand like that caressed her. Such a thought had not bothered him before. Now, suddenly, it seemed all-important. That was because the thing was done, the die was cast. Tonight had marked a crisis in his life.

Ellison began pacing his narrow quarters again. This was the room of a man who had been a soldier. It was neat, plain, bare. Bulky law books were piled on the glass-covered table that served as a desk. Drawers and closets were tightly closed and no articles of clothing protruded from them. Nine conservatively patterned neckties hung from a rack on the closet door. Ellison's overcoat, jacket and gray felt hat, however, had been tossed carelessly on the bed as if he planned to put them on again very soon. The maid always left the green and white bedspread dangling to the floor. Daily Ellison tucked the spread under the mattress, army-style. The only decorative notes in the room were a frilly shade on the bridge lamp and a monochrome of sheep grazing in a meadow, both supplied by the hotel, and a silver-framed photograph beside the law books on the desk. The photograph showed the face of an impishly pretty girl. Her eyes laughed under arched brows, her nose tilted provocatively and the mouth was childishly soft. The photographer had not eliminated a small area of attractive freckles about the nose. It was a photograph of Patricia Linton whose grandfather now lay murdered less than half a mile away.

Ellison looked at the framed photograph. Then he looked down at his right hand. He balled the hand into a fist, as if he were concealing something. Pat had gone out with another man tonight. Pat had gone out with a cop named Walters. Oh, well, Ellison thought, it will be the last time she's ever out with him.

Abner Ellison kept glancing at the cradled telephone as if he expected it to ring momentarily. He felt warm. The small room was overheated. His right hand unclenched and fumbled with his loosely knotted tie. He unbuttoned the collar of his shirt. He crossed to the window and was in the act of raising it when something on the street below attracted his attention. He turned hastily and snapped off the light of the bridge lamp with the frilly shade. He stood by the window, partly concealed by the drapes, gazing out into the light-pricked night. A big car was parked across the street, some twenty yards away. A man stood beside the car. The car and the man were only thicker shadows in the darkness, barely discernible, yet Ellison had a distinct feeling that the man was watching the hotel, was even looking up at the room. Abner stood by the window for several moments. Finally the man walked off into the deeper shadows. Ellison began his pacing again.

The clangor of the phone split the silence of the little room.

9

Ellison picked up the phone, said, "Hello." There was a click at the other end as if the receiver had been hung up, breaking the connection. There was a muted humming on the wire now. Abner slammed the knuckles of his right hand up and down on the receiver button and there was a crackling like static in his ears. Then the room clerk said, "Mr. Ellison? There was a call. Didn't you get it?"

"Nobody on the line. Sounded as if they hung up."

"I'm sorry. It was a man's voice. A very low voice."

Ellison was irritated. "You must have pulled out the plug or something. I was rather expecting a call."

"No, sir. I did not. There's still an outside connection."

"Okay. I guess they'll call again."

The phone rang again very soon. This time it was the room clerk. "A man just left a note at the desk for you and hurried out," the clerk said. "I'm sending the note up by the elevator boy."

"Note?" asked Abner.

"Not a special delivery or telegram. The fellow who left it looked like one of those bums who hang around the corner. Seemed in a big hurry. Just tossed it on the desk and shuffled right out again."

Abner answered the door, found coins for the elevator operator. The envelope was made of cheap paper. On it was printed in pencil, "Mr. Abner Ellison, Heights Hotel." He closed the door, slit the envelope open. He read the penciled note. His expression was blank. He read the note over again. Then he crushed the note in his right hand. He stood looking down at the fist doubled over the note. He seemed to regard either the note or the right hand that held it as something obscene. At length he smoothed the note out again, replaced it in the torn envelope and slipped it in the pocket of his trousers.

Ellison turned off all the lights in the room at the central switch. He crossed to the window again and stood motionless, peering out into the darkness. He could see the massed shadow of the big car down the street. The man had returned and was standing beside the car. The man's figure was little more than a murky outline, like the wraiths that float in a fog. The upturned face could barely be discerned, pale and faintly luminescent against the thickness of the night. Were the eyes staring at the window? Abner Ellison thought they were.

Ellison closed the window and lowered the shade over it. He switched on the lights of the room. He glanced nervously at his wrist watch. What did you do when a murder was committed?

What had his father done that time some twenty years or more ago when he had killed a man? He must have run, even though there was no place at all for him to hide. He must have run and kept on running until a relentless cop named Linton tracked him down.

Abner had to run, too. But first there was something he must check. He picked up the phone, asked the night clerk to ring the number of the Linton house. For long moments the receiver trembled with the bee-buzzing sound of the ringing phone. At length Abner hung up. The police had not arrived, then, and dead men cannot answer telephones.

Sweat plastered the curly ringlets to Abner's forehead now. He pushed them back impatiently. For a moment he felt nauseated with fear and helplessness, as he had felt that time when Rundstedt struck back in the Ardennes and Patton's tanks had not crashed through. He'd had to run, then, too. But thousands of others had been running with him. Now he must run alone. He wanted a drink desperately. He did not often drink, but there was a bottle in the drawer because Ricky Sperber sometimes visited him in the room and Ricky liked a little drink. He opened the drawer of the dresser and took the bottle from beneath a pile of shirts. He drank directly from the bottle. He replaced the bottle and remembered something else that was hidden beneath the pile of shirts.

He had brought the army .45 back as a souvenir of war. Now he was glad that like many other soldiers he had never gone to the trouble of getting a license for it. He crossed to the bed, picked up the topcoat and stuffed the .45 in the deep pocket. He also put a few handkerchiefs, a razor, a toothbrush, toothpaste, brushless cream, a comb into a pocket of the coat. This was his luggage. He donned his jacket, coat, hat. He buttoned the collar of his shirt, pulled the loose knot of the tie into place. He was ready to run.

He turned off the lights. Before he left, he pulled back the window blind and glanced out furtively. The car was still there and the shadowy man was still beside it, watching, waiting. Waiting for Abner Ellison, perhaps.

The wait for the elevator seemed interminable. When he tossed his key on the desk, the night clerk said, "You going out late tonight, aren't you, Mr. Ellison?" Abner merely nodded. The Heights Hotel was a quiet family hostelry. The clerk thought there must be some funny business going on for a guest to get phone calls and letters in the middle of the night, then to hurry out looking pale and worried like that.

11

The electric sign of the hotel shone on Abner as he stood looking for a cab. Traffic on this side of the street was headed uptown. Across the street, the car and the man still loomed darkly unidentifiable. A few seconds after Abner emerged from the hotel, the shadows of the man and the car melted into each other. The man had entered the car. Abner hailed a passing cab.

"Turn around and head downtown," Abner told the driver.

The driver said, "Ain't suppose to make a U-turn, mister. But at this time of night . . ."

He made the U-turn at a corner. By the time the cab was headed downtown, the other car had moved off. Abner saw a tail light disappearing into a side street.

When they reached the street where a man lay murdered, Abner said, "Turn right here and slow down."

The driver obeyed. Seconds later Abner saw what he was looking for. A small knot of people with coats thrown over nightclothes stood outside Linton's house. Two uniformed policemen stood stolidly in front of them. Police cars were parked in the street.

"Trouble down here," said the driver.

"Step on it," said Abner urgently. "Take the ramp to the highway and head downtown."

The driver swerved past the parked cars, steered for the entrance to the West Side Highway, said, "Slow down, step on it. Make up your mind, mister. And tell me where we're heading. I gotta make out a call sheet."

"Head downtown," Abner replied. "I'll tell you when we get there."

As the car mounted the ramp, Abner took the gun and a handkerchief from his pocket. Concealing the gun under the flap of his coat, he wiped it hard with the handkerchief. He lowered the taxi window. Still holding the gun beneath the handkerchief, he tossed it out the window with a hard backhand motion, over the highway railing into the little park beside the river.

The driver said, "You throw something outta this cab, mister?"

"Only an empty cigarette package," Abner answered.

"You want a smoke?"

"I've got another pack," said Abner, lighting a cigarette to prove it.

He glanced back out the rear window of the cab. Few cars were on the highway at this time of night. None was in pursuit of the cab.

12

He could see the south tower of the Mad Hatter's castle looming darkly against the pale winter moon like a grim sacrificial altar of the ancient Druids.

3

It was two o'clock in the morning.

One hundred and eighty city blocks south and east of the street where a castle stood and a man lay murdered, J. Dabney Ashton sat in the basement bar of the ancient Washington Square Hotel playing chess. His opponent was a thin, ascetic looking man named Thomas Pirtle who was an architect. Behind the small zinc bar the white-haired barkeep nodded sleepily. The Washington Square Hotel was one of the last buildings in the neighborhood to resist the encroachments of expanding New York University. It had been built during the administration of Rutherford Birchard Hayes, and, judging from their appearance, most of the present employees had been in service at its opening.

Dab Ashton had no false modesty. He was proud of a great many things, justifiably proud, he believed. He took quiet pride in his blooded Virginia ancestry. He was proud of his reputation as one of Broadway's most dependable character actors. He was convinced that few men the shady side of sixty carried themselves so erectly, had such slim waists, or such a fine head of wavy white hair. He was vain of his mustache, which he considered dashing and tended carefully with French wax. He thought his taste in such matters as tweeds and Havana cigars and Bourbon whisky was excellent. He was glad that one of his minor accomplishments—a facility at solving puzzles—had been of some small service to his country during the first World War, when he had been assigned to Yardley's Black Chamber charged with breaking enemy codes. He also believed himself to be an outstanding exponent of the ancient game of chess, an opinion that the position of the pieces on the board now confirmed.

Dab was about to move a chess piece when Charles, the night porter, limped into the barroom. He seemed to be of an age with the waiter and the barman.

"There's a man here to see you, Mr. Dab," Charles called

13

out in a cracked voice. "I told him you were playing chess and couldn't be interrupted but he wouldn't wait. Says he's a police officer."

The big, dark man directly back of the porter obviously had no compunctions whatsoever about interrupting such a serious matter as a game of chess. He was swarthy, bulkily built. In profile, his heavily defined features had an almost classic look. There was a dead-serious air of brooding intensity about him. This made his method of speaking, which was usually a form of cynical raillery, distinctly shocking to those who did not know him well. He addressed everyone except the very highest brass of the Department as "honey boy" or "baby doll." He was Detective Lieutenant Romano, attached to Homicide at Manhattan West.

Dab had met Romano before at Philip Linton's home. He recognized him, said, "Lieutenant Romano! What brings you out at such a witching hour?"

"A police officer?" said Pirtle. "What have you been up to, Dab?"

"I'm not quite sure," Dab replied. "But if John George Arthur, the critic, has been found slain, I'm justly suspect. He once refered to me as 'that moldy old Virginia ham.' "

"Well, I can give you an alibi from nine o'clock on," said Pirtle. "You've been beating me at chess since then."

Romano said, "Can I see you privately, honey boy?"

"Of course," Dab answered. "We can go to my rooms. This must be serious, Lieutenant."

"Kind of serious, I guess," Romano replied. "Matter of murder. That ain't a misdemeanor, honey boy."

"Good Lord!" exclaimed Dab. "How on earth can it concern me?"

"Privately, baby doll. Privately," Romano answered.

"You'll excuse me, Pirtle?" Dab asked, rising.

Pirtle nodded, obviously swallowing questions he wanted to ask.

Dab led Romano up a short flight of steps to the lobby. Enormous, inscrutable old Madame Sorel, proprietress of the hotel, acted as night manager herself, because she suffered from insomnia. She sat behind the desk, adding figures in an old-fashioned ledger. She wore a rusty black dress, her rough-hewn face was pallid, she had keen dark eyes and a shock of bright red hair. Dab knew the hair was dyed. The woman was over seventy. She always reminded him of one of those calculating concierges dressed in bombazine whom Van Gogh loved to paint.

14

Dab lived on the second floor and did not use the elevator. Upstairs, the carpeting of the hall was threadbare and the plastering bald in spots. Madame Sorel was frugal. Dab occupied a corner suite that overlooked the park. He had occupied the same suite for more than a quarter of a century. The living room was so large it was barnlike. A crystal chandelier was suspended from the high ceiling. A coal fire was laid in the grate. The Washington Square was the last hotel in New York with fireplaces that really worked. Hotel furniture had been moved out to make room for gracious Sheraton pieces that Dab had shipped from the family home in Virginia when his mother died. One wall was covered almost completely by photographs of actors and actresses and framed theater programs. Over the mantel was an heroic oil of a handsome bearded gentleman in the gold-laced gray of the Confederacy—Major Joshua Ashton, of Lee's staff, Dab's grandfather.

Romano made himself comfortable in an overstuffed chair, accepted a drink of Bourbon that Dab poured from a crystal decanter.

"Tell me what this is all about," Dab asked.

"I will," said Romano. "Prepare yourself for a shock. Then don't interrupt me with a lot of foolish exclamations. To get it over fast, your friend Phil Linton's been murdered. Shot through the belly with a .45. Assailant unknown. One prime suspect. More about that later. Take a drink now, and I'll give you what facts we have."

"I—I can't believe it!" said Dab inadequately.

"Nobody believes murder until it happens," the swarthy detective answered. "According to the statistics six out of every hundred thousand persons living today are going to die from a slight case of murder. But no one believes murder can happen to him or anyone close to him."

Dab opened his mouth. Romano raised his hand. He said, "A little after midnight a call came in to an uptown precinct station. It was a man, unidentified, call untraced. He said there'd been trouble at a certain address and the police had better investigate. Then he hung up. It was Phil Linton's address. Prowl car reached there about twelve-twenty. Lights on downstairs. Door locked. French window to porch closed but unlocked, with a pane knocked out. Cops went in, found Linton shot to death, called Homicide. We found Linton lying beside a little coffee table. Carpet had soaked up a lot of blood. Pretty obvious he'd been shot by man standing just inside the room, in the window.

"Medical evidence Linton probably killed somewhere be-

15

tween eleven-thirty and twelve, may have lived some ten minutes after bullet hit him. Linton had those little fingerprint-symbol cards he uses in his lectures on the floor beside him. Some of them he'd arranged into a kind of order or pattern. A display, you might call it. Evidently he wanted you particularly to see this display, thought it would mean something to you. Something special, maybe. Anyway he'd propped a letter addressed to you against the leg of the table, like he wanted to attract your attention to the cards. We read the letter, I'm afraid. It didn't seem very important. Said he couldn't dine with you at the hotel Friday night. You were to come to his place instead, because there was going to be a kind of family dinner and his granddaughter had an important announcement to make. We're pretty sure now what the announcement was."

"This is awful. Awful!" exclaimed Dab. The actor's face was drawn, bloodless.

"It's worse than awful," replied Romano. "I'm afraid there's an even greater shock coming for you, Mr. Dab. Murder's not the worst thing in the world, not from a cop's standpoint, anyway. We like to solve a murder fast, but there's no real urgency. The victim's already dead. There's no statute of limitations on murder. We can take all the time we want in tracking down a murderer. Years, sometimes. But kidnapping's a different matter. In kidnapping, time's the all-important factor. We have to solve a kidnapping in a matter of hours, days at most, or we almost always find the victim dead."

"Kidnapping?" Dab's expression was blank. "What's kidnapping got to do with Phil's death?"

"Patricia Linton, Phil's granddaughter, has been kidnapped," Romano said flatly.

Dab sank back in his chair. "Oh, no!" he cried. "Oh, my God, no! Not little Pat, Lieutenant! Not my little girl! When? How, man?"

"Don't get impatient, honey boy," said Romano. "It's a tough story to tell, because it's screwy. A little before one, while a dozen or so cops were stewing around at Linton's house, another call came in to headquarters. It was from Detective Allan Walters. He was at a gas station, on a little country side road off the main highway in Westchester, just across the New York City line. He was pretty frantic. He'd had a date with Patricia Linton. It was a very important date. He was going to ask her to marry him. So he took her 'way up in Westchester to one of those farmhouse restaurants with candles on the table and prices high as a camel's hump. Pat said yes, so they took a long time over dinner. Didn't finish until

16

nearly ten. They decided to do a little more celebrating at a roadhouse with a big-name band that was even farther up-country, but when they got there all the tables were taken, so they left and just drove around. The car had a heater, so they were cozy. Just after midnight, on the way back to town, they stopped at a roadside stand for hamburgers and coffee. Walters parked his car outside in a dark space near some trees. When they finished, he took a short cut, a side road, back to the main highway. He hadn't got far when the car began to cough and spit, and then it stopped. He'd had a full tank when he started but he was out of gas. He figured somebody had siphoned his gas while he was parked at the hamburger joint. He remembered that he'd seen a gas station a few hundred yards back on the side road. It was closed, but it looked like one of those places where the proprietor combines his home and his business. He thought he could wake up the proprietor. He asked Pat to walk back with him. She said it was cold, the road was rough and she was wearing high heels. Pat's a rugged girl who's not afraid of the dark. She said she'd sit there in the car while her boy friend went back for a can of gas. Said she could keep the heater on. He didn't argue too much. The road was deserted. One car came toward him while he was walking back to the gas station. He stood and watched it until it made a turn in the road, past the place where his own car with Pat in it was parked. He had some trouble waking the gas-station people and took a little abuse, but finally got a can of gas and went back up the road. The front door of his sedan was standing open. Pat wasn't inside. She wasn't anywhere. Walters threw in the can of gas and drove back to the station. He called the Westchester police from there, which was proper, then he called his own people. Headquarters was to send men up to work with the county boys. Walters didn't know about Linton's murder, of course. He couldn't have. They're going to bring him to the house to tell him. He's probably there by now."

Dab poured himself more Bourbon. "This is fantastic, Lieutenant," he said.

"Yeah, honey boy," replied Romano. "Murder and kidnapping and things like that are always fantastic. But they happen. One thing, the cops, especially the fingerprint men, think they've read those little cards that Linton arranged without any trouble. They're pretty sure they know who killed him. But they want you to take a look at them before they're disarranged."

17

"They think they know the murderer? Who, Lieutenant? Who?"

"Linton's foster son. Abner Ellison."

Dab's mouth fell open. His eyes stared. An expression of complete amazement that any actor might have envied was written on his face. The expression faded. Now there was nothing in the old man's face but the blank, shocked look of death itself.

Inside his head there was an insistent sound like a whispering *My son! My son!* said the whispering voice. *The little boy with the great, wide eyes that held so much of fear and hurt. The little boy I tried to comfort. The little boy who became the only son I ever had. Abner. Little Ab. The human being I love most in the world. They're telling me my little boy is vile, a murderer.*

Dab shook his head, fought to regain control of himself. He said, "With all due respect, Lieutenant, are you quite insane? Ab? Impossible! Phil was a father to Ab from the time he was eight years old. He brought him up, housed him, fed him, educated him. They were devoted to each other. What possible motive could Ab have had for killing Philip Linton?"

Romano said, "Take it easy, baby doll. Who knows what grudge Ellison might have had sticking in his craw? For one thing, Ellison's father copped a Murder Two plea more than twenty years ago and went away to Dannemora. He died there while Abner was being a hero in the Battle of the Bulge. Linton's evidence helped send the elder Ellison up. That's the reason Phil took pity on the motherless child and adopted him. Another thing, you and I and everybody who knew Phil Linton and his family realize that Abner Ellison's been in love with Pat ever since she was a little girl in pigtails."

"Yes," said Dab. "I've always hoped she'd marry him. I'm very fond of Ab. And I love Pat as if she were my daughter."

"But she wasn't going to marry him," said Romano. "She was going to marry Walters. More motive."

"For killing Philip Linton?"

Romano nodded. "The police have reason to believe Phil Linton knew something very bad indeed about Abner Ellison. He moved out of Phil's house a couple of months ago, remember, took a room in a hotel. Maybe Phil influenced his granddaughter's decision."

"Have the police questioned Ab?"

"The police can't find Ab," replied Romano. "They haven't

18

yet, anyway. He's not at his hotel. But when we started checking his license-plate number, a bright young cop remembered something that happened during the afternoon. About five o'clock Abner Ellison called to say his car had been stolen. The police got a lot of phone calls in the last few hours."

Dab said, "Do you mean to imply that you suspect a man of murder because he reported a stolen car?"

"No," said Romano. "I don't mean that at all, honey boy. But look at it this way. If your car happens to be seen at the scene of a murder or kidnapping, it would be mighty convenient to have it on record that the car'd been stolen from you quite some time before."

Dab gave Romano a look so witheringly contemptuous that it was worthy of Cyrano at his most arrogant. "There is not a shred of real evidence against Ab," he said. "I've never heard such moonshine. I'm surprised that competent police officers would put any credence whatsoever in any of it."

"Let's be getting up to the Linton place," replied Romano, "and you'll see the evidence. The real evidence, I mean. We've got what amounts to a deathbed statement. Like the fortuneteller says, it's all in the cards."

4

For the most part Dab and Romano were silent as the Departmental car carried them uptown. But as they sped along the West Side Highway, Dab said, "Lieutenant, I've been thinking about the timetable. The same man couldn't have done the murder and the kidnapping could he?"

"It's possible, just possible," replied Romano. "The murderer might have had as long as forty-five minutes to reach the hamburger stand where Walters' gas was siphoned. A fast driver, with any luck, could have made it in twenty-five or thirty. But how on earth would the man know he'd find Walters and Pat at a certain roadside stand at that exact moment? Answer is he couldn't have, not possibly. Whoever snatched Pat had been following Walters' car all evening. That seems certain. Theory is the murderer had confederates who pulled the snatch while he was taking care of the

19

kill. We've got reason to believe Abner Ellison knew plenty of muggs who wouldn't shy at a snatch."

"That's a lot of damned nonsense," said Dab shortly. After that there was no more conversation.

It was after three when they reached Linton's little house. In sharp contrast to the grim, dark bulk of the castle across the street, the small dwelling blazed with lights. The mortal remains of Philip Linton had been carried out in a basket some time before. The body reposed now at that great clearing house of violent death on East Twenty-ninth Street—the City Mortuary. Dark stains on the carpet and chalk marks showed where the body had been found. The house was still filled with police officers, some in plain clothes, some in uniform. Most were there on official business. Some had been friends of the murdered man and had come when they heard the news. Among them was a huge, red-faced old man with hamlike hands, Detective-Inspector Sansone, long past retirement age. He had once walked a beat with Linton. Dab recognized Sansone and Captain Haas, the Identification Bureau's fingerprint expert since Linton's retirement, and a Homicide aide of Romano's named Grierson. He had played poker with these men in this same house.

Every man in the room looked grim. A cop had been killed. Murder is mostly routine business to hard-bitten veterans of the force. But when a cop-killer is on the loose, it's a very different matter.

And Phil Linton had been a great cop. One of the best the Department had ever known.

Dab saw young Allan Walters standing miserably in a corner. The old actor's heart went out to the boy. He was shocked by Walters' appearance. The large, usually ruddy young man was corpse-white. He was shaking like a drunkard. Even his lips were trembling. Dab had always liked Walters, although he had felt much closer to Pat's other suitor, Abner Ellison. Ab had a spark of sheer brilliance, a kind of incandescent charm that was lacking in the simple, sober Walters. Dab walked over to the young detective, put his hands on his shoulders.

"Allan, my boy," he said. "This is a terrible thing, I know. But you have to pull yourself together. You must help us find Pat."

Walters sobbed, broke down completely. "Oh, God, Mr. Dab, why did I leave her alone in the car like that?"

"It wasn't your fault, boy. Nobody blames you."

Captain Haas spoke. "Mr. Dab," he said, "if you'll be good
20

enough, please take a look at those cards that are spread on the floor. Linton must have arranged them while he was dying. He seemed to want to direct your attention to them especially. We have a pretty good idea of what they mean, but we'd like to know what they convey to you."

Somewhat hesitantly Dab crossed the room. He stood looking down at the cards. It took only a few seconds for their meaning to stab into him like a knife. He knew now what Romano had meant when he had said "It's in the cards." But Dab didn't want to admit that this could be the only meaning. He stalled. He tried desperately to make his devious mind bring forth another answer.

"Well, Mr. Dab," said Captain Haas. "What do you see?"

"Not much I'm afraid, not right off," Dab replied. "I know what the cards are, of course. The fingerprint symbols Phil used to illustrate his talks."

"Just tell us what you see," the captain prompted.

Dab resorted to a little ad-libbing and wished he might depend upon an off-stage prompter. "Well," he said, "Phil taught me the rudiments of fingerprinting from time to time. I know the names of these symbols, I think. The first is a simple arch. The second's rather odd. It's a loop shape, all right, but it's not inclined or marked in any way, so it can't be called either ulnar or radial. It just goes straight up and down, and loops don't do that on the fingertips. They have to be one thing or the other. Loops are the patterns most frequently encountered in fingerprinting, I believe."

Dab paused.

"Go on," urged Haas.

"Well, after the space . . ."

"After the space," snorted Inspector Sansone. "The space is the only important thing, sir. Keep that space in mind."

Dab groaned inwardly. There could be no doubt that they had seen it, too.

Dab named the cards that appeared after the space—the whorl, the accidental, the lateral pocket, the tented arch, the exceptional arch. He paused when he came to the eighth card, said, "The next to last is another loop, but this time the way the markings are inclined show plainly it's a radial type loop, one that points toward the thumb, since it's the eighth card and would be on the left hand. The final card is very strange indeed. It's not a symbol for a pattern. It's a symbol for one of the five characteristics of fingerprints. It's called a ridge fragment, isn't it?"

21

"You pass one hundred per cent," commented Captain Haas drily. "Now tell us what all this means."

"I'm afraid I really don't know," Dab lied.

"Come on now, Mr. Dab," growled the inspector. "You're supposed to be good at puzzles, aren't you? The meaning's plain as the nose on Jimmy Durante's face. Think of the space, man."

"How many cards do you see on the floor?" asked Haas. Dab pretended to count. "Nine," he answered.

"How many fingers do most people have?" asked Haas.

"Ten, of course," said Dab.

"You see a space between the cards?"

"Yes."

"Where?"

"Between the second and third cards."

"Assuming that a fingerprint man arranged those cards, he would begin with the right hand. So the card for what finger would be missing?"

"The middle finger of the right hand," Dab answered miserably.

"Exactly," said Haas. "In fingerprinting that missing card would be called an amp. Meaning an amputation, of course. What we have are cards that point out a nine-fingered man, a man with the middle finger of his right hand amputated. Do you know such a man, Mr. Dab?"

Dab wiped his brow with a linen handkerchief. "Yes," he said softly. "Yes, of course I do."

"And his name?"

"Abner Ellison," said Dab. "He lost the middle finger of his right hand in the war."

"See what I mean about a deathbed statement, honey boy?" asked Romano.

"Convinced, Mr. Dab?" the inspector asked. "We're lucky in a way. Most of us were Phil Linton's friends. Had been for years. We'd visited his house, knew his family well. That's why he was able to leave evidence he was sure we'd understand. That's why we've been able to clear this thing up in a matter of minutes insteads of days or weeks."

"We've still got to find the girl," Romano reminded him. "Finding the girl's what counts. We can't save Linton now, but we can save the girl—maybe."

"We'll find her." The old inspector wagged his big head. "When we find Ellison we'll find the girl and pray to the Almighty that she's still alive. Questioning suspects is supposed to be a lot of psychological rot, these days. But me, I'm an

22

old-time cop. Just find Ellison and leave me alone with him in a locked room." The inspector held out his two enormous, hair-spiked hands. "When I get these meat-hooks of mine on him, he'll talk."

Oh, God, thought Dab, they're talking about my boy. Yes, he was my boy, almost as much as he was Phil's. I remember when they first brought him here. He was such a little fellow with such big eyes and so much terror in them. We used to walk together then when I came up here, and sometimes when we were coming up the hill he'd put his hand in mine. Phil used to laugh at us. "Dab and Ab," he'd say. "You remind me of Mike and Ike, They Look Alike." We'd sit out on the front steps in the summer and I'd make up stories for him about the Mad Hatter's Castle and the beautiful princess in the tower. Was it his tenth birthday or his eleventh that I gave him the baseball uniform and the Louisville Slugger bat? He always had a front-row seat for the Wednesday matinée when I was in a play, and I'd look down and wink at him. Then there was the first night of the Lonsdale play, he was about sixteen then, and he wore his first tuxedo, the one charged to my account at Brooks Brothers, and Pat was beside him, no more than a child of twelve wearing a frilly dress, and Allan Walters, wearing his first tux, too, and looking scrawny and all Adam's apple. And then the news from the War Department when Rundstedt struck back in the Ardennes and we didn't know if he'd lost a leg or an arm or his eyes and how relieved we were when we found it was only a finger.

Only a finger!

A damnable, obscene, amputated finger that points to him and calls him "Murderer!"

Dab thought a long while before he spoke. He had to read these lines right. He couldn't afford to muff them. These were the most important lines he'd ever read and he'd been an actor nearly forty years.

Dab said, "I insist there is some other explanation for the meaning of these cards."

"Suppose you give us a better one!" challenged the inspector.

"I'm afraid I can't," said Dab. "Not right now. Not at just a glance. I'll have to study them. I suppose they've been photographed. Could I have a set of prints?"

"Of course," Romano answered. "We'll send them to your hotel first thing in the morning."

"Why the devil are you trying to make a Chinese puzzle out of this, Mr. Dab?" Inspector Sansone asked irritably.

"Why try to do it the hard way? Inside of five minutes or less the dumbest cop here saw what Phil Linton was trying to tell us, saw that those cards meant one thing and one thing only—a nine-fingered man, a man with the middle finger of his right hand amputated."

"That's just the point," declared Dab. "It's *too* simple. If Phil had had anything like that in mind, he would have known you cops could read the message. But the message wasn't directed to you. It was specifically pointed out to me by that envelope that's standing against the table leg. Phil tried to teach me the more advanced phases of fingerprinting, but he gave up. I couldn't get beyond the elementary stuff. He often said that I'd never make a fingerprint expert even though I was a crackerjack at puzzles. He knew I was good at puzzles, so he left a puzzle for me to figure out. He wouldn't have left me a problem in fingerprinting. He'd have left that for you fellows. I contend that these cards constitute a puzzle and that it's pure freak coincidence that considered as fingerprint patterns they point out a man with an amputation. I claim the symbols on those cards are ideographs, forms meant to convey an idea to me, and that they have nothing whatsoever to do with fingers or the science of fingerprinting."

"I say you're nuts," said the inspector.

Captain Haas said, "Look, Mr. Dab. We can all understand why you're so anxious to find a different meaning. We know how close you were to Abner Ellison. But I'm afraid you can't come up with anything that's more convincing than the evidence that's right before our eyes."

Dab turned to young Detective Allan Walters. "Allan," he said, "you're a neighborhood boy. You grew up with Ab and Patricia. Do you believe that Ab killed Phil Linton and made off with Pat?"

"No," said Walters. "I don't. I don't believe it for a minute. He just couldn't have."

Inspector Sansone snorted. "You're letting personalities affect your judgment, Walters," he said. "You're not talking like a cop."

"I'm not through arguing," persisted Dab. "Not by a long shot. I don't pretend to know much about fingerprinting except a few things Phil told me. But I know this. On fingerprint cards, the impressions of the fingers are arranged in two rows, with the prints of the right hand at the top and the prints of the left hand at the bottom. If Phil had meant to convey something about fingers or fingerprinting to us, he'd

24

have arranged these cards in two rows. He didn't. They're spread out in a single row."

"The answer to that one's easy, honey boy," said Romano. "Linton had a gut wound and he was bleeding to death. The slightest unnecessary movement of his body would have made the hemorrhage worse. He would have had to shove back on the floor to make room for another row of cards between his own body and the coffee table."

"There's another thing," the old actor continued. "Why did he use certain cards and discard others? There are several he didn't include scattered about on the floor. Why, for the last card, he went to another pile entirely! He had plenty of the cards with patterns on them left, but he reached for one showing a characteristic, that snaky looking symbol called the ridge fragment."

"Are you trying to tell us that Linton died from snake bite?" Inspector Sansone asked.

"The answer, of course," said Romano, "is that he simply picked up the first cards he touched. He needed nine cards with fingerprint symbols on them. It didn't make any difference whether they were symbols for patterns or characteristics and it didn't make any difference what the symbols looked like."

Dab fingered the waxed ends of his mustache nervously. He decided to try another tack. "Let's forget these cards on the floor for a minute," he said. "I maintain that you can present only the flimsiest sort of motive for Ab killing his foster father. Ab's father, James Ellison, was fired from his job. Rightly or wrongly, he believed he was done a great injustice, that he had been fired solely to make room for one of his employer's relatives. He was deprived of the means of supporting not only himself, but his child, and Ab became a charge of the city. One night, when he was drunk and desperate, James Ellison went to his employer's home and killed him. It was a clumsy and an amateurish crime. Ellison left fingerprints all over the place. Phil Linton was the fingerprint man on the case. His evidence convicted Ellison. But because of the man's psychotic addiction to alcohol and his unbalanced, desperate state of mind, the D.A. allowed him to take a second-degree plea. He was sent up for life to Dannemora with the worst, most hardened criminals of the state. He died there of cirrhosis of the liver while his son was fighting overseas."

"I don't give a hang what these modern criminologists and psychologists and so forth say," put in the old inspector. "I believe in blood. Bad blood and good blood. Like father like son. Crime runs in families. I've seen it happen too often."

"Nonsense, man!" snapped Dab. "I'm very proud of my blood. The Ashton family is rated F.F.V. But one of my remote ancestors was a Louisiana pirate under Jean Lafitte. Do you think that means I'm likely to board the Queen Mary some night brandishing a cutlass?"

"Abner Ellison's disappeared," said Romano. "We've had men in his hotel room. Clerk says he took off right after Linton was chilled."

"There's probably some perfectly rational explanation for that," insisted Dab. "But to continue. Phil did what he could. He adopted James Ellison's son, brought him up. Ab and Phil Linton were devoted. I've been very close to this family and I know that. Ab held no grudge against Phil because of his father. Why, Phil often took the boy up to Dannemora on visiting days. Ab lived in this house for some twenty years. Do you suppose that all of a sudden, years after his father's death, Ab is going to kill Phil because he identified his father's fingerprints once in the line of duty? Such a notion is plain absurd."

The inspector said, "He lived here for twenty years, but he moved out two months ago. Don't you think that might mean he and Phil didn't get along as well as they used to?"

"Ab lived here and paid board after the war while he was going to law school under the G.I. Bill of Rights," said Dab. "He continued to live here and to pay more board when he graduated and got a job with a law firm. His moving out was purely a matter of old-fashioned propriety. About three months ago Phil Linton signed up with a lecture bureau to give talks on the history and practice of fingerprinting. Some of those lectures were in other towns and he had to stay away overnight. That left no one in the house but Ab and Pat. So Ab moved into a little family hotel not more than ten blocks from here."

Dab saw the policemen exchange glances. They were holding something back from him, he knew. They had a trump card. But he felt compelled to go on, to state his case, to press every possible point that might be to the advantage of the young man he loved as a son.

"Now," he continued, "of course I know that Ab was in love with Patricia. He's about four years older than she. She was a baby when he came here as a child. But I think he always loved her, just as young Allan here did. Since childhood they've been friendly rivals. For a while it was anybody's

26

guess which suitor Pat preferred. I think she was very fond of both boys. They're very different, but they're both decent, good-looking young men. However, in recent years I believe even Ab knew that it was going to be Allan she would choose in the end. I doubt that Ab even proposed to her. I think he felt—wrongly, I'm sure—that being the son of a murderer cast a stigma on him in the eyes of a policeman's daughter. In any event, even granting that he went into a jealous rage when Pat finally accepted Allan Walters last night—providing Ab knew of it—why would he kill her grandfather? Why didn't he kill Allan Walters instead? Phil Linton would never have done anything to influence his granddaughter's decision. I'm very sure of that."

"He might have," said Inspector Sansone, "if he'd known that Ellison was a crook."

"Ab a crook," exclaimed Dab. "Abner Ellison never did a crooked thing in his life!"

The policemen again exchanged glances.

"We've got good reason to believe Abner Ellison was a crook," said Inspector Sansone, "and that Phil Linton knew it and was about to expose him."

The inspector looked doubtfully at Lieutenant Romano.

Lieutenant Romano said, "This much is fact that we can prove. Abner Ellison was with Philip Linton last night. He was with him half an hour or so before Linton was murdered. Patrolman Bellinger saw the two of them come out of this house about eleven o'clock. They spoke to him. They walked down the hill toward Broadway together."

"But Phil was killed inside the house by someone who forced an entrance. He must have been killed after Abner left him."

"Ellison could have followed him back here and forced the window so it would look like an intruder," replied Romano. "We have reason to believe that Ellison's conference with Linton last night convinced him he had to kill Phil to save his own skin."

"Why? Why on earth should you think that?"

Romano looked inquiringly at Sansone.

"Take over if you want to, Inspector," he said.

Inspector Sansone regarded Dab with narrowed eyes. His big, spatulate fingers played over his square chin.

"I shouldn't tell you this, Mr. Dab," he said, "but I think I'll let you have it. It's top-echelon police business and mustn't be repeated, but you're peculiarly concerned in this affair and I think you have a right to know. Phil Linton knew something. Something that was hot as a firecracker. He told me two or three months ago that he'd talked to the new commissioner—he's an old-time cop Phil had known well—and told him he'd blundered on to something and that in time he might be able to offer the Department some information that would knock the town wide open. Right after that, Ellison moved out of here. Things seemed kind of cool between Ellison and Linton from that time on.

"I guess you remember the Grand Jury probe into the numbers racket a year or so back. Evidence was presented to indicate that some Manhattan police officers had been taking graft from the Lenny Fassio mob that's got the numbers and a lot of other enterprises sewed up in this town. Well, I remember the investigation, all right. There were some dirty hints in the papers that I was one of the 'high officials implicated.' I've got thirty-five years on the force and am due for retirement. The reason I'm still here is I wouldn't quit under fire.

"Main witness against the cops was a former Fassio gunsel named Mike Stella. The Grand Jury returned indictments but before the case could come to trial, Stella disappeared. He stayed disappeared. Theory is he was bumped and packed in cement. So the case fell to pieces and the D.A. wound up grinding his teeth down to stubs. A few cops retired, some of the brass got busted, half a dozen detectives were put back in uniform and sent out to walk beats in Canarsie. That's all there was to it, so far as the public was concerned. But very quietly a departmental investigation continued. That's why I'm still around. I'm going to take a pension only when I'm free and clear of any charges, actual or implied.

"The numbers racket went merrily on, of course. There were whispers that somebody connected with the law firm of Burke and Holmquist was the payoff man. Burke and Holmquist acted as counsel for Lenny Fassio when he was called before that senatorial television show a while ago. Abner Ellison works for Burke and Holmquist."

"Good Lord, man!" interrupted Dab. "Are you trying to imply that working for a law firm that accepts criminal cases makes a man a crook? Burke and Holmquist are one of the most respected legal offices in the city. Besides, Ab is mighty small potatoes. He's only been working for the firm a few years, since he got out of Columbia Law School. He's never even tried a case. He's just a kind of glorified clerk who looks up precedents and points of law."

"Nevertheless," declared Sansone, "his connection with

28

Burke and Holmquist would give him an opportunity of meeting Lenny Fassio and Lenny's boss mobsters. And his connection with Phil Linton would give him access to a lot of cops, including some top brass in the department."

"This is plain damned silly!" flared Allan Walters. "Everybody knows that Mike Stella himself was payoff man in the numbers. That's what the whole investigation was about!"

"You're forgetting your rank, Detective Walters!" Sansone barked' like a martinet on the drill field. "But under the circumstances, I'll overlook the breach of discipline. Stella may have been payoff man. But he broke with Fassio and turned pigeon. That's why he's got a cement overcoat or is cut up in little pieces and stowed away in trunks. With the heat on, it was a lot safer to use a respectable lawyer as payoff man than to use a known mobster. Even Fassio hasn't got enough money to corrupt the top men of Burke and Holmquist. But Ellison was a little man, with just the right contacts, and Fassio's money would look mighty big to him. One cop even intimated that he'd been approached by Ellison in person, but that cop was under a cloud himself and nobody would take his unsupported testimony. When Phil Linton, who'd been retired for years and out of touch with departmental business, said he might have information about the payoff, it was a different matter. How would he get such information except through personal contacts? And who was he closer to than Abner Ellison, the boy he'd brought up, who had lived with him up to a couple of months ago?

"Now I can tell you something that I can vouch for. I saw Phil four days ago. He seemed mighty unhappy. He said he was going to see a certain person on Wednesday night. That was last night, the night he was murdered. He said he had to make sure, but he'd be sure after he saw this person, and he'd lay what he had before the commissioner. Well, he saw Abner Ellison last night and he won't lay anything before the commissioner, because Phil Linton's on a slab in the morgue right now.

"The way I figure it, it all ties in. The Fassio mob thought maybe Phil's granddaughter knew something, too. Did she say anything last night to you that would indicate she knew, Walters?"

"No," said Walters in a choked voice. "No, I'm sure she didn't know anything."

"You'd better be careful in dark alleys just the same, young man," warned the inspector. "The mob must know you were with her and they may figure she talked to you. They may try
29

to keep you quiet. But they probably think having the girl is enough assurance that you won't squeak, even if you know something.

"Here's what I think. Murder's a lot simpler than kidnapping. They left chilling Linton to Ellison. But Fassio's still got a few old-timers around, some of them just sprung from stir, who were experts in the snatch racket even before the Lindbergh law was passed. Those are the guys who got the girl. It was neat, siphoning the gas tank and all. Maybe they figure having an ex-cop's granddaughter will help 'em make a deal with the police. Anyhow, they've got her where they can keep her quiet.

"We know from the hotel people that Ellison got in before twelve, that there was a telephone call for him, but that the party disconnected and a few minutes later a seedy-looking bird came in and left a sealed note for him at the desk. Soon as he got this note, he took off. It was probably word that the snatch was set and told him to meet somebody somewhere."

The old man looked at Dab. "That's it, Mr. Dab. I've let you have it."

Dab was silent for a long while. "Tell me," he said at last, "if I can find another meaning in these cards on the floor, will you give my version serious consideration?"

"Sure we will, Mr. Dab," replied Romano. For once he wasn't flippant. "We'll get photos of these cards to you first thing in the morning, and we'll listen to anything you have to say."

"You needn't bother sending me home in a police car," said Dab. "I want to walk a piece. I can get a cab on Broadway."

Allan Walters accompanied Dab to the front porch. He was a large young man with wide shoulders, but somehow he appeared to have shrunk, to have wasted in a matter of hours. His taut face accentuated the size of his eyes which seemed to burn feverishly. The cheekbones were pronounced, the flesh glove-tight over them. *His face is like a death's head*, Dab thought. *He's like a skeleton wearing a coat with absurdly padded shoulders. He's dazed. I'm dazed, too. We're both in a state of shock. Panic, even.*

Walters laid a hand on Dab's arm. He said, "Can you solve that puzzle another way, Mr. Dab? Can you, sir? She's my girl. She'd have been my wife in just a few more weeks. I've loved her since we were kids. You've got to solve it, Mr. Dab. It's up to you. If we find the murderer, we find the kidnapper

30

and that means we find Pat. I'm a cop. I know about these things. When there's a snatch, you have to catch them right away. Kidnappers wait twenty-four hours, forty-eight hours, maybe a little longer. But if you don't find the victims quick, you find them dead. It's Pat they've got, Mr. Dab. Can you find her? Can you solve that puzzle Phil Linton left for you?"

The dandyish gentleman with the waxed mustache looked suddenly very old and very tired.

"I don't know, boy," he answered. "It's the toughest job I've ever tackled. I've not only got to do it the hard way. I've got to prove the easy, obvious answer is the wrong one. But maybe, if I have time . . ."

The big clock across the river flashed

TIC

TOC

It was four o'clock in the morning.

5

SHE AWAKENED to mote-swirling gloom and to silence that was almost complete.

A murky shaft of light, trembling with dust particles, stabbed down from a small, grimy skylight in the high ceiling. The place was cold, yet insufferably close and musty. There was a smell of old wood and dry rot that reminded her of the attic in her own home. Suddenly the silence shivered with the slightest of sounds. It was a fluttery, frightening little noise, the soft sound that the padded feet of rats make in woodwork.

Her head ached intolerably. A faint and cloying smell seemed to linger in her nostrils and her throat was very dry. She was nauseated. Her neck ached as if the muscles had been twisted. As the faint light swirled in front of her eyes like a smoky curtain, her head cleared a little. She became more acutely conscious of pain, discomfort, but now she could remember, and the disembodied, floating sensation was passing. I am Patricia Linton, she told herself. A while ago—or was it an age ago?—a young man named Allan asked me to marry him. We were in an old farmhouse and there was a checkered tablecloth and a candle was stuck in a wicker-covered bottle

31

and the tallow had dripped down over the bottle's neck in fat chunks and made fascinating basket-weave designs. Our dinners were very expensive because I peeked at the check and with the cocktails and the wine it came to nearly eighteen dollars and that didn't even include the tip. You see, I can remember even small details very clearly. Then we were driving in the car. We were on a very dark and a very rough road and suddenly the car began to spit and cough and inexplicably we were out of gas. So I waited there inside the car where it was warm while Allan went back up the road to the darkened station to get a pail of gasoline to start the car. I thought how still and how dark the country was and how even the daughter of a cop and the granddaughter of a cop who knew something about judo might be just a little frightened.

Then there was a slight noise, as if the back door of the sedan were opening but before I could turn around, there was a strong arm around my neck, forcing back my head, and there was a piece of cloth pressed over my face, and the cloth had that hospital smell to it, that smell I could remember from the time when I was very little and Daddy was dying in a place that was all white and sanitary. And then I didn't know anything at all. But once, it seems, I remember a sense of movement as if I were riding in a car again. I stirred and tried to open my eyes and see something, and I *did* see something, something small and faintly familiar, before the cloth was on my face again, stifling me. The thing I saw, or thought I saw, was swinging to and fro, and it was white and fluffy. I had seen a thing like that many times before, but there must be a lot of them in the world. Or maybe I didn't really see it at all. Maybe I just dreamed I saw it. Anyway, it simply couldn't be *his.* I've known him nearly all my life and I'm sure he loved me even though I was going to marry another man. And he's good and kind, I know he is, even if he was cruel sometimes when he was a little boy. He used to make me scream and cry when he tore the wings off butterflies or that time he shot a sparrow with his B-B gun and it didn't die for a long time but just floundered around on the ground while he stood watching it, running his tongue over his chapped lips. No, I mustn't remember things like that. I must remember how good and kind he really is, and how well he's done in the face of a great handicap, and how he loves me even though I'm going to marry another man.

Pat tried to rise. For a moment she felt giddy and sat on the edge of the bed, clutching the side of the bed with her hands, shaking her head. In the dim light she could see that besides the cot there were other articles of heavy, old-fashioned furniture in the room, all of them draped with ghostly sheets. Then she realized with a start that this room was almost perfectly round in shape.

Besides the skylight there was a window, but it was boarded over. There was a chink in the boards, however, and a twisted taper of wan light thrust through it. There was a heavy door. Pat rose on unsteady legs, paused as dizziness assailed her, put her hand to her forehead. Then, when she was sure she would not fall, she crossed to the door and tried the knob. It was securely locked, of course.

"The room I'm in is round," she told herself, "like a room in a tower."

She went to the window and pressed her eye against the pane so she could see through the chink in the boards. It was a gray and misty day. Below her flowed a sluggish river. Across the river she could see an enormous clock. The lights of the clock were not lit now, for the great hands pointed to a few minutes before eight in the morning.

But she knew the clock. It was the Tic-Tok clock.

Patricia Linton began to laugh hysterically.

I'm in the tower, she thought. I'm in the tower of the Mad Hatter's castle. I'm just across the street from home.

I'm the princess in the tower.

She remembered how Mr. Dab used to make up stories about the princess in the tower when she and Abner had sat on the front porch with him those summer evenings when she was a child.

6

He had slept for only a few hours upon a hard and unfamiliar couch. His brief sleep had been troubled and fitful with dreams of a soft young girl whose eyes were bright with stark and naked terror. In his dreams he saw the young girl in a dark and dreadful place with the bars and padlocks of an ancient donjon keep, and on the edge of the darkness lurked the shadowy figures of evil men who watched the girl and waited. Sometimes enormous hands, gnarled and heavy-knuckled, furred and taloned, would reach out of the darkness

33

toward the girl, seeking to touch and bruise and outrage her. Once he had awakened with a stifled scream pulsing in his throat and his body slimed with sweat because one of the hideous hands he saw had had a missing finger.

Abner Ellison would not have slept at all except for the unaccustomed alcohol he had consumed after he had fled and found sanctuary in the bleak tenement rooms of a former convict. Now, in this half-wakeful state, his senses lulled by the after effects of whisky and restless sleep, he fought against consciousness, against the enormity of facing brutal reality. He kept his eyes tight-closed, for briefly the lowered lids afforded him a shield, just as they had on those other mornings when he had awakened on cold, damp ground and had known that as soon as he opened his eyes he must crawl back into the horror-stricken reality of shrieks and thunder from the protecting womb of his foxhole.

This suspended consciousness had been a bulwark for his sanity then and it was a bulwark now. It was a false euphoria in which the animal took over entirely. He was pleasantly conscious of his strong body, the power of his muscles, the steady breathing of his lungs, the hunger in his belly and the lusts in his loins. The nightmare events and the nightmare dreams of the past hours had receded from his mind. He was content to let his body have its way with his brain, to think of hot food and warm womanflesh, to give full sway to his body's needs and urges.

It was strange, the defenses that the body built when horror was too much for the mind to bear. He could recall a day in a gutted Norman town when German 88's and machine guns had cut a whole platoon of men to bloody shreds in the village square. He had burst through a door that hung on one hinge and had crawled over a wooden floor of a darkened room, his carbine ready. He had seen no Germans. He had seen two American soldiers. One was using a knife to shovel food into his mouth from a ration can and was taking great gulps from a wine bottle. The other was in the actual act of love with a writhing, wild-eyed peasant girl. On all sides of them the masonry was crumbling from the reverberations of the guns.

The picture of Pat Linton was still very much in Abner's drowsy mind but he no longer saw a pale face with fright-dazed eyes. Her face was flushed and her eyes danced with excitement and her mouth was soft and inviting. That had been the time it almost happened. He had lived in the same house with her for many years and he had loved her always,

34

he supposed, in that fierce, possessive, yet oddly secretive way of his, but it had never really happened between them, not even that time it almost did. He had come home from basic training at Benning for his first furlough—it turned out also to be his last—and he'd been proud of his uniform and of his brand-new corporal's stripes. He had orders for Fort Meade when his ten days and travel time were up and everybody knew that Meade was a port of embarkation, so this was it. Maybe that was what had made the difference. Or maybe it was that Pat, who was barely seventeen, had suddenly become a woman. In the few weeks he'd been away, the legs that had been bare and spindly above bobby socks now filled out nylon stockings and filled them very well indeed. The breasts that had been mere quivering points beneath her sweaters were now rounded to a melon ripeness. Her face still was prettily innocent and the eyes were young and laughing and the mouth was soft and immature, but it was a woman's body, the kind of body that G.I.s dreamed about in lonely barracks. And when she had kissed him hello it had been a different sort of kiss than they'd ever had before, not a childish peck or a cool, sisterly salutation but a kiss from lips that were warm and moist, lips that clung to his a moment longer than was necessary and that promised more.

During that furlough Pat had broken all her dates, even her dates with Allan Walters, who was Abner's rival, so that she could be with him every minute. One night Phil Linton had gone to a banquet and Pat and Abner had been alone in the softly lighted living room. She had asked him to build a fire, although the room was warm enough, and when the fire blazed, she had turned off the lights and suddenly she was in his arms. Her lips sought his and her young body entreated him. Her dress became disarranged. Shoulder straps slipped down her arms and for the first time he touched her bare, warm flesh. Nothing in the world seemed real then but their desperate wanting. Her small hands dug into the muscles of his arm and back and she tore her lips away and said in a voice that was not Pat's voice at all, but a hoarse, almost inaudible whisper. "I want you, darling. Let's be married . . ."

"When I come back from overseas . . ."

"No, now! Tonight! Let's pretend we're married. Carry me up to my room. We'll lock the door. . . ."

And then the telephone had rung.

Allan Walters had never learned how well-timed that call of his had been.

Abner had always marveled at the self-possession of women

35

in any situation, however young they were. Pat was cool and calm and poised immediately. She rose and shrugged her dress and slip back on her shoulders, smoothed out her skirt and answered the phone in a normal, casual voice, leaving poor Abner there on the sofa, rumpled, red-faced and perspiring.

They had never come that close again, although Patricia Linton had remained the one woman that Abner wanted. It was the thought of that night when their bodies had strained together that had come to him most often when his mind and nerves could no longer stand the sights and sounds and smells of battle. It was the thought of that night that his half-awakened consciousness clung to now to blot out the awful fact of murder.

He had returned from war self-conscious over a minor deformity, realizing that long years of law school were ahead of him before he could hope to make a living for a wife. He had found that Pat and Allan Walters, who was drawing the pay of a first-grade detective now, had gone together fairly steadily during the war and they continued to see much of each other while Abner was attending law school. Abner had erased himself more and more in those years, although his love for Pat and his fevered desire for her had not abated in the least. Pat had accused him of drawing back into his shell like a turtle. Why shouldn't he? She was the daughter and the granddaughter of a cop and he was a murderer's son. He had been maimed in war, not only by losing a finger but by the shock and bitterness war leaves on the mind. Her other suitor was whole and handsome and had a ringing laugh. He was a schoolboy and her other suitor was a cop who had a gun and a badge and authority and a monthly paycheck.

There was much bitterness in him during those years of loneliness and study. Bitterest of all was the thought of Pat in Allan's arms, straining her body against him, whispering "Let's pretend we're married." He tried to reject such a thought. Deep down he didn't believe it. But it recurred and it was torture. Even worse was the feeling that the old relationship between Pat and him had vanished, that he was no longer her protector. No longer would she skip along beside him, her small hot hand, clutching his.

Then he'd graduated and had a job and it seemed that Pat and he were back together again when Phil Linton heard the charge that Abner was an errand boy for mobsters. He wondered if Pat had heard, too.

He was fully awake now. No longer could the fragile shield of his eyelids shut out the clamorous present or obscure

36

his desperate situation. He must awaken to the fact of murder and even greater horrors. It was the second time in his life that murder had been waiting there beside his bed when his eyes came open. On the other occasion he had been in a children's shelter, a small boy with moist eyes and tremulous lips, when they came to tell him that his father had been arrested for a crime so fearful they would not name it.

Abner pulled himself to a sitting posture and shuddered. His host had lit the small oil stove, but the room was clammy with damp cold. Plaster peeled from the walls, the few furnishings were old and dark and scarred, the window glass was filmed with dirt and admitted a murky shaft of light into the chamber's gloom. It was a fitting place to awaken after murder had been done. The room was almost as small as a cell at Dannemora.

Abner heard a door open and shut, footsteps in another room. He jumped and glanced about him for a hiding place. The ex-convict came into the room. He was a small, chubby man. His arms were full of bundles and newspapers.

"Take it easy," said Abner's host. "It's only me. I went out and got food for breakfast. I bought the papers, too. They're full of the murder and the kidnapping. The police have found the shot was from a forty-five, fired from about ten feet away. They haven't found the girl, of course. Linton lived a little while. Long enough to put some cards down on the floor. They've got fingerprint symbols on them. The cops think they're a clue, that Linton wanted your friend Ashton to see them."

"But he couldn't have lived long enough to put any clues on the floor!" Abner exclaimed. "A forty-five fired at that short distance knocks you off your feet, kills you instantly!"

"Maybe Linton was extra-tough. It was a belly wound and belly wounds are tricky sometimes. Anyway he lived to put those cards down on the floor."

"They must have been the little cards he uses in his lectures," Abner said. "They were piled on the table last night, I remember. But they couldn't mean a thing. They're simply symbols for different types of fingerprint patterns. You can't point out any individual set of prints with them." Abner suddenly raised his right hand, looked at it. "Unless . . ."

Abner stood staring at the hand, like an infant that is fascinated by the sight of its fingers.

"Unless," he said, "he meant to point out a man with a missing finger."

"You think he did?" the small man asked.

37

Abner didn't answer. He began to don his clothes hastily.
"What's the rush?" the chubby man asked. "You're not going anywhere, my boy."

"I've got to. I've got to go to Pat. I dreamed about her. There were hands, horrible hands reaching for her."

"Take it easy, son. You can't leave here. Not now. There's a town full of cops, with their hands on their guns, waiting out there for you."

"Listen, I've got to go, I tell you. She's my girl, can't you understand? I've got to get to her. She's locked up and those muggs of Fassio's must know where she is, along with——well, along with whoever put her there. You've seen those mobsters, dealt with 'em. So have I. You ever see the way they look at a woman? I've seen them there in Burke and Holmquist's office, sitting, waiting, not saying a word, with those hard, dark eyes of theirs undressing the women in the place, right down to the skin. I don't want their dirty hands on Pat."

"You listen," said the little man more sternly. "You listen to me. I'm an ex-con. I know about cops and muggs and murder. You can't leave here, I tell you. You've got your orders. Maybe you got 'em straight from Fassio. You don't leave here, not if I've got to put a gun on you to keep you."

"Damn it, man, I can't just sit here doing nothing! Christ knows what they're doing to Pat right now!"

The small man spilled liquor into a glass, handed it to Abner. "Take this," he said. "You need it. You're forgetting something. We don't know which way to jump until this old man you know joins those other three old men tonight."

Abner gulped the liquor, gagged, shook his head. "I've got to get to Pat," he said.

"Just how far do you think you'll get?" the small man asked. "How far do you think you'll get with a cop like Sansone and a killer like Fassio both gunning for you, kid?"

7

It was nearly noon when J. Dabney Ashton fought his way out of the fog of troubled sleep. He draped a purple silk robe about him and picked up the telephone. Paul, the day man, who was as ancient as the other employees of the Washington Square Hotel answered.

"Mr. Dab? There's a package come for you. From the police, I think it is. And a special-delivery letter. But I didn't wake you up. The Madame said you come in awful late, so I said the poor man needs his sleep, he's not so young as he was any more, and . . ."

"Thanks for your consideration, Paul," Dab interrupted. "You can send the package and the mail up with my breakfast. Give me the restaurant, please."

Old Pierre, the waiter, answered the room-service phone and took Dab's order for eggs Benedict and a large pot of coffee.

Room service, like all service at the Washington Square, was a leisurely affair. Before Pierre shuffled in with the tray, Dab had time to shower and shave.

Pierre said, "I brought the mail, Mr. Dab. And a package from the police department. And the morning papers. It's all over the papers about the murder of your poor friend, Lieutenant Linton."

He lifted the cover of the eggs Benedict. "I do hope Michel hasn't made the hollandaise too tart again," he said. "I'm always telling him he's too heavy on the lemon."

Pierre was a frustrated cook. For nearly forty years he had hoped to succeed the hotel's excellent chef in time. The old waiter shuffled from the room.

Dab slit open the Police Department envelope. There was a large photograph showing all nine cards. Dab rose and crossed to the mantelpiece. He set the large photograph in the center of the mantel. Then he arranged the nine smaller pictures in front of it in their proper order, careful to leave a space between the second and the third. Despite the sizzling and hissing of the old-fashioned radiator, Dab found the room chilly. He applied a match to the fuel that had been laid in the fireplace and returned to his breakfast.

As the flames in the grate leaped up, light flickered and sparkled on the glossy surface of the photographs.

The coffee table on which Dab's tray had been placed was near the fireplace and all during his breakfast the old actor gazed somberly at the cards upon the mantelpiece.

"I've got to get it," Dab said desperately. "I've got to save Pat. And I've got to save my boy."

As Dab drank his coffee he glanced through the mail. He did not open any of it. All advertising, he thought. Even the special delivery. A Broadway tailor, who designed a modified

39

sort of zoot suit, had taken to circularizing members of the theatrical profession with special-delivery appeals to come in and view his merchandise. Dab turned to the *Times* and the *Tribune*. The murder was on page one, of course. But the police had not given out any information regarding their version of the fingerprint symbols. There was a mention of the fact that authorities were seeking Linton's foster son, Abner Ellison, for questioning.

There was a knock at the door. Dab called, "Come in."

Pirtle, Dab's chess opponent of the night before, who was also a long-time resident of the hotel, came in.

"Dab!" said Pirtle. "I've just heard about this horrible thing. I didn't know the lieutenant too well, of course, but I liked him very much the few times I saw him here with you. And this kidnapping of his granddaughter, it's awful, Dab! Awful!"

"It may be even more awful than you know," said Dab.

"Are there any clues?" asked Pirtle.

Dab gestured toward the mantelpiece. "Only the clues up there," he answered. "Coffee, Pirtle?"

Pirtle shook his head. "What in the world is that display on the mantelpiece?" he asked. "I noted you were staring at it like a man transfixed when I came in."

"Clues," Dab answered. "The *only* clues."

"Solving this is very important to you, isn't it, Mr. Dab?" asked Pirtle.

"It is," Dab answered. "It is one of the most important things I've ever been asked to do. A man's fate and a young girl's life may depend upon it."

"I think I know what those pictures are now," said Pirtle. "I read that Lieutenant Linton left a set of fingerprint cards of some sort spread out on the floor. Are those photographs of the cards?"

"They are."

"Have the police any idea of what they mean?"

"They think they have," said Dab. "That's the trouble. I have to disprove their solution as well as offer a better one."

Dab crossed to the sideboard, picked up the liquor decanter and a glass and returned to the fireside. "I'm not a morning drinker," said Dab, "but it's a little after noon. Have some Bourbon, Pirtle?"

Pirtle nodded. "Just a touch."

Dab poured Bourbon in the glass, handed it to Pirtle. He splashed more Bourbon into his cup of coffee, sipped from it. Suddenly he regarded Pirtle, snapped his fingers.

40

"Pirtle," he said, "you're an architect. You work with forms, shapes. You are concerned with the interrelation of curves and angles. Forget for a minute that those photos are fingerprint symbols. Just look at each of those pictured shapes, starting at the left, and tell me what each one means to you."

Pirtle said, "There was once a great teacher named Charcot. His pupil, Sigmund Freud, is known to everyone, but the master is forgotten. Charcot said a profound thing once. He said, 'We see only those things we are prepared to see or those things we have been taught to see.' As you say, I'm an architect. I'm likely to see architectural forms in those symbols—or in any other designs that attract my attention, even if I make a conscious effort not to do so."

"Make no conscious effort!" Dab urged. "I believe those symbols are ideographs meant to convey a simple meaning to me. But the terrible personal responsibility I feel in this business has fogged my mind, dulled my wits, distracted me completely. Please, Pirtle! Look at those cards. Tell me what they mean to you."

Pirtle said, "Well, if you insist, of course . . ."

He studied the cards for a moment. He said, "It's rather like the Rorschach test, relating the accidental shape of ink blots to familiar objects."

"Exactly," said Dab. "Don't think about 'em too long. Just give me your first impressions."

Pirtle drank his Bourbon, settled back comfortably and regarded the first photograph. He said, "Right off, that inverted V-shape is like an architectural arch, or it resembles a pediment even more closely. Now, if I tear myself away from thinking like an architect, I might say it was a corporal's chevrons. But that would be very personal thinking. I was a corporal in the A.E.F. in World War One. Of course, it could represent a simple incline, a hill. . . ."

"It's actually *called* an arch in fingerprinting," Dab put in.

Pirtle chuckled at the second print. "At least," he said, "this one's most certainly on the phallic side. Of course, the Phallus symbol is used throughout art and architecture. There I go again. Architecture. It might be one of those rounded, narrow towers used on some buildings. Old castles, for instance."

Dab's eyes regarded Pirtle speculatively. "That's very interesting," he said. "And very odd. It's strange you should mention a hill and a castle. In fingerprinting that second symbol is a straight up and down loop, used by instructors solely to

41

show the shape of the pattern. On the fingers themselves the loop is always tilted one way or another."

Pirtle said, "You're quite an expert. You must have studied hard under Lieutenant Linton. Is that space between the second and third cards important?"

"Forget the space," flared Dab. "That space is a sore subject with me right now."

Pirtle contemplated the card that depicted a whorl. "No hesitation about this one," he said. "It conveys spinning motion, a wheel going round and round. Architecturally it might be the top of a Grecian column, but the spinning wheel is a much stronger impression. That next card, though, the fourth, is nothing out of architecture or anything else, unless it's an abstractionist's nightmare. A snake poised to strike, maybe, and a Figure 6."

Dab said, "Even fingerprint men have a hard time defining it, so they just call it an 'accidental.' "

"The fifth card's as much of a puzzle," Pirtle continued, observing the lateral-pocket symbol. "No architectural form is like that unless it's one of those weird buildings they erected at the World's Fair on Flushing Meadows before the war. Looks like a walking stick enclosing a tilted phallic symbol. The sixth, though, is very similar to the first. Architecturally it's an arch or pediment. Or it's just a rise, a hill."

"It's known as a tented arch," said Dab.

Pirtle showed no hesitation about the seventh card, the exceptional arch. "It's a fork in a road," he stated. "It's almost exactly like symbols on maps for roads that suddenly divide in two, with a kind of safety island in the middle. Dozens of 'em in Long Island, Westchester. . . ."

"Road! Westchester!" Dab exclaimed. "Well, I'll be dam'."

"The next to last card is the old phallic symbol again," Pirtle declared. "If it's a tower this time, it must be the Leaning Tower of Pisa."

"It's a loop," Dab said. "It's tilted that way because it's a radial loop."

"The last card looks like a snake," Pirtle went on. "But I'm not seeing snakes on one shot of Bourbon. So I'll say it's a road. A winding road."

"In fingerprinting, it's a ridge fragment," said Dab. "Pirtle, you've seen some rather remarkable things in those cards, do you know that?"

"Right out of *Alice in Wonderland*, I'm afraid," Pirtle replied.

"At least you saw something," asserted Dab. "You give me some hope, because I saw nothing at all. Do you realize that your interpretation of these symbols could be highly relevant? You saw hills. Phil Linton's house is on a hill. You saw a castle tower. There's a castle with rounded towers just across the street from Linton's. You saw a spinning wheel, like the wheel of a moving car. Pat Linton was taken out of one car and carried off in another. You saw a road fork, like those on Westchester highways. You saw a winding road. Young Walters described the scene of the kidnapping as a dark, winding road! Pirtle, this could be interpreted to mean that Pat Linton was kidnapped in Westchester, abducted in a fast-moving car and is held prisoner in the tower of a deserted castle on top of a hill!"

"Good Lord, man!" Pirtle exclaimed. "Do you mean I've blundered into solving a murder and a kidnapping?"

Dab shook his head sadly. "I'm afraid not. When Phil Linton left those cards on the floor he couldn't have known all that. He was dead an hour or more before his granddaughter was kidnapped."

Pirtle rose and smiled ruefully. "Time, the inexorable master of us all," he said. "For a minute you had me thinking I was very smart, a hero, even."

"You are in a way," Dab assured him. "You've given me hope. You've snapped me out of the fog I was in. I can see now there are ways of reading those cards differently from the police version. Thank you, Pirtle."

After Pirtle left, Dab sat in front of the fireplace, the cards winking down at him mockingly. But he no longer felt old, confused, beaten. His mind was working now. His cheeks were flushed. *Time. If I only have time enough,* he thought. Occasionally he scribbled notes on a pad.

Castles, hills, cars, he mused. *But of course no kidnapper would be fool enough to imprison Pat in a castle right across the street from home, anyway.*

The fire crackled, hissed. Dab started at the cards, rubbed his chin, scratched his ear. Suddenly his eyes flew wide open, his mouth hung slack, as if he had made a startling discovery.

"No!" he said aloud. "No! It couldn't be!"

He rose, paced nervously about the huge room. "It's not like Phil," he told himself. "Why, if that's it, it's actually a pun. Phil was a simple, sober man. He would never try to convict a murderer with a pun."

He paused directly in front of the cards, still speaking aloud. "But it's a chance," he said. "It's another way of inter-

43

preting the damn thing! It—at least it's worth investigating."

He sank down in a chair.

"Sansone!" he whispered. "Inspector Sansone!"

8

Dab felt excited, elated. The problem wasn't hopeless after all.

"You see only those things you are prepared to see or those things you have been taught to see," Pirtle had quoted. The police had been prepared to see fingerprint symbols, a tool of their trade, and those symbols had meant a nine-fingered man to them. But an architect had seen entirely different things. Towers, hills, spinning wheels, forking roads, winding roads. Despite their apparent relevancy to the case, these things could really mean nothing because of the time element. Dab thought of the big, bright clock across the river from Phil Linton's house, ticking the minutes and the hours away. The clock was a sort of symbol, too. Time. That was the all-important thing. He must read the message right in time to save Pat Linton's life. "Twenty-four hours, maybe forty-eight. Kidnappers don't wait long," Allan Walters had said.

But there was hope now. The things Pirtle had seen in the cards meant nothing. Dab accepted that. There was still the other interpretation that had suddenly occurred to him—the almost incredible pun that pointed out an equally incredible suspect. An inspector of detectives. One of the highest ranking officers of the New York police.

Dab had no real faith that such a wildly improbable interpretation of the symbols on the cards offered the correct solution. But the mere fact that the symbols could have such a meaning, that they could have yet another and seemingly pertinent meaning to Pirtle, showed that the police version implicating Abner Ellison could be at fault. To Dab, this established what lawyers term "reasonable doubt." It furnished him an incentive. It offered a means of direct action, and direct action was a catharsis that he needed badly.

The old actor stood looking out the window at the park. Suddenly he was conscious that it had begun to snow. His excited, hopeful mood now became one of sheer euphoria.

44

Big, fat snowflakes were floating down indolently outside his window, and to Dab this was a personal sign from Heaven that all was right again in the best of all possible worlds. Dab loved snow. He had always loved snow. He could remember snows of fifty years and more ago on the sloping hills of Virginia and a red sled he had owned and the family sleigh with dappled horses and bell-tinkling harness. There just couldn't be anything wrong in a world that was soft with snow. What more does a man need than snowsheen outside the windows and a crackling fire in his grate to convince him of the eternal rightness of things?

The feeling of fatigue and futility that he had experienced earlier was completely gone now. He was a man again. A man with the wisdom of age and the quick alertness of youth. A man who could take care of the people he loved.

Dab began to dress. While he was attaching his braces to his trousers, a sudden idea struck him. He dropped the braces and they trailed behind him as he crossed to the telephone. He called the Eighth Precinct Station on Mercer Street, just a few blocks from the hotel. Allan Walters was attached to the detective squad there. Dab was informed that because of his special connection with the Linton case young Walters was on temporary duty with Lieutenant Romano, of Homicide, at Manhattan West.

Dab couldn't reach Walters at Manhattan West, but Romano came on the line. He said Walters had gone out for a sandwich and coffee.

"Can you have him call me when he returns?" Dab asked. "I think maybe I'm on to something."

"If you're on to something, honey boy," said Romano, "I'll come down and see you. Me, I haven't been to bed since night before last, and what I'm on to is nothing at all."

"Don't come now," said Dab. "Just have Walters call me."

Dab finished dressing. He caught a glimpse of himself in a gold-framed mirror. He moved to the mirror and examined his face closely, grimacing.

"By golly," he said aloud. "You look pretty good. Just a little while ago when you were shaving I thought how old and tired and beat-up you were. But you're really not bad at all. Your belly's flat and you've got your own teeth and there's plenty of hair left on top. You can still cross foils with the best of them once a week at the fencing club. Maybe the girls don't say you're handsome any more, but at least they call you 'distinguished looking.' And you're the best damn chess player and puzzle solver in Lower Manhattan."

45

Dab grinned. "By golly," he said, "I think I'll wax my mustache."

Mustache waxed and bristling, Dab was drinking Bourbon and smoking a Havana cigar when the phone rang.

It was Allan Walters calling. His voice sounded flat, hopeless.

Dab said, "Allan, would it be possible for you to check the movements of a certain person last evening without him finding out and without you asking me any questions right now?"

"I—I suppose I could," Walters answered. "I could try."

"Even if that person were an important man, a policeman?"

"A policeman, Mr. Dab? What on earth are you on to? Did you see something in those cards Lieutenant Linton arranged?"

"Maybe," Dab replied. "Maybe I did. But don't press me now, boy. And for both our sakes, be discreet. Don't let on what you're up to. Can you do it, boy?"

"I'll get on it right away. Do you think this person can lead us to Pat, Mr. Dab?"

"I don't know. It's a long shot. But maybe it's worth trying."

"Who?" Walters asked eagerly.

"Sansone, Allan. Detective Inspector Sansone."

Dab could hear Walters exhale his breath in amazement. There was a long period of silence. That knocked him for a lateral pocket loop, Dab thought. He's probably at the station and other cops are listening.

At length Walters answered. He obviously chose his words carefully.

"I'll check the matter, sir. I'll call you back." ·

"Careful, now, boy," Dab urged.

"Don't worry," said the puzzled Walters. "I'll be very careful."

For nearly an hour, Dab Ashton sat alone with his thoughts.

Finally the phone rang again and it was Walters. A rather breathless and excited Allan Walters this time.

"Mr. Dab? I'm calling from a pay booth, so I can speak freely. I checked up on Sansone downtown as carefully as I could without attracting too much suspicion. Sansone went off duty at six o'clock last night. He mentioned to the desk sergeant, a fellow I know, that he was going to eat at Luchow's on Fourteenth Street. He's a regular habitué of the place, I know that. Fancies German cooking. I went to Luchow's. They know him well. They said he was there last

46

night, all right, but he didn't eat. He had a drink at the bar first, as was his custom. Then he got a phone call. He'd told the captain he'd be eating later, but after he got the call he canceled his table. He went out in a hurry, looking excited. Even left a full drink on the bar, and that's not like him if you know his drinking habits. I can't get any trace of him between then—about six-thirty—and around midnight. He stopped by headquarters then. He often does late at night when he's off duty. They told him about the Linton murder squeal. He rushed right uptown to Linton's house. Had 'em send him in a car."

"Hmm," said Dab. "Not very conclusive, I'm afraid, but decidedly interesting. Do you suppose you could make further discreet inquiries, Allan, and find out where the inspector was between the time he left Luchow's and the time he visited headquarters?"

Walters hesitated. Then he said, "Mr. Dab, maybe I better tell you. I'm afraid I wasn't too smart. It's kind of ticklish for a detective to check up on an inspector, you know. When I got back to Manhattan West, Lieutenant Romano called me in. Said this desk sergeant had phoned wanting to know why I was inquiring about Sansone. Said there'd be hell to pay if the old man found out I'd been asking questions. He wanted to know why. I told him you had some kind of lead, I didn't know what, and you'd asked me to make a routine check on some of Lieutenant Linton's associates, including Sansone. Romano's an easygoing guy usually, but he was pretty burned up. He wants to bring me down to your place right away. I made an excuse so I could get out and call you, tip you off. But I expect Romano and I will be calling on you pretty soon."

"Good Lord, boy!" exclaimed Dab. "I am a blundering old fool! I've got you into trouble!"

"Don't worry about that, Mr. Dab," Walters said. "If checking on Sansone means finding Pat, I'll tail him to the North Pole. I'll hand in my badge if necessary. I don't give a damn about anything except Pat. . . ."

"I'm sorry, boy. I didn't mean to get you into a mess. Forget the whole thing, Allan, you hear?"

"No. I'm not forgetting it. I'll do anything to find Pat," Walters answered. There was a buzz on the phone indicating time was up and more coins needed to continue the conversation. Walters said, "I've got to get back now. Good-bye, Mr. Dab. You'll probably be seeing us in a few minutes—unless Romano's changed his mind."

Romano hadn't changed his mind. In twenty-five minutes

47

exactly, the two detectives knocked at Dabney Ashton's door.

Romano appeared a rugged and healthy man who was heavy-lidded for want of sleep, but was so accustomed to this hazard of his profession that he had developed a philosophical contempt for minor discomforts. The younger man was still death-gray of face, Dab noted. The fevered eyes seemed to have sunk far back into his head and were rimmed with great dark circles. *The boy is suffering*, Dab thought. *He's suffering terribly. And like the old fool I am, I've added to his problems.*

Romano did not show active displeasure with Dab. He seemed merely bored and tired. A quarter of a century on the force, many years served in Homicide, had accustomed him to the strange behavior of persons concerned with murder cases. Nothing much could surprise or even irk him any longer.

The dark-faced lieutenant glanced at the photographic prints on the mantelpiece. "Honey boy," he said, "I see you've got Exhibit A right out in full view of the jury. Made anything out of it?"

"Maybe," said Dab shortly. "Maybe I have, Lieutenant." He spoke brusquely because he felt a gnawing sense of guilt.

Dab busied himself serving Bourbon to his visitors. Romano thanked him, smacked his lips over the aged whisky, said, "Baby doll, Papa's come to spank. You've been right naughty. It's not nice sending a young detective like Walters here to ask questions behind an inspector's back. The inspector might get mad. Especially if he's a rugged character like Sansone whose temper's about as even as a hydrogen bomb's. Why'd you do it, honey boy? Did those little cards up there tell you Detective Inspector Sansone's a kidnapper, a murderer, maybe?"

Dab shifted uncomfortably in his chair. He despised himself heartily because this confident, cynical man could make him feel like a small boy caught with his fingers in the cookie jar. With more asperity than he intended, he replied: "To be frank with you, yes! That's just one of numerous constructions that can be put upon those cards, Lieutenant. Viewed properly, it is just as logical for me to assume they point out Inspector Sansone as it is for the police to assume they point out Abner Ellison."

Romano said, "Now that's right interesting. Tell us how these cards point out Inspector Sansone."

Dab wavered. For a second he was on the verge of blurting out his conclusion. But under the circumstances his theory about the pun seemed very weak and far-fetched. He imagined the lieutenant would laugh at him. *And I don't like being*

48

laughed at unless my lines are supposed to be funny, Dab told himself.

He said, "I don't think I care to discuss that right now, Lieutenant."

"Why, honey boy?" Romano inquired.

Dab's voice again sounded more sharp and quarrelsome than he meant it to be. *I'm blowing up in my lines,* he thought. *I've got to watch out.* He said, "I'm not like the police, Lieutenant. I don't want to jump at the obvious and cast suspicion on a man without making some preliminary inquiries, at least. I think that one possible solution of the puzzle Phil Linton left me to solve fully justifies my interest in Inspector Sansone's movements last evening."

The lieutenant was less amiable now, less bantering. He said, "But why involve young Walters? He's got enough grief without having old Sansone down on him."

Dab was flushed with guilt again. "It's the only way I could think of to obtain the information I wanted. I know Allan better than I know you or any other police officer except Phil Linton, and I need hardly remind you Phil is dead," he answered stiffly.

Romano said, "You could have asked the inspector a straight question. He'd have answered you." The lieutenant chuckled. "He'd have cussed a lot, but he'd have answered you."

"If he's guilty," Dab retorted, "he'd not only cuss a lot, he'd lie a lot. That's why I needed someone to check. I'm truly sorry I've involved Allan if it's going to mean more trouble for him. But I'm trying to make a point. Sansone, Captain Haas, even you, Lieutenant, assumed the symbols on those cards could only mean a nine-fingered man. I've read them another way—to mean Sansone—and in my book this interpretation is just as logical. And I'll tell you something else. Yet another person has seen those cards, and he has read another message in them. This person doesn't know any of the facts of the case and isn't acquainted with anyone connected with the murder except myself. Yet most of the things he saw in the cards *could* have a direct connection with both Phil's murder and Pat's kidnapping."

"Well, well," said Romano. "Who saw all this? Some tea-leaf reader in a green silk turban?"

"The man who examined the cards is a competent citizen and a brilliant architect. His name is Pirtle. Here are some of the things those figures conveyed to him. A fork in the road, like the forks in Westchester County highways . . ."

49

"That place we stopped for hamburgers was right at a fork in a Westchester highway," Walters interrupted excitedly. "That's where they must have siphoned my tank!"

Dab couldn't resist smirking a little bit at Romano. He continued, "This architect saw a winding road, too, and spinning wheels, like a motor car in motion. Since one of the adjoining symbols is called an 'accidental,' this message in the cards could mean a motor accident, like running out of gas on a winding road. Also this man kept seeing the loop designs as architectural forms similar to towers on ancient castles."

"This last I don't quite get," Romano interposed.

"The Mad Hatter's Castle!" exclaimed Walters. "It's right across the street from the Linton house. It could mean the murderer is hiding in one of the towers—or that he's got Pat prisoner there."

"Now we got a Mad Hatter in the act," Romano said sourly. His eyes narrowed shrewdly as he regarded the young detective.

"The Mad Hatter," Walters continued. "It could mean something, Lieutenant. Everybody knows he was a goofball and that his disappearance off the face of the earth is an unsolved mystery. . . ."

"I've read about him," said Romano, "and I've heard Phil mention him, but I've kind of forgotten . . ."

"But . . ." Dab attempted an objection, but was interrupted.

"His name was Frank Tocci," Walters said eagerly. "He came here years ago as an immigrant from Albania. He used to say all Albanians are barbers or brigands and he'd been both in his time. First he worked as a barber, then as an apprentice hatmaker. He got the idea of making cheap hats after expensive models, opened up his own factory and cleaned up a fortune. Millions. That's why he called himself a brigand. Claimed all millionaires were bandits. He called his product Tic Toc Hats because his own name was Tocci. A clock's his trademark. Big clocks all over the country advertise his hats. After he'd made millions, he built himself a castle modeled after one he'd seen in Europe as a kid."

"But I've been trying to tell you the Mad Hatter and his castle couldn't really be involved in this," said Dab, "because . . ."

Romano held up a hand to silence Dab. "Let the kid go on," he said. "It's a good story."

"Well," Walters continued, "Tocci'd been in semiretirement for years. He must have got bored. After the war in Europe he decided to become a king-maker. Maybe he wanted to put Zog back on the throne of Albania. Some folks say he

50

wanted to be king himself. That's not too fantastic. The throne of Albania was once offered to an American for a price and the last queen was an American heiress. Anyway, Tocci announced he was going to use his fortune to re-establish a monarchy in Albania. He went to Europe a few years back and held some high-level top-secret negotiations in Greece. Then he left, presumably for Tirana, the capital of Albania. At that time the country was in the hands of the Tito Commies. A few days later the Stalin Commies took over and the Mad Hatter simply disappeared. Our State Department was never able to find a trace of him after he left Greece. Neither could the private investigators hired by the estate. Tocci was a bachelor and the castle's been vacant ever since except for old Groscz, the watchman, and Groscz's nephew, who lives in the caretaker's cottage with him. Real-estate companies have tried to buy the place for an apartment development. But Tocci's will leaves it to the city for a museum and instructs the executors never to sell."

Romano nodded. He said, "Well, Mr. Dab, I told you the cops would do all they could to help you if you found another meaning in those cards. This is a screwy lead, but we'll take your architect's word and investigate. Anything to oblige, that's the motto of New York's Finest. Walters, you know old Groscz, don't you?"

"Sure," Allan replied. "He used to let Pat and Abner and me into the castle grounds sometimes when we were kids. Inside those walls, it was just like in our picture books."

"Okay," said Romano. "Get up to the Heights. See old Groscz. Question him, rope him. Get him drunk if you have to."

"I will!" Walters declared. The therapy of hope had worked a miracle with him. "I'll go right now! And we can get a search warrant." He picked up his overcoat, struggled into it.

Dab looked incredulous.

"Easy on the search warrant," Romano warned. "There are angles to be considered. Just rope Groscz."

"But there's no possible point . . ." Dab protested.

Walters' back was turned. Romano shook his head violently at Dab, put a finger to his mouth.

"Get going, kid," the Lieutenant urged Walters.

Walters was at the door. He turned to the others, said, "I'll call you at Manhattan West, Lieutenant. I'll call you, too, Mr. Dab."

He left the room. The heavy door slammed behind him.

Dab said to Romano, "I don't see any meaning in this grand

51

gesture, Lieutenant. It might help some if you trace Sansone's movements. But you know damn well that Allan's trip uptown is a waste of time. Phil Linton left those cards on the floor. And when he died he couldn't possibly have known his granddaughter had been kidnapped on a road in Westchester."

"Sound observation," Romano answered calmly. "Fortunately young Walters is too addled, under too much strain to think clearly. The trip serves a purpose, though. It gives Walters something to do. He's about to crack up. That's why I got him temporarily detached from Mercer Street. They send him out on some precinct squeal, the shape he's in, he'd foul up so bad he'd be walking a beat again next week. Even old Sansone, the toughest cop in the department, agreed we should wet-nurse him a little. Sending him to rope old Groscz is a bright idea. I been trying to get him to go to bed all day. He'll be right close to home and maybe he'll be smart enough to get some shut-eye. He's taking it hard, that kid."

Dab said, "You send Allan off on a wild goose chase on the pretense you're humoring me. But you won't do anything about checking Sansone's movements last night, will you?"

Romano rose, donned his coat and hat. "Honey boy," he said, "you haven't given me any reason for your suspicions. I'm a lieutenant. Sansone's an inspector and a very tough cop. I like my job, maybe because I'm too dumb for any other work. Besides, Sansone's sure to find out about those inquiries Walters has been making. And if I know the inspector, he'll be down here in person before long. You can question him yourself."

Romano noted that Dab seemed to be slumped down in his chair. Even the waxed mustache appeared to droop despondently. The lieutenant lingered a moment at the door. "Believe me," he said, "I'm not trying to knock over your little house of cards, baby doll. I liked Abner Ellison. I hope he's not guilty. But I can't waste too much time on red herrings. If we don't find Pat Linton alive in the next few hours, we're going to find her dead." Romano left without the formality of a good-bye.

As the door closed, Dab roused himself. He got to his feet, said, "Good-bye, Lieutenant."

But the lieutenant was gone.

Dab sat down by the fire again. The breakfast dishes had been cleared from the coffee table, but the unopened advertisements that had arrived in the mail cluttered it. One by one, he tossed them into the fire. The last was the envelope with the special-delivery stamp. He noted idly that the Broadway tailor had no return address printed on the envelope. And his

52

address were printed by hand. It seemed to him
…al-delivery ads he'd received before had had a
…without a name on them. He raised his hand to
…lope into the fire.
…ason that was apparent to him, he changed his
…it the envelope open.
…s no advertisement inside.
…as a note, on cheap, crumpled dime-store stationery,
pencil. There was no salutation, no signature.
…te read: "Join the three old men who have no wives
…ht."

9

NIGHT CAME early in the strange, round room where dust
swirled in the awesome silence.

There had been hardly any light at all from outside since
two o'clock. By that time the sloping skylight set in the high
ceiling had been completely covered by snow. The chink in
the boarded window was less than an inch wide and no more
than three inches in depth.

But Pat Linton had not been sitting there in darkness. Now
that the real evening had descended, the round room seemed
almost cheerful. Fire glowed red in a small kerosene stove. An
old-fashioned kerosene lamp made a small circle of yellow light
in the swarming shadows. Her grandfather, noting her tend-
ency to rearrange the furnishings of the house periodically,
had called her a frustrated interior decorator. Even in this place
she had done what she could to make her surroundings less
fearful. She had ripped the ghostly garments from the heavy
furniture and she had used one of the swaddling sheets to wipe
off the worst of the dust.

She had been amazed by the consideration that her kidnapper—or kidnappers—had shown for her basic comforts. Groscz
lived on the grounds in a separate caretaker's cottage and there
had been no electric current or heat in the castle itself since
the Mad Hatter had departed on a king-maker's errand. The
stove and the lamp were obviously newly purchased and must
have been brought there in anticipation of her arrival. There
was a small bathroom. There was no tub and no hot water and

the stream from the cold tap in the bowl ran a rusty
at least it furnished her a means of elementary c
There was a new cake of soap and a roll of paper tow
And there was food. A large grocery carton was fill.
cans of meat,· vegetables, soup that could be heated a
fashion on the small kerosene stove. There were two loav.
bread and a jar of instant coffee. The groceries made her th
of letters she had received from Abner when he was oversea
He had complained that C-Rations and K-Rations were th·
worst part of war.

There was something else in the grocery box. It was a very
common and a very homely thing but it made her feel queer
when she saw it. It was a large, cellophane-wrapped jelly roll.
When she was very young, jelly roll had been her special favorite food. She remembered how she used to place her hand in
Abner's and he would take her up to Broadway and Klaus's
Bakery. They would purchase a seven-cent jelly roll and would
return home with their faces smeared with reddish goo and
crumbs.

Pat estimated that the food in the box would last a girl with
a healthy appetite about a week. What would happen after
those seven days were passed? Certainly, her grandfather, who
owned only the small house and had no income except his
pension and occasional fees for lectures, could hardly ransom
her for a sum worth the risk of a capital offense.

The alternative was not pleasant.

The alternative was that a person, suddenly crazed, was
going to kill her in his own good time.

She looked at the paper plates, the paper cups, the paper
forks and spoons, that had been laid beside the groceries. There
were six of each. Perhaps, she thought, he doesn't even plan
to keep me seven days.

He—or they—had left her pocketbook on a table beside the
cot. She examined the contents. At first she thought that everything was there. She found her compact, the small amount
of cash she always carried, an orange stick, keys, spare bobby
pins, a book of stamps. Then she realized that two things were
missing. Her lipstick and a small memo book with pencil
attached.

They were afraid she might write a note!

She took stock of the means she might have of writing a
note and getting it out of the sealed room. Writing it, she
decided at once, would be no problem at all. She considered
the skylight. There was no possibility of her reaching it in an
attempt to open the catch. The desk was the highest article of

furniture in the room. The Mad Hatter had apparently used this place as a kind of retreat, an ivory-tower study. There was only one chair. That was the chair to the desk. If she piled the chair on the desk, she estimated that she would still be some four or five feet short of reaching the skylight. Pat was five feet four. She judged the skylight to be at least fourteen feet above the floor.

But something could be thrown through the skylight. True enough, it could not possibly land outside the grounds of the castle, but old Groscz might find it and she could hardly believe that Groscz was implicated in this mad business. The broken glass would let in drafts of frigid air, and the small stove was hardly sufficient to take the chill off the room at best. That discomfort she would simply have to endure until help arrived.

She got the paper toweling from the bathroom, tore off a sheet. She picked up the lamp and the box of kitchen matches that had been left beside it and placed them on the desk. She struck a match. When it had charred down halfway, she blew out the flame. She knocked off the small bulbous head and had a kind of pointed charcoal stylus. She began to print large letters on the paper towel. It took two matches to complete the message.

HELP

I AM IN CASTLE TOWER

PAT LINTON

She selected a can of pork and beans. She had never liked pork and beans, anyway. She got the book of stamps from her pocketbook. She used several stamps to stick the piece of paper towel to the can, with the message outward. Then she stood in the middle of the round room, grasped the can firmly, and swung her arm back, like a pitcher winding up. I'm glad I used to play ball with the boys in the neighborhood, she thought. I'm glad I was a tomboy. I could pitch better than Abner, even. Right in the groove now, Linton! She gauged the skylight with her eye. It had not yet begun to snow. A shaft of noonday light streaked through the grimy skylight. Suddenly she stopped herself just as she was about to hurl the can, stood rigid in suspended motion. There was a checkered pattern visible outside the dirty panes. The skylight was covered with chicken wire! The can would never go through that.

She wasn't beaten. She turned to the boarded window on the river side. She wondered why the Mad Hatter or his caretaker had even bothered to board the window. Even the ace hurler of the Yankee pitching staff couldn't throw a rock that high. The Mad Hatter was a fantastic fellow, though. Maybe he was afraid of meteorites, or fearful of having his castle grazed by flying saucers. In any event the boards that had been set into the window frame were at least an inch thick and were nailed securely. There was no chance whatsoever of prying them loose with her only tool—the can opener that her abductor had left her. For that matter, there was no chance of opening the window. It had been nailed shut.

She regarded the small chink in the boards through which the thin rapier of light was thrusting. If she broke the window glass she might be able to work folded tapers of paper through it. Perhaps the paper would float down to the courtyard and old Groscz would find it when he was making his rounds. It was worth trying, anyway. She detached the note she had printed from the can of pork and beans. She folded it carefully into a three cornered shape that came to a sharp point, like the airplanes she and Abner Ellison had made when they were kids. She sat down at the desk again, burned more matches, wrote more notes. Maybe at least one of them would be found. She used twenty-two matches printing eleven more notes on the toweling. When she had an even dozen, she picked up the can of pork and beans. She would use that for smashing the window pane.

Then she knew that this scheme wouldn't work at all. She knew because now she remembered the architectural details of the castle. These round towers did not rise directly from the ground. They were set on other towers—square towers. And at the base of the round tower, the square tower formed a kind of wide gallery on all sides, with a railing. She supposed that such eminences had been used in ancient times as platforms from which great cauldrons of hot oil were poured down on attackers. Some said that the Mad Hatter had copied his castle from that of another madman, Ludwig of Bavaria. King Ludwig had had no more need of a medieval castle than Frank Tocci, but he had built one just the same. She could remember now seeing the Mad Hatter, a speck against the sky, standing on the gallery at the base of this very tower, looking up and down the curving river like a feudal lord surveying his vast domains.

At any rate, her pathetic paper airplanes would fly no farther than the porchlike structure at the base of the tower. And no one would ever find them there. She bit her lips in rage.

She opened a can of meat loaf and made a sandwich. She put water in a little saucepan her kidnapper had thoughtfully left

56

for her, and placed it on top of the kerosene stove. It would take a long time for it to get hot enough for the powdered coffee.

After she ate, she fell asleep again for awhile, physically and mentally exhausted. When she awakened, the skylight was covered with snow. She thought wildly of breaking the glass of the skylight by hurling a can at it, then building a fire directly beneath out of the sheets that had swaddled the furniture, the blankets on the cot. Maybe the smoke would attract attention. She decided that she would only end by suffocating or burning herself alive.

And so she waited.

She waited for long hours while the snow fell on the sky-light.

Her granddaddy was a good cop. He'd have every police officer in town looking for her.

They'd find her in time.

She waited in the silence. Then she heard a sound. A very soft and furtive sound. A creak. A step on the stairs. This brick-walled, wood-paneled room was almost soundproof, but she felt sure there was some movement just outside the heavy door.

She was looking so intently at that heavy door that there were painful little pin-pricks in her staring eyes.

A tiny speck of white was appearing under the crack of the door. It grew larger. It moved toward her until all of it was in the room.

There were faint sounds again, fading now.

She waited a long while. Finally she went to the door and picked up the piece of paper. Printed words were on the paper.

"Warning—The room you are in is watched from outside every minute. Don't try throwing anything through window or skylight. Don't scream or make noise. One false move and you will be killed at once."

The note was printed in pencil on cheap dime-store stationery.

10

The afternoon had been filled with frustrations.

When he threw more coal upon the fire in the grate, the flames licked up and glittered on the glossy surfaces of the pictured symbols, and they seemed to wink at him sardonically, mockingly.

In his hand was the printed note that had come by special delivery. He knew exactly where to go at midnight to find the three old men who had no wives. They had been in the same place for many decades. But J. Dabney Ashton had no idea at all of what might be in store for him when he joined the three old men who have no wives.

Romano had called a little after four.

"Listen, Mr. Dab," the lieutenant said. "You started something with that business of yours about checking Sansone and seeing castles and towers in those fingerprinting symbols. Young Walters just called. He's about to blow his top. He's asking for plenty of trouble. He's been to see Groscz. That was my idea, of course, but I didn't know it would turn out this way. I was just trying to give the kid something to do. Occupational therapy, you might say.

"Well, anyway, he saw Groscz. And of course there's not even a possibility that somebody caught Groscz when he was blotto and persuaded him to let them in the castle. Groscz claims he took a pledge with the priest six weeks ago and he's been riding the wagon ever since. He swears he hasn't had a drop. Groscz says absolutely nobody has been inside those high walls in the last month except himself and his nephew who lives in the caretaker's cottage with him, and an agent of the estate who was making his regular monthly check on the locks, the condition of the premises and so forth.

"Walters must have acted like a wild man, though. Groscz threatened to call the Department and report him, I understand. Walters flashed his badge, which was a bad mistake, and demanded he be allowed to search the castle without a warrant. Groscz told him that he didn't even have a key to the castle itself. The only keys are kept in the offices of the estate's executors. They've been there about five years now,

58

ever since the Mad Hatter took off. The castle is still filled with valuable paintings and art objects, of course.

"So Walters demands that the police or the D.A. issue a search warrant for the premises and serve it on the Tic Toc people. I don't have to tell you that the Mad Hatter and his millions mean something in this town, or that his attorneys and bankers and managers are pretty important people. They wouldn't like being accused of complicity in a kidnapping through furnishing the hideout for the victim. And nobody is going to issue a warrant on such meager grounds as the fact that an architect thinks maybe the fingerprinting symbol for a loop looks a little like the tower on a castle. That's a cinch.

"So Walters has gone completely nuts. He's threatening to force an entrance into the castle on his own, if necessary! He says he'll intimidate Groscz, break through a window or blow the lock off a door with his police revolver if he has to. Maybe he's crazy enough to do it, too. If he tries, he'll be bounced right off the force."

"No, no," said Dab. "Allan mustn't do that, of course."

"He mustn't," agreed Romano. "And you're the one who's got to stop him. I told him you were going to call him at his house. I figured that was one way of getting him home. He might listen to you."

"I'll call," Dab replied. "I don't know what I'll tell him, but I'll call."

"Also," said Romano, "if we're going to save Walters' skin we've got to pray old Inspector Sansone doesn't get wind of this. He wasn't too fond of the idea of my baby-sitting the boy anyway. The relationship between Inspector Sansone and old Groscz makes this thing particularly nasty."

"A relationship between Groscz and Sansone?" said Dab. "What relationship?"

"Didn't you know? I thought Phil Linton would have told you. Groscz was a cop for a very short time a lot of years ago. It was during Prohibition and he had the itchiest hands of any rookie in town. He knew Sansone in those days, when the inspector was still walking a beat. Also he married Sansone's sister. The sister is dead, but Groscz is still Sansone's brother-in-law. And Sansone is one of those stubborn old birds who believes his kin, even his in-laws, can do no wrong. If Walters spouts off to him that he thinks Groscz is implicated in a kidnapping—well, honey boy, it's curtains for young Walters."

"I'll call right away," Dab promised.

What an old fool I am, Dab thought, as he waited for his
59

call to Allan Walters' house to go through. I try to help one boy who's in trouble and all I do is get another lad in a mess. A damned, futile old busybody, that's all I am.

Allan's mother answered the phone. She sounded vague and slightly incoherent. She's drinking again, Dab thought. Poor Allan. As if he didn't have enough grief already. Dab knew from Phil Linton that Mrs. Walters had been a problem drinker for years. One of those housewives who hide bottles of cheap sherry in closets. She'd taken pledges in the church from time to time and once had even been sent away quietly for a cure, but nothing seemed to help. Dab knew that one of the strongest bonds between Abner Ellison and Al Walters was that both had reason to be ashamed of their parents. After some hesitation and a few completely irrelevant comments, Mrs. Walters called her son to the phone. Dab tried to remember the stage roles in which he had played stern, convincing characters. He said, "Listen, Allan. You're not to do anything more about the castle, understand? I've made a very great mistake. I'm just not thinking right, that's all. Neither are you. If we'd used our noodles, we'd have realized that Phil Linton couldn't possibly have known of Pat's kidnapping because of the time element that's involved. So he couldn't have possibly left cards with symbols meaning roads and castle towers. That silly theory of mine about the Mad Hatter's castle is out completely. Don't make any more inquiries there, boy. It will only mean trouble."

"Where does that leave us, Mr. Dab?" Walters asked. "Right back where we started from? Does it mean Abner or possibly Sansone are the only suspects, that we have no way at all of finding Pat before they kill her?"

There's that sixty-four-dollar question, Dab thought.

"I can't answer that now," the old actor replied. "But there's still hope. I have an appointment at midnight. I should know more after I keep it. Promise not to do another thing until I call you or see you tomorrow. Go to bed and get some sleep."

The phone was silent for a moment. At last Walters spoke hesitantly, miserably. He said, "Inspector Sansone knows everything. He called me here just before you rang up. He's raging mad. They told him about my checking his movements last night, and old Groscz, his brother-in-law, must have called him about me going to the castle. I told him Lieutenant Romano sent me to the castle. He really blew up then. He started cussing me and Romano and you. Especially you, Mr. Dab."

"Swear words won't hurt me any," said Dab. "I've been

60

cussed by experts. Go to bed and stay there. That's the best way of keeping out of trouble."

Dab expected it, of course, but it came surprisingly soon.

The phone was no more than cradled when it began to ring. The desk informed him that Inspector Sansone was in the lobby and wished to see Mr. J. Dabney Ashton.

When the inspector came through the door, Dab thought, *He's one of the most fearsome-looking old men I've ever seen. I wonder why? Maybe it's that bright red face under the snow-white hair. Or those hands. They must be fully as big as Carnera's.*

Inspector Sansone didn't waste time in greetings. He said, "I've come to talk turkey to you, Ashton. I want you to listen and listen good."

He took off his hat but he did not remove his overcoat. He seated himself on the sofa by the fire. Dab realized how angry the old man must be when he refused a drink. Liquor never showed on Sansone, but Dab knew he was a heavy drinker.

"I'll get right to the point and no beating around the bush," said the inspector. "You're a damned nuisance. I don't want any more of you and your damned silly puzzles, understand? The police know who murdered Phil Linton. He's on the lam, but we'll find him. When we do we'll find out who kidnapped Pat Linton, and if she's still alive, we'll get her. We don't need any damned play actors to help us, either."

Dab started to protest. The inspector silenced him.

"Get this, Ashton," he said. "I won't tolerate any interference with the police by damned amateur detectives. I loathe amateur detectives, private citizens who want to play cops. Amateurs don't solve crimes. Cops solve crimes. That's what they're paid to do. And they don't solve 'em with a lot of lie-detecting machines and psychological hogwash, either. They solve 'em by putting the fear of God into muggs and making 'em talk." The old man clenched his wrestler's fist, hit the coffee table a hard blow with it. "Get this, then. You're out of this case. You've got nothing to do with it. We don't need your help and we don't want your meddling. Stay away from the cops. Stay away from me and Lieutenant Romano and Detective Walters. Stick to your play acting and your crossword puzzles."

Dab had always prided himself on his self-control. He realized now that he was dangerously angry. He could feel the flush burning his cheekbones. He delayed for a minute before

61

he answered the inspector. Trying to keep his voice down, to control his rising gorge, he said, "I am not playing amateur detective, Inspector. Phil Linton was my friend. I've known him for a quarter of a century or more, ever since he was a cop on the theatrical-district beat. I liked him and I admired him. It's too bad there aren't more cops like him. Phil Linton left some cards on the floor when he was killed. He directed my attention to them. He thought they would mean something to me. I intend to discover what they mean."

"The cops already know what they mean," said Sansone. "They mean a nine-fingered man named Abner Ellison. You're trying to protect Ellison, Ashton. The cops know that, too. You're willing to have a young girl killed, even, to save Ellison's skin. So you're throwing red herrings at us to delay the investigation. You've even gone to the extreme of implying that my brother-in-law or I myself might be involved, and you persuaded a detective on the city payroll to waste his time in checking your damn fool theories. You wanted to know where I was last night, did you? Well, I'll give you my alibi. I'll hand it to you on a silver platter, and then I'll tell you off for good, mister. I went to Luchow's restaurant, where I planned to eat my dinner. I'd just ordered a highball at the bar when I got a phone call. It was from the police commissioner, Ashton. He wanted to see me at his house right away. I went there. I ate dinner with him. I stayed with him until nearly midnight. Then I went to Headquarters, heard about the Linton squeal and beat it uptown to the murder scene in a department car. You want a signed affidavit from the commissioner, Mr. Meddler? Or maybe you think the commissioner and I were accomplices in a murder and a kidnapping?"

Dab Ashton was completely deflated. The little house of cards had really tumbled down about his head.

It's a battle between two old men now, he told himself. *Only this old man has lost all his fighting pieces before the game begins.*

The silence was heavy in the big room except for the crackle and sputter of rosy coals. Dab knew a feeling of awful emptiness that he had experienced only once before in his life. On that occasion he had walked onto a brightly lighted stage and for a horrible moment had completely forgotten his lines. Hundreds of eyes had gazed upon him expectantly during those seconds that seemed a lifetime. Now only one pair of cynical, hard, red-filamented eyes regarded him. But these eyes were far more terrible than the hundreds that had peered from the cavernous gloom of a theater. They were the eyes of

62

a man who wanted to destroy a boy Dab loved, the eyes of a man who would exult in seeing Abner strapped helpless in a crude, thronelike chair with cathodes pressed against his shaven skull. *He's going to destroy Abner,* Dab thought, *and it pleases him to know that he'll destroy me, too.*

With a supreme effort, Dab found his voice, but he spoke the first words quaveringly. *I'm scared,* he thought. *I'm scared to death and my fear is naked before this grim old man.*

Dab said, "Lieutenant Romano knew quite well that I did not seriously believe those cards on the mantel mean that Pat is held prisoner in the Mad Hatter's castle. He sent Allan Walters there on a pretext, to give him something to do. The poor boy is cracking up. I did not give too much credence to the theory that you might be involved, either. But there's a perfectly logical assumption to be drawn from the cards—an assumption that Phil meant to leave your name there on the floor."

Sansone laughed. His laughter was not pleasant.

The inspector said, "How do the cards spell my name, Ashton?" He spread his huge, hairy hands out in front of him. "I've got all my fingers. They're a little knotty from old age and arthritis, maybe, but all ten of 'em are there."

"That's just my point," Dab answered. "The cards don't have to mean a nine-fingered man, as you assume. There are other ways of looking at them."

The inspector snorted. "The amateur detective again. Never do it the easy way. Never accept the obvious truth. Blame it on the butler's illegitimate son who's disguised as the prime minister. Never blame it on the guy who's caught with a smoking gun in his hand. Well, I've got news for you amateur detectives. The suspect all the evidence points to is the one who's committed the crime, ninety-nine out of a hundred times. And the cops, not meddlesome private citizens, are the ones who catch criminals."

Dab was thoroughly angry now. He said, "You complain about private citizens interfering in police routine. Yet when you fail to solve a case you complain that the police have been unable to get co-operation from private citizens who might have information that is vital to the case. Do you want to know why the average private citizen hesitates to go into a police station with information that might be pertinent? I'll tell you why, Inspector. Because there are too many cops like you! The citizen knows he's likely to be treated as if he were a moron or a suspect when he exposes himself to police questioning."

63

"So we've got dumb cops," said the inspector. "I'm kind of dumb myself, maybe. I never had a college education, and I'm an inspector. There's nobody but you private citizens to blame for dumb cops, mister. You pay a rookie who's maybe got a wife and four kids to support thirty-seven dollars and fifty cents a week and you expect him to have the I.Q. of a genius and to be incorruptible. I've got news for you, mister. A lot of good cops have taken a little graft now and then when they didn't think it would hurt anybody.

"I couldn't blame the boys who took a little here and took a little there from the numbers racket too much. Everybody likes to bet a little and win a lot. Numbers are like booze. Popular with you private citizens. So some cops took a little without figuring they were contributing to the support of Fassio and all his other rackets, including dope and murder. Oh, I got some detectives fired off the force, all right. I put some others back in uniform."

The inspector rose and crossed to the door. "There's one detective in particular," he said. "Used to be first-grade. He's walking a beat out on Staten Island now. That's a long way from his home up in the Bronx. I didn't recommend firing him because he gave me some information. He told me who paid him off."

The inspector waited, hand on the doorknob.

Dab said nothing.

"The man who paid him off was Abner Ellison," the inspector said, seeming to savor each word. "What have you got to say about that, mister?"

"Since the source of your information was admittedly corrupt, I would doubt the veracity of the information," Dab replied stoutly. "I would say your detective was a damned liar."

The old inspector grinned. "How do you amateur detectives arrive at a conclusion like that?" he asked. "You never saw the man and never heard of him before, but right off you say he's a liar. Did some architect tell you the man was a liar? Or did you see evidence that he was a liar in those little cards up on the mantelpiece, along with my name and the towers of the Mad Hatter's castle?"

"Abner Ellison is no crook," declared Dab. "And he is not a murderer."

"Pretty cocksure, aren't you?" baited the old detective. "A cop tells me that Ellison bribed him on behalf of Lenny Fassio. I need corroboration. Phil Linton, who's close to Ellison, is

64

going to give us important information in connection with the numbers racket bribes. But he's killed right after he's been with Ellison. Ellison disappears. To me, it adds up. But of course I'm just a dumb cop. I'm not a smart amateur detective. I'm no good at working puzzles, either."

"You despise me, don't you, Inspector?" Dab asked.

The inspector shook his big head. "No," he answered. "No, I don't despise you. You don't want to believe anything wrong about someone who's close to you. That's human, like cops taking bribes. But I still don't want any more of your interference. You've got one cop in trouble. That's enough."

"Certainly you aren't going to discipline Allan Walters for something that's entirely my fault?" pleaded Dab.

The old man nodded. "For his own good. I'm suspending him. Not for too long. Just long enough to teach him a lesson. To teach him to take orders from his superiors on the force instead of from amateur detectives. Besides, he's overwrought. He needs a rest or he'll flip his wig completely."

Dab bit his lips. He looked white and sick. The inspector regarded him with narrowed eyes. He fumbled with the doorknob, started to open the door, hesitated.

"You say you want to help the cops as a private citizen," said the red-faced old man. "Okay, I'll give you a chance to help. Will you answer a couple of questions?"

Dab nodded miserably.

"Have you been in touch with Abner Ellison since last night?"

"No," said Dab.

"Do you know where we can find him?"

"I've no idea where he may be," Dab replied.

"If you found out where he was, if he got in touch with you, would you inform the police?"

Dab hesitated. "I might not," he said at last. "Not if I believed he was innocent. I might try to find proof of his innocence first. I think you're prejudiced. I don't think you'd give the boy a fair deal if you found him now."

Inspector Sansone snorted. He opened the door. "That," he said, "is what you upstanding private citizens mean by co-operating with the police. Shielding a murderer. Refusing information about a cop-killer." He left. The door slammed behind him.

Dab sat down on the sofa by the fire. Through the window he could see the night shadows lengthening over the snow of Washington Square, black as the mood of dejection

65

that consumed him. The fire hissed and little purple flames spurted like blown feathers. The glossy, inscrutable faces of the little cards on the mantelpiece winked tauntingly.

On an impulse, Dab crossed to the desk, consulted a small notebook in which he had jotted down odd facts. He found the scribbled note "4,660,337 centuries." Phil Linton had told him that a South American authority had estimated that the same fingerprints in two individuals might occur every 4,660,-337 centuries. That, then, was the margin of error against which fingerprint experts worked. Once every 466,033,700 years they might possibly be mistaken.

The certainty and the exactness of fingerprinting were what had appealed to Phil Linton. He was a man who had liked a well-ordered life in a well-ordered world. He was impatient of guesswork. He wanted to deal with facts, undeniable facts.

Yet the murdered police officer had bequeathed to Dab a maddening piece of guesswork in those symbols for arches and loops and whorls and their composites that should have made up an exact science.

The evening was as long and as frustrating as the afternoon had been. Dab had no appetite for his excellent dinner. This fact delighted the jealous waiter, Pierre, who took the food Dad left upon his plate as an implied affront to his rival the chef, Michel. Michel himself, a towering starched cap on his head, strode into the dining room to demand the reason for M'sieu Ash-ton's displeasure with his culinary skill.

Dab tried playing chess in the barroom with Pirtle and lost three straight games in record time.

He returned to his rooms and brooded by the fire for a long time. A few minutes before midnight he bundled himself into a burberry and a heavy woolen scarf and descended to the lobby. He opened the street door and wind-driven, grit-hard snowflakes slashed his face.

Madame Sorel at the desk called to him, "Where are you off to at such an hour on a night like this, you old fool, you?"

Holding the door open, with wind and snow sweeping into the lobby, Dab paused, took the shaggy Borsalino from his head. He made a low bow, worthy of the Sieur de Bergerac sweeping an azure portal with his unblemished plume.

"Madame," Dab declaimed, "I go forth to keep a rendez-vous with the three old men who have no wives."

Madame Sorel shook her head until stray strands of dyed red hair fell over her high white brow.

"But definitely," she declared, "he has misplaced his wits, this old one."

66

11

It was dark and cold in the round room now.

This was not the soft and friendly darkness of a winter night. This was the still and frightful darkness of the tomb. And this. was not the bracing cold that bites the cheeks and tingles in the nostrils. This was the dank, dead cold of moldy grave soil.

For the first time in her life Pat Linton knew what terror was as she lay there in the stifling darkness and felt the lizard touch of cold upon her flesh.

Fearing a fire or asphyxiation, she had turned off the lamp and the stove before she tried to sleep. Now her teeth were chattering and her hand shook as she reached for matches. She had seen poor Allan Walters' mother shake like that at times. Mercifully, it had been termed a nerve condition. Actually it was the effects of the sweet wine the woman drank.

At last she found the matches and the lamp flamed up. Shadows like dancers in dark drapery shivered on the walls. Pat wrapped a blanket tight around her slim, trembling body. Then she fumbled with the matches again and lit the stove. The warm red glow through the porthole was small solace in this place where shadows trembled.

Pat warmed her frigid hands at the little stove. Then she crossed to the grimy window and pressed her face against the cold glass of the pane. She peered through the tiny chink that afforded her her only view of the world outside the tower.

Through the flickering curtain of falling snow she could barely discern the big, bright clock across the river, the Tic Toc clock.

The light flashed TIC then TOC.

It was two minutes to midnight.

What time are they going to kill me? she wondered. What day? What hour? Will they kill me before the groceries that they left are gone? If not, I have five days more, maybe six if I am careful.

How are they going to kill me? she asked herself. Will they slip in through the cold darkness some night when I'm asleep and slash a knife across my throat? Will they press the smelly rag upon my face again? Or will the door open some time when I'm awake and will they merely walk right in and say, "The time has come," and point a gun at me and pull the trigger?

She was nauseated with fear. There was a sharp pain inside her. She thought of that time when she was a little girl and she'd had a stomach ache and they'd called the doctor because the pain was on the right side and they feared appendicitis. The doctor had kneaded and punched and prodded her and in the end he'd decided it was nothing except too much jelly roll. Mr. Dab had given Ab a dollar and Ab had spent it all for jelly roll and she and Ab had eaten every bit of it.

I could write a note, she thought, and push it under the door. They came here once and they're sure to come again. They may even be here now, just outside the door, waiting, listening. I could write a note and say I have acute appendicitis and they have to get a doctor right away or my appendix will burst and I'll die.

Then she began to laugh hysterically. A lot they would care about her precious appendix. They were going to kill her anyway, they'd warned. If she made one false move. They were going to kill her.

Unless . . .

Unless her grandfather found her first. Her grandfather was a good cop. A great detective. He was respected and loved by the highest-ranking police officers on the force. He'd find a way. He'd find a clue. . . .

She thought of the one pitiful clue that might point to her abductor. The white, fuzzy thing that swung to and fro, the one thing her clouded eyes had briefly seen when she roused from the stupor in a moving car. But the one she'd seen couldn't belong to him. There were hundreds of such things. Thousands. Millions, probably. Ironically enough, the thing she'd seen was supposed to be a good-luck symbol.

The thing she'd seen had been a rabbit's foot attached to a little beaded key chain and the key was in the ignition of the car that must have brought her here.

But it couldn't have really been his car, of course.

She pressed her face hard against the window glass, trying to will herself out of the room, out of the cold, the cavorting shadows, the grim terror.

TIC

TOC

The big hand jumped forward again. It was exactly midnight.

68

"It's midnight," she said aloud. "They've let me live one day at least."

12

Mr. Dab made his way through the swirling snow to the little section of park on the east side of the towering memorial arch. He came to the runtish statute of Giuseppe Garibaldi and paused, taking his bearings. The snow was sticking. Already it was deep beneath the feet. Garibaldi seemed to wear a white fur collar on his coat.

There was no one at all in Washington Square Park. A few pale lights gleamed in the old buildings of New York University to the east. There were shimmering islands of snow-flakes beneath the park's street lamps. Dab turned left, took a path that ran in a southeasterly direction. He stopped beside a snow-covered bench. Here three old trees with twisted limbs stood side by side.

Nature study, along with chess and puzzles, had once been a hobby of J. Dabney Ashton's. He knew the name of every tree in Washington Square Park. There were, he knew, seventeen gingko trees from Eastern China in the park. But only three had been planted side by side.

How many years had it been since he and a boy of nine or ten named Abner Ellison had sat on a bench just across this path? The boy had said, "Mr. Dab, those three old trees look just alike."

"They are just alike, son. They're gingko trees."

The boy had said, "They look like three old men all twisted up with rheumatism."

Dab had chuckled. "You're right, son," he had replied. "They are very old. The oldest species of tree of which there's any record. Some folks say the gingko is a living fossil. In China they are kind of sacred. They're always planted beside temples. Also, you're right about them being men. Those trees are males. The female gingko is never planted in this country. Those are three old men who never will have wives."

"Why?" the boy had asked.

Dab laughed. "I hate to have to say this, because it isn't

69

gallant," he had answered. "But the female gingko has an awful smell."

On fine days the actor and the boy had often sat in the shade of the three old trees and talked of the wonders of nature and of Dab's small victories in deciphering enemy codes during the First World War and of the prospects for the Yankees and the Giants.

Dab glanced at his watch.

It was exactly midnight.

A figure was moving through the snow now, moving down the very path where Dab was waiting. Dab said, "Damn!" It was a cop approaching him. At least, Dab thought, he can't believe I'm some old masher, not on a night like this. As the cop drew closer, Dab recognized him. Ferguson, a beat man from Mercer Street. Dab had visited young Walters at the precinct house and knew many cops there.

Ferguson said, "Evening, Mr. Dab. Fine night you chose for a stroll in the park."

"I love snow," Dab replied weakly. Oh, go away, he prayed. *Get away from here. Go on before Abner comes, you fool.*

"Terrible thing about the lieutenant," said the cop. "I hear Detective Walters is taking it pretty hard."

"Yes," said Dab. "I understand they're going to give him a vacation, a rest."

The cop nodded. "He needs it, I guess. They'll get the guy. They always get cop-killers. Always. Romano's on it. So is old Sansone himself. Those two, they're tough. They'll get him. Cop-killers never get away."

"No," said Dab. Vaguely, through the snow and darkness he saw another figure approaching.

Ferguson said, "You'd better get home to your fire. It's no night to be out, not for anybody but dumb cops. Fact is, if I didn't know you I might think you were up to something, being out on a night like this."

Dab attempted a laugh. The other figure was moving closer, coming on to the path. "I just like the snow," he said. "I won't disturb the peace, Ferguson. Good night."

"Good night, sir," said the cop. He moved away with a maddening slowness.

But the other figure wasn't Abner after all. The man was short and chubby, wore a light-colored camel's hair coat and a beret. He was leading a cocker spaniel on a leash. The cocker kept getting snow between its toes and holding up its paw in mute appeal to its master. When the little man reached Dab's

70

side, he paused deliberately, took out a cigarette, said, "Excuse me, could I have a light?"

Dab cursed under his breath. He brought forth matches. He never used a lighter. He thought the fuel made a good cigar taste bad.

As the flame flared up the chubby man said, "Don't I know you?"

Dab shook his head. "I don't think so."

The man inhaled, snapped his fingers. The dog began to jump against Dab's leg, pawing and whining.

"I've got it!" said the little man. "You're an actor, aren't you? Seen you on the stage and television."

Dab said, "I didn't know my face was so familiar. I'm flattered."

"J. Dabney Ashton! That's it, isn't it?"

"That's it," said Dab.

"Down, Danny," the man said to the dog that was making frantic love to Dab's leg. The little man looked Dab full in the face. "I see you kept your date with the three old men who have no wives," he said.

"Who are you?" Dab asked.

"The name is Ricky," the chubby little man replied. "Ricky Sperber. The dog that has developed such an affection for you is Danny. He's named for my alma mater."

"You mean there's a college called Danny?"

The little man named Sperber chuckled. "Short for Dannemora," he replied. "I spent twenty-four years there. I was in the cellblock with James Ellison. In prison I used to think about what it would be like to have a woman again and what it would be like to own a dog. By the time I was paroled my interest in women was purely academic, so I got a dog. Nice little fellow. Friendly. What the world needs is more friendliness. Will you walk west with me, sir?"

"Where are you taking me?" Dab asked.

"There's someone wants to see you."

"Where is he?"

The little man kneeled down and scraped snow from between Danny's toes. "This way, please," he said when he straightened up. "Do you ever read science fiction?"

"No," said Dab, "but I see a lot of space cadets at the television studios. They seem to dress in diving suits and pinwheel beanies."

Sperber said, "I held the illustrious post of librarian at my alma mater. I'm of a literary turn, you see. Escape literature

71

such as science fiction is staple diet for prisoner reading. Sound psychology. A kind of sublimation of the escape impulse. Instead of taking off over the walls, they take off in rockets for Venus. Characters in science fiction are always propelling themselves ahead in time as well as in space. They skip from the twentieth century to the twenty-fifth century by taking a pill or turning a crank. Good trick. In the older samples of the genre, such as H. G. Wells, characters propelled themselves backwards in time. That's what Abner Ellison has done. He has to hide out for awhile. So he's hiding out in another era. I'm taking you back into the 1920's sir." He laughed loudly. "I sound quite mad, don't I?"

"Mad as a science-fiction writer," Dab agreed.

Danny was again holding up his paw and looking appealingly pitiful.

"Excuse me," said Ricky Sperber, bending down. "Danny hasn't accumulated enough snow since my last ministration to be suffering. But he wants attention. Everyone wants attention, of course, and we adopt various poses to gain it. My generation posed as the sad young men, the disillusioned. We identified ourselves with characters out of Scott Fitzgerald. We championed free love and acute alcoholism to gain attention. When I was young I came to Greenwich Village to write the great American novel. Or at least the great American short story. Instead I drank and talked. I wound up an indicted murderer."

"A murderer?" asked Dab. "Were you guilty?"

"In a technical sense, I was," Sperber answered, rising. "We will cross the Square to the other side of the park and take the walk to the Fourth Street exit, if you please. About the murder. There is no accessory before the fact under New York law. An accessory before the fact is treated as a principal in a crime and punished accordingly. Perhaps I should have been a mechanic instead of a writer. I loved fast motor cars. I anticipated the present hot-rod generation. I had a chance to get a job as driver for a gang of rum-runners. It appealed to me. I wanted thrills. I thought, in my innocence, that this was life, that I could gather material for my novel. I never did anything but drive. I didn't even own a gun. But one day we ran into cops and one of the boys got trigger-happy. The great Lenny Fassio was a member of the gang. He was just a punk then. He wasn't with us when the cop was killed."

Danny was putting on his act again, but Ricky Sperber jerked the leash impatiently. "Come along, now," he said.

72

"You can carry a good thing too far, you know." Danny reluctantly responded to the leash, limping dramatically. "About the cop," Sperber continued. "It was a senseless killing and we were caught. I was lucky in a way. The other three got the chair. I was allowed to cop a Murder Two plea. They gave me life. I may say I served the best years of my life. Two dozen of them to be exact. Still, I got a break. Cop-killers seldom get a break, you know. Even the ones who are principals in a purely technical sense. Mostly only very tough men with gun raps go to Dannemora. Neither Jim Ellison nor I belonged there. But we shared a cellblock and our memories and our hopes for many years. Jim died before I was finally released last year. He might have been paroled except for the fact he could not resist the raw alky that the trusties and even some of the screws peddled to the inmates."

They had reached the Fourth Street exit of the park and Sperber finally knelt down again to answer Danny's anguished whimpering. "I wonder if there's such a thing as overshoes for dogs?" he said. As he busied himself removing snow from Danny's paws, the little man went on, "I was paroled after three unsuccessful tries. It takes the law a long time to forget when a cop is killed. I looked up Jim Ellison's son. I doubt Abner has ever mentioned me to you. He doesn't like talking about his father or anything connected with him. It makes him bitter."

"No," said Dab, "he never mentioned you to me."

"Abner was very good. He got me a job as chauffeur for one of his employers, Mr. Holmquist. When Abner found himself in trouble, he looked me up, and I have hidden him in another decade."

The little man rose, said, "We walk south on MacDougal Street."

Dab said, "I take it the 1920's must lie south of here."

"Exactly," Ricky Sperber answered. "Did you ever hear of Gipsy May Daroff?"

"Lord, yes," Dab replied. "I knew her twenty-five or thirty years ago when I could still play juveniles if I had to. She used to operate a speakeasy on Minetta Street. It had a most delightful name. 'Gipsy's Cosmic Tea Room.' Only the stuff in the teacups wasn't tea. It was Prohibition booze. Don't tell me she's still alive?" `

Sperber nodded. "Very much alive," he said, "and she still operates a speakeasy on Minetta Street. In fact, it never closed."

73

"I thought those swanky after-hour bottle clubs uptown were the only speaks left in New York," Dab said.

"By no means," Sperber declared. "This very neighborhood is full of speaks. They're in the back rooms of little fruit stores, candy stores, barber shops. The Italians in the neighborhood like a cozy atmosphere when they drink and they have no respect at all for Internal Revenue. But Gipsy's place is just the same as ever. The old bohemians still go there, the ones who haven't succumbed to delirium tremens or cirrhosis. Macey Reed, the white-haired young prodigy of poetry back in the early twenties, is a fixture there."

"I occasionally see the poor old fellow trying to peddle hand-written copies of his poems on street corners," Dab said. "He was a great lyric poet once."

"Once," said Ricky Sperber. "What a wonderful place Once is. It's the only place you ever talked about or heard about in prison—Once. I consider Gipsy May a public benefactress. She provides a Once to which beat-up, boozy has-beens can retreat and become young geniuses again for a little while."

They crossed the street and turned up Minetta Lane. Danny was again demanding attention, but his master informed him sharply that he could wait until they reached their destination. They turned left into Minetta Street which bent into a perfect V exactly at its middle. At the recess of the V Ricky Sperber opened the unlocked door of a very old house. He reached high to ring the bell of a first-floor apartment.

They were surveyed through a peephole. Then Gipsy May Daroff opened the door. She was a plump and wrinkled caricature of a John Held flapper. She wore her gray hair in a boyish bob. She smoked a cigarette from an absurdly long holder. Her skirt hung above her knees and the waistline of her dress began only a few inches above the border of the skirt.

"Hello, Ricky," Gipsy May said cordially. She closed the door behind them, bolted it, discovered Dab. She threw her arms around him and screeched happily.

"J. Dabney Ashton!" she exclaimed. "Ricky told me he was bringing you, but I'd have known you anyway. You haven't changed a bit, only your mustache bristles more, I think. Darling, did you know I used to be in love with you? It must have been five or ten years at least since you were here."

"Nearer thirty years, I'm afraid," said Dab.

"Really?" said Gipsy May, with a fine contempt for time. "Well, anyway, you're here again, so let's have fun!"

Gipsy May gestured toward the few customers in the room,

74

most of whom were drinking from teacups and looking disconsolate. "The same old crowd," said Gipsy May.

"Crowd," thought Dab, was something of an overstatement. A wild-eyed man with a beard that hung down to his chest stood by a pot-bellied stove. Dab recognized the man as Macey Reed, the poet who had outlived his time. Reed appeared to be conversing with the pot-bellied stove. He pointed an accusing finger at the stove, cried, "Fascist!"

"Dear Macey," said May fondly. "He's always accusing my poor stove of being a Fascist or a Nazi or something. Maybe because it's fat like whatshisname, Goering." She shook her head. "Sometimes I think Macey drinks a little too much Pernod. It's the nearest thing to absinthe he can get. They don't let them make real absinthe any more, you know, because it comes from worms."

"Wormwood," Ricky Sperber corrected her.

"Really?" said May. "I always thought they made it out of worms. Anyway, Macey says he has to have absinthe because all the decadents like Verlaine and Baudelaire and Rimbaud drank it. I stock Pernod especially for him."

A chubby little woman with close-cropped white hair advanced on Dab. She was clad in a loose dress that seemed to be made of an India print. Barbaric metal jewelry clanked on her neck and arms. She said, "I hear you're a famous actor. Perhaps you'd like to see my new play when it's finished. Did you see *Spring Blossoms* when it was on Broadway? I'm Alma Trent. I wrote it, you know. But there was some argument with the Shuberts about the theater, I never quite understood what."

Dab could remember no play called *Spring Blossoms*. When Miss Trent moved away, Ricky Sperber informed him the play had run for four days in 1926. Macey Reed discovered the new arrivals, regarded them covertly for a minute. He started toward Dab holding out a sheet of yellow foolscap. He hesitated doubtfully, tugging at his beard. The old poet reminded Dab of a bashful child at a party. With typical childishness, he covered his embarrassment with bluster. Thrusting the sheet of yellow foolscap at Dab, he said, "Are you a Philistine who squanders his money on gawds and bawds, or will you buy my poetry? Written by hand and signed. One poem by a genius for a dollar, the price of two cups of absinthe!"

Dab smiled, accepted the yellow foolscap and gave Macey Reed a dollar. "May the absinthe inspire you to greater flights of poetic fancy," he said.

75

The poet obtained his cup of absinthe and returned to his belaboring of the pot-bellied stove.

The poem was little more than a phrase.

The new moon is a slender, shining scimitar,
Dangling from the girdle of a warrior in sable armor.

"The old boy's still a phrasemaker," Dab said to Ricky Sperber. "He hasn't lost his gift for imagery."

Sperber read the lines and chuckled. "Poor Macey," he said. "He's plagiarizing himself. This is from *Dreams and Demons,* first published during the administration of Warren Gamaliel Harding."

Sperber said to May, "Has our young friend arrived?"

May said, "That handsome boy with the long eyelashes who came here last night? I love men with long eyelashes! Yes, he's here. He said you wished to be private so I put him in the back room. That's where my anarchist group used to meet and plot things, though they were quite harmless, I'm sure. I don't think anarchists are fashionable any more, are they? Everybody seems to be Republican or Communist nowdays."

She pushed aside a curtain and led them to a small room in the rear. Abner Ellison sat alone at the single round table.

Ellison said, "Mr. Dab! I'm so glad you could come."

Dab said, "Didn't you know I'd come, Abner?"

Ellison nodded. "Yes," he answered, "you've always come when I've needed you."

May took their orders for drinks. She served the drinks in teacups, a relic of the early Prohibition era that amused Dab greatly. Gipsy May Daroff had found the giddy 1920's to her liking and she had managed somehow to stand still in time.

When the speakeasy proprietress left the room, there was a long, strained silence. Both Dab and Abner seemed to wish to speak. But neither wished to speak first.

Danny tried frantically to crawl into Dab's lap, his eyes moist with affection and his paws wet with melting snow.

Ricky Sperber was merely an interested spectator. He sat twirling a little beaded key chain in his hand.

Spinning around on the end of the chain was a charm, a white rabbit's foot.

13

"You're in trouble, boy," said Dab. "What can I do to help you?"

Abner Ellison said, "I didn't kill Uncle Phil. I didn't kidnap Pat. You know that, don't you?"

"Of course, boy. Of course I know that."

"So why am I in hiding?" Abner asked the question that Dab had not wished to ask. "If I don't stay in hiding—or go to the police and confess the crime—Pat Linton will be killed. The one—or the ones—who've got her mean business. They'll stop at nothing. I'm the only chance she has."

"You know who they are?" asked Dab.

Abner said, "I think so. I think I do. But I can't prove it. If I even tried to prove it, if I even showed myself and got arrested they might kill her."

"It's Lenny Fassio's mob?" asked Dab.

Abner Ellison shook his head. "I can't tell you," he repeated. "I can't risk the slightest slip. It's Pat's life, Mr. Dab, and I love Pat."

"Pat was going to marry Allan Walters, Abner," said Dab. "She accepted him the night that Phil was murdered."

Abner said, "Even if she was, I love her. I have to save her life. You can see that, can't you, Mr. Dab?"

Abner pushed dark curls back from his brow, said, "I even hesitated getting in touch with you. But then I thought of a message that no one but you could understand. I had to know what the police were doing, know more than would be printed in the newspapers, so I took a chance. It wasn't such a big chance. If you'd been followed or if there were anything suspicious, Ricky would have noticed. He had you under observation for quite a while before he approached you, I suspect."

Sperber said, "The years spent in prison at least teach you a certain amount of guile."

"I'll tell you as much as I can of what happened last night," Abner went on. "There are certain things I can't tell you, for safety's sake. I spent the evening with Uncle Phil. Pat was out on a date with Al Walters. Uncle Phil and I discussed a very important matter. I can't tell you now what we discussed."

"The police think you talked about the numbers racket and the bribery of cops," Dab interrupted.

"That's one of the things I won't discuss with you or anyone, for Pat's sake," said Abner. "Anyway, I got up to leave a little before eleven. Uncle Phil walked a piece with me. It was after eleven when we parted. I stopped off at a bar and had a beer or two. Then I went to my room."

Abner told Dab of seeing the shadowy figure outside the hotel. He said that he had thought Pat might call him when she returned from her date with Walters but that when the phone rang there was no one on the line. Then the vagrant had delivered the anonymous letter at the hotel. Abner took the note from his pocket. "When I'd read this I called the Linton house and got no answer," he continued. "I knew that Ricky stays here at Gipsy May's place late every evening. He'd brought me here several times. So I took a cab and came down here and found him. I had a gun, a war souvenir. It wasn't licensed and I didn't want the cops to find it. I threw it out of the cab window on the way downtown."

Abner handed the note to Dab.

Dab took the piece of paper. It was one-half of dime-store note paper that had once been folded. The paper was jagged where the sheet had been torn off. It was crumpled. Dab looked at the paper a long time. It was exactly like the paper on which the note instructing him to join the three old men had been written. Finally he read the message, which was printed in pencil.

"Linton has been murdered. We have Pat Linton. You will be suspected. Unless you disappear at once—right now—the girl will be killed. Go hide now and stay hid or the girl dies. We mean business. Destroy this note."

"The only instruction I didn't follow was to destroy the note," said Abner. "I wanted you to see it. It's not very convincing, of course. The police wouldn't take it as evidence of my innocence. I could easily have written it myself and paid the bum to deliver it. I see even you're a little suspicious," he added, smiling. "It's the paper, isn't it? Well, my note to you was written here last night, or early yesterday morning to be exact, and Gipsy May didn't have a piece of paper in the house. She doesn't even write out checks for the customers. Just remembers their bills, or takes cash when she serves 'em. For once, Macey Reed, who always has that foolscap pad with him, wasn't around. I did have stamps, including a special

78

delivery, in my wallet and May finally managed to find one envelope at the bottom of a drawer, so I tore the piece of paper I had apart, used the blank sheet and wrote you. Ricky went right out and mailed the letter."

Dab looked relieved. The similarity of the two pieces of paper with the jagged edges had troubled him.

"Where are you staying?" asked Dab.

Abner hesitated. "I guess I can tell you that," he said. "I'm staying with Ricky. He has a little cold-water flat not far from here. I shouldn't compromise a man with a record, but it's hard to find a room without exposing myself to cops. I can hide in Ricky's place, lay low, but I'll have to move out as soon as possible."

"Nonsense," said Sperber. "You're Jim's son. You can stay as long as you need to. No one knows about our connection except the bosses at the office and they would never suspect I'm hiding you."

Dab said, "Boy, you can go to the cops quietly. They'll protect Pat. They'd listen to your story, read that note. That's the way of helping Pat. Her kidnappers don't have to know."

Abner shook his head. "They'd know," he declared. "They'd know the minute I went to the cops. You don't know how involved this thing is. The cops, especially old Inspector Sansone, suspect me anyway. A detective—he's a patrolman now in the sticks—put the finger on me as the man who paid him off for Fassio! I never even saw the man, Mr. Dab! But I found out about what he told Sansone through Uncle Phil and Al Walters."

Dab said, "Abner, did you know that Pat was going to accept Allan Walters' proposal that night?"

Abner Ellison was silent a long while. Finally he said, "I don't think I'm going to answer that. That's one of the things I can't discuss right now. I'm sorry, Mr. Dab." He smiled wryly. "If I did know, it would be a good motive for murder, wouldn't it? But why wouldn't I have murdered Walters?"

"The police have an answer for that," Dab said. Then he told Abner of everything that had happened since the murder. Abner interrupted him once. He said, "I think you ought to know this. Uncle Phil didn't trust old Inspector Sansone too far. Like a lot of tough cops, the inspector took a lenient view of what he considered harmless graft."

"Sansone," said Dab as if the name were gall in his mouth.

When Dab finished his story, Abner said, "It's in those cards, Mr. Dab. The murderer's name is in those cards, and it isn't my name. It can't be. Uncle Phil was a clever man.

79

He was resourceful. He left you a puzzle to solve. You've got to solve it. For Pat's sake. For my sake, too. I'm completely helpless. All I can do is hide."

Dab sighed. "God knows I've tried," he declared. "And I'll keep on trying, of course. As I told you, I even had an architect take a look at the cards."

"It's funny about that tower he saw," said Abner. "You remember the story you used to tell Pat and me about the princess in the tower? Pat was always the princess. She loved that story." Again his mouth twisted into the wry grin. "If the cops knew about that story and Pat was found in the tower, I suppose it would be more evidence against me," he added. "Psychiatrists could probably make something of that."

Macey Reed's poem was on the table. Dab glanced at it. He said, "Our Mr. Reed is quite an imagist. Maybe I should take him over to the hotel and determine what images he sees in those cards. But I have no Pernod. Only Bourbon."

Ricky Sperber laughed. "Poor Macey never sees but one thing any more," he declared. "Most alcoholics see snakes. He sees Fascists. I saw him waving an accusing finger at Garibaldi's statue up in the park the other day and shouting, 'Fascist scum!' at the old boy."

"Well," said Dab, "if the fine theory my architect had about the tower hadn't proved untenable, we'd have the Commies involved already. They're supposed to be holding the Mad Hatter prisoner if they haven't shot him."

Sperber said, "Puzzle books were among the literature considered harmless enough for the Dannemora library. I became quite a puzzle addict while I was in stir. Maybe I should have a look at those cards on your mantelpiece. Also, I like good Bourbon."

"Unless you don't wish to leave Abner alone, why not come up right now?" Dab invited.

"It's better for Abner and me to go home separately anyway," Sperber said. "He has a key. But first I'll go out and scout around to make sure the coast is clear. If it is, Abner can leave. We'll wait for a few minutes."

Danny had managed to climb up in Dab's lap and was licking his face with an enjoyment that seemed to verge on the lascivious. There was adoration in his swimming cocker eyes and his bushy tail spun like a whirligig in a hurricane. Dab stroked the dog, smiled at Abner.

"It's going to be all right, boy," he said. "We'll solve the damn thing somehow."

80

When Sperber returned, his face was troubled. "I'd bet my beret nobody followed us," he said. "But there's a character standing in a doorway across the street I don't like. He's not one of the bums who slink in doorways to drink Sneaky Pete, either. Gray hat, dark coat with collar turned up. Big guy."

They waited for ten minutes. Then Sperber reconnoitered again. "He's gone," he said, when he came back into the room. "It wasn't anybody that concerns us, I guess. You can dust, kid. But be careful. Go straight home and don't stand under lamp posts."

As Abner rose, Dab asked, "When will I see you again?"

"You and Ricky arrange how to keep in touch," said Abner. "He'll know where to find me."

Dab squeezed the young man's hand. "I'll get it, boy," he declared with an optimism he did not feel. "Don't worry."

"Try hard, Mr. Dab," urged Abner. "Try hard for Pat's sake." He laughed. "You know something? I'm not much of a drinker, but right now I'm half stiff. I only had a couple here, but there was a bottle at Ricky's and I drank a lot of it before I came. I'm going to drink some more, too, so I can sleep a little, maybe."

Ricky Sperber and Dab had another highball in a teacup. Then they, too, left, much to the disgust of Danny, who had fallen asleep in Dab's lap. Gipsy May kissed Dab on the cheek and urged him to come back soon. As the door closed, they heard Macey Reed hurling epithets at the stove. "Fascist! Fascist swine!"

They could not find a cab that was vacant. Danny's foot trouble finally became such a nuisance that his master capitulated and carried him most of the way to the old hotel at the edge of the park.

As they entered the hotel, Madame Sorel regarded them impassively. She was still bending over her ancient ledger, adding endless figures. She said to Dab, "Someone has been calling. Every few minutes since about twelve-thirty. It is now two o'clock in the morning."

"Was there a message?" Dab asked.

The old woman shook her bright red hair until more wisps streamed over the chalky white forehead. "No message. No one I could recognize. An unpleasant person. A gruff voice."

"An odd hour to call," said Dab.

"Actors," stated Madame Sorel, "lead odd lives, I believe."

They mounted the stairs and entered Dab's rooms. Dab

81

built a fire and lit it, much to the delight of Danny, who stretched out upon the hearth and extended his cold paws toward the warmth.

Ricky Sperber sampled Dab's bottled in bond and approved it with a nod of his head and a smacking of lips. He sat for a long while contemplating the cards on the mantelpiece. On the hearth, the outstretched Danny made contented sounds.

"Make anything of 'em?" Dab asked at last.

Ricky Sperber shook his head. "Nothing very helpful," he replied. "They remind me of the symbols used by ancient alchemists."

"Don't tell me they teach alchemy in prison trade schools!" said Dab.

Sperber chuckled. "Strange men get into prison cells and strange books get into prison libraries," he replied. "We had three copies of Jonathan Edwards' Collected Sermons, for instance. And there was a history of alchemy. Fascinating. The book on alchemy, I mean, not the Reverend Edwards' sermons. I used to study the book a lot. I remember some of the symbols quite clearly. Take that first card . . ."

"In fingerprinting it's called an arch," said Dab.

"In alchemy, there's a symbol that resembles it," said Sperber. "The symbol for alcohol." He reached for a pad and pencil that lay beside the telephone, drew a hasty sketch. He handed the sketch to Dab.

Dab said, "The alchemic symbol seems to point out a drunkard as the murderer."

"Any tosspots among the suspects?" Sperber asked.

"Old Groscz, the watchman at the castle, is definitely a lush," Dab replied, "but he's hardly a suspect. I understand that Inspector Sansone is a two-bottle man when he gets going. And there's a little neighbor woman who hides bottles under her bed. But I can hardly imagine her blasting Phil Linton with a forty-five or kidnapping his granddaughter. Also, I doubt that Phil Linton ever wasted his time with such fascinating and esoteric matters as alchemy. Certainly he had no reason to believe I could interpret alchemic symbols, and he left the puzzle for me to solve."

Suddenly Dab began to laugh.

"This is getting a little too fantastic," he said. "Those cards point out a nine-fingered man. They point out a castle in a fairy tale. They point out such madly assorted Lewis Carroll things as poised serpents and walking sticks and corporal's chevrons. They point out an inspector of detectives. And now we have them as symbols of long-dead alchemists who sought

82

the philosopher's stone. About all we need is to have Kali, the Hindu Goddess of Murder, walk into the room, waving all four of her arms at us."

Kali, Goddess of Murder, did not walk into the room. But there was a knock on the door.

14

THERE WAS a knock on the door.

The knock surprised Gipsy May and the other occupants of the speakeasy. Gipsy May's customers didn't knock. They rang the bell. The bell, in fact, was Gipsy May's main protection. She had a poor memory for faces, unless the faces were those of young men with long eyelashes, and even those blended into a sort of composite, idealized dream face of the romantic young man she had always wanted for a lover and had never really found. She allowed anyone who rang the bell to enter her place. Her theory was that if a person knew where the bell was located, he must be an old customer. The bell was placed inside the door frame, high up on the right where no uninitiated person would ever think of looking for it.

Gipsy May stood for a moment looking about her helplessly. Finally she slid back the panel that covered the peephole. She clapped her hand to her mouth and uttered a startled exclamation when she saw the policeman standing there. A raid! After all these years! Why, she hadn't been raided since Prohibition, and then they always warned her in advance. It was just sort of a matter of form that the cops had to raid you now and then in these days. Of course the police knew she'd stayed in business without going through the bother of getting a license. Why, a cop from the Mercer Street station often dropped in for a drink when he wasn't on duty. She really did nothing wrong except avoid the license fee that she couldn't afford to pay at the prices she charged.

The liquor she bought wasn't bootleg. The tax on it was paid. She didn't even get it wholesale. She bought it at retail price at the corner liquor store. There had never been any trouble in her place. It was a refuge for people who weren't wanted in the more legal resorts and who would hardly feel comfortable in them. Macey Reed, for instance. Regular café

83

proprietors would never put up with him calling their bar stools and juke boxes "Fascists." Her customers were a little eccentric, perhaps, but they were really quite harmless.

The policeman was a young man. He said, "Don't be frightened, ma'am. I don't mean you any harm. I'm Officer Ferguson. I was here the other night with Patrolman Gaines, but I wasn't in uniform, remember?"

May said nothing. She still looked doubtful.

Ferguson gulped and reddened. He added, "I'm the one you said—you said I had nice eyelashes, ma'am."

May was fumbling with the latch. She said, "Eyelashes." She opened the door, said, "I don't like your coming in uniform. It doesn't, well, look right, you know. And uniforms always offend poor Macey, too."

That remark about his eyelashes had made Officer Ferguson feel pretty foolish. It had been hard to get it out. But he was a very ambitious young cop and he wanted to get into this place. It was a lucky break, running into J. Dabney Ashton earlier and connecting him up with Phil Linton and Abner Ellison. He'd done what he thought was proper at the time, but he had begun to wonder if he'd done enough. Now, through sheer luck, he might get another break, even though he had to walk a bit off his beat for it. It might be the break that would mean promotion to detective.

When the policeman entered, Macey Reed turned his attention from the pot-bellied stove and snarled at the new arrival. "I knew it!" he exclaimed. "The police state has arrived at last! Fascist! Gestapo!"

"Now, now, Macey," Gipsy May said placatingly. "This is a nice young man. He isn't going to hurt us. He has long eyelashes. No one with long eyelashes is ever mean, you know."

"I remember you!" declared Alma Trent. "My, but you're handsome in your uniform! I like policemen. So large and dependable."

Ferguson was painfully embarrassed but he was dogged. He said, "When Gaines brought me here the other night there was a plump little man wearing a beret at a table by himself. He had a cocker spaniel dog."

"Ricky Sperber!" cried May. "No, I will not tell you his name, young man. Certainly you're not going to put him in jail again? He was there a long time. And he never did anything anyway. Not anything really bad, I mean."

"So his name is Ricky Sperber and he's got a record," said Ferguson with satisfaction.

84

"You know his name?" asked May, astonished. "How did you find that out?"

Ferguson grinned. "We have our methods, ma'am," he said.

"He lives right next door to me on Sullivan Street. He just left here a little while ago," put in Alma Trent. "He and that actor he was with."

"J. Dabney Ashton?" asked Ferguson.

"How did you know *that?*" May inquired.

"Like I say, ma'am, we have our methods," Ferguson answered.

"My goodness," said May. "I don't care what you say about them, Macey, the police are awfully smart!"

15

THERE WAS a knock on the door.

The whisky that Abner Ellison was pouring into a glass spilled as his body lurched. Abner put the bottle down on the little table beside him, lowering it carefully. He switched off the one light in the small room. He leaned down and untied his shoelaces. He removed his shoes, sat tense as the knocking was repeated, louder this time.

Ricky Sperber's tenement flat was called a "railroad" because it consisted of three small rooms in a straight row, like railway coaches hitched together. The only room that gave on the hall of the house was the kitchen. Someone was knocking on the kitchen door. The kitchen was on the front of the house. The tiny living room where Abner was sitting was at the extreme rear, overlooking a fire escape and an alleyway. The room that Sperber used for sleeping quarters was between the kitchen and the living room. There was no light at all burning in the apartment now.

The knocking became a continuous, determined pounding that had a kind of urgent rhythm to it. Abner rose and walked softly into the bedroom on his stockinged feet. He felt his way around furniture and entered the kitchen. It sounded now as if the person at the door were determined to break the panel with his fist. Street lamps and electric signs cast a dim radiance into

85

the darkened kitchen. A straight chair stood beside the door. Above the door was a transom. The transom had been painted over, but in spots the paint had chipped away and little beads of light from the hall glowed through the panel.

Abner placed a stockinged foot on the chair, raised himself slowly, carefully. He was thankful for the cascade of sound that the knocking made, for the chair was rickety and it creaked as he put his weight on it. He pressed his eye to a tiny spot where the paint had chipped away, looked down. The young policeman loomed enormous in his greatcoat. He had begun to call out now to punctuate his knocking. "Anybody home? Open up, here! This is the police."

A door opened across the hall. An old man's voice said, "What's going on, officer? What's the matter?"

Abner climbed down from the chair. He made his way back to the rear room as rapidly as was possible in the darkness. On the way he picked his coat and hat up from a couch. In the living room he donned his coat and hat. He found his shoes on the floor, put them on, laced them. He started to raise the window of the fire escape. As an afterthought, he groped for the bottle he had placed on a small table. He found the cork, jammed it in the bottle's neck, put the bottle in the pocket of his overcoat. It was a cold night. He was going to need all the bottled warmth and courage he could find. He raised the window higher, stepped out on the narrow ledge of the fire escape and paused to lower the window again. The deep well of the alleyway gaped three stories below. Abner looked down. The distant ground glowed with a kind of dim phosphorescence that was the reflection of light behind the blinds of a few windows in the adjoining building. He could distinguish no objects at all in the hazy twilight beneath him. He knew that another cop might well be waiting at the bottom of the fire escape. But there was no other way out. No other way at all.

Abner felt for the railing of the ladder and began to descend the fire escape. The snow and ice on the railing thrust needle stabs of cold into his hand. Beneath the crusted snow rust flaked off into Abner's moist palm. His legs were shaky as they had often been in combat. His feet were unsure on the iron slats that were the ladder's steps. He descended into darkness. Wind-borne snow lashed softly against his face. The raw wind that sighed out of the darkness made his lungs ache. As he reached the landing of the second floor, his foot slipped and made a ringing sound against the iron platform. Abner froze motionless against the wall of the house, beside the window. A light had suddenly winked on behind the window's blind.

Abner flattened himself as close as possible to the wall, longing to melt into the masonry. He glanced sideways at the window, waiting for a head to appear. For moments he hardly dared to breathe. The blind remained down. Perhaps the occupant of the flat had not heard the noise at all. Perhaps he was a restless sleeper who had turned on the light to banish some figment of a troubled dream. Or perhaps he was telephoning the police.

The light went out again. Abner waited for seconds, the slow, slow seconds that seem loath to pass when a man is full of fright.

The final stage of the descent was the most dangerous of all. He did not know what might be waiting for him down there. And the last ladder, of course, was suspended high above the ground by counterbalances. It would descend only when he placed his weight on it. Abner knew that it would creak and rasp.

It creaked and rasped as he had expected. He seemed to float down as if he were descending in a parachute. As he neared the ground he was rigid, waiting for the brawny arms of a policeman to stretch out of the darkness and encircle him. He reached the paved area at last. He took one cautious step away from the creaking ladder. Something brushed against his leg and there was a howling fury of sound that surged and shuddered in the little courtyard. He had disturbed a sleeping alley cat. Abner stood statue-still, not even daring to back against the house. But apparently such tigerish caterwauling was no novelty in the dead of night in Greenwich Village. No windows were raised in the surrounding buildings.

Abner began to feel his way around the areaway, seeking an exit. Finally he risked striking a match. There was simply no way out. The building from which he had descended blocked him on one side. There was a door, but he did not even try it, for he did not wish to meet police inside the house. There was a door in the house across the way, too, but that was locked securely. To his right and his left were high board fences. He finally found a gate in one of the fences, but it would not open. It had been nailed shut on the other side. Abner had to force back bitter laughter. It was an irony of these old tenements that their fire escapes led only to a cul-de-sac. It was irony that he had been running since the night before only to reach a place from which there was no escape.

He stumbled into a metal object. It was a garbage can without a top. He placed the can against the fence and turned it upside-down. It was wobbly, but it supported his weight. Standing on it, he could reach the top of the fence with his hands. As he gripped the fence, he suppressed an outcry. Splinters of glass had been placed on the fence to discourage intruders. Abner had no gloves. He reached in his pocket and brought forth a handkerchief. He wrapped the handkerchief around his hand, brushed fragments of glass from the top of the fence directly above him. The glass tinkled as it fell to the ground. To Abner the tinkling was an enormous sound.

Abner pulled himself to the top of the fence, dropped immediately to the other side. As he did so, the garbage can was tipped over. It fell with a loud crash. A light went on in one of the buildings and a window slammed open. Abner lay on his belly, shielding his face with his arms. A woman's voice was screaming.

"Who's that? Who's that in the yard? I hear you!"

Abner raised one outthrust arm ever so slightly, peered out from under it. He could see the woman's face framed in the lighted window. It was a first-floor window, only a few yards distant from where he lay. The pool of light from the window lacked only feet of reaching him. The woman was young and husky and looked Italian. She leaned far out the window, still screaming. She wore only a low-cut nightgown. Her heavy breasts almost spilled from the scanty covering as she bent her body out into the yard.

Another window opened. A man's angry voice shouted, "Shaddup! Shaddup you crazy fool! People got to sleep!"

"There's a burglar in the yard!" the woman shouted back. "I heard him kick a trash can over!"

"Burglars! Trash cans!" the angry voice retorted. "It's only the cats, you crazy fool!"

Abner had shifted his position slightly. He could see the woman quite plainly now. She was bathed in light. Her eyebrows were thick and dark. Her screaming mouth was large. In her excitement she was heedless of her nakedness. The nightgown had slipped lower. Abner could see the dark splotches above the nipples of her sagging breasts. The man across the way was fully aware that the woman was scantily clothed. He yelled, "Go back to bed with your husband, you crazy woman! Quit doing strip acts for the neighbors in the middle of the night!"

The woman clutched at her nightgown. She forgot the burglar in her anger at the man. She screamed, "You dirty, stinking crumb! My husband'll pull you out of bed and beat you up, you dirty crumb, you!"

The window closed with a crash. The woman disappeared. The light remained on, flowing over the paved yard. Abner

88

waited a few moments more; then he began to crawl toward the house with the lighted window. He had spotted a narrow passageway beside the house. The house was next door to the one in which Ricky Sperber lived. The passage must lead to Sullivan Street. Abner crawled on his elbows and his knees, as the army had taught him to crawl, until he was at the very edge of the little pool of light that glimmered on the dirty snow. Then he rose and ran, head-down and crouching, for the uncertain sanctuary of the dark passage. When he reached it, he leaned against the wall, gasping for breath and trembling. At the far end of the passage there was faint light from the street and he knew that he had not reached another dead end. When he regained his breath, he began to brush snow and filth from his overcoat and trousers. He had forgotten the bottle in his pocket. He found it was not broken and he drew it out and drank from it. Then he took a handkerchief from his pocket and wiped moist grime from his face and hands. There were tiny bubbles of blood on his palms where the glass shards had pricked him when he gripped the fence. Pressed against the wall and moving sideways, he began to inch toward the distant exit. Each time before he moved, his left foot reached out to seek any obstacles that might impede his progress. The sound of the crashing garbage can still rang in his ears. At last he reached the end of the passage.

He moved his head slowly to the side until the street came into view. He ducked back quickly. He had seen a policeman standing in front of Ricky Sperber's house. He thought it was the same policeman who had pounded on the door of the flat. He moved back into the darkness a few feet. Then he crossed the narrow passageway and flattened himself against the wall of Ricky Sperber's house, his eyes riveted on the narrow segment of street at the mouth of the passage. Long moments crawled by. At last the figure of the policeman appeared briefly at the head of the passage, moved out of sight, walking south. Abner shielded the luminous dial of his wrist watch with his maimed right hand. He had decided to wait two full minutes before venturing out into the street. That should give the cop time to walk some distance. The jittering sweep hand that marked the seconds appeared to lurch forward with such maddening slowness that Abner pressed the watch to his ear to make sure it was ticking. When the two minutes were finally up, Abner went to the head of the passage again and glanced quickly up and down the street. Across the street revelers from a night club were shouting for a nonexistent taxi. Far down the street he could see a policeman's back. The cop was still heading south. Abner ducked out of the passage and began walking rapidly northward. At West Third Street he turned left and headed west.

Midway along the block, Abner stopped abruptly. A little knot of people blocked his way. They were assembled around a drunken, dirty old man who lay upon the soot-speckled snow. There was blood on the old man's face. Labored breath wheezed through his gaping, bloodied mouth. Abner turned to cross the street. A green and white police car drew up to the curbing directly in front of him. Abner moved away hurriedly in the direction from which he had come, as uniformed policemen dismounted from the car within feet of him. Then glaring light blinded his eyes. Another prowl car was shrieking to a stop. The old vagrant, who had known a lifetime of neglect, was suddenly the object of lavish municipal attention as he lay dying.

Abner stood stone-still for a moment. He knew he was about to panic. There was a police car on each side of him, policemen shoving the bystanders back. *No place to run*, he thought. I wonder if it was like this with my father, too.

He was in front of a doorway. The doorway seemed to lead to a cellar drinking place. Drinking in cellars is a Greenwich Village custom. Abner descended steps and pushed the door open. There was a small lobby and then another door. This was a noisy resort. Abner could hear shrieking laughter, shrill conversation, snatches of a song through the second door.

Abner opened the second door. The interior of the drinking room was softly lighted and thick with smoke. Abner sensed at once that something was wrong. The minute he stepped into the dim room all laughter, conversation, singing ceased. The silence was so completely dead that it was frightening.

Abner glanced around him, seeking a mirror. He found none. He had vaulted a fence and a splinter had ripped a small tear in his coat. He had lain on his belly in the snow. But he had brushed himself off and soaked clothing should not be so startling on a snowy night. There were small lacerations on his hands, but his hands were thrust deep into his pockets. He could not account for such a reception, for the awed silence that greeted his appearance in a barroom. The wild thought came to him that his photograph as a wanted man might have just been flashed on a television screen, but he saw no television set in this place.

There were perhaps a dozen men at the bar. There were no women. The men had each looked full into his face when he entered, then they had rapidly averted their heads and had

90

stood staring into their drinks. Only the bartender continued to gaze at him. The bartender was a plump, rosy young man with the cherubic, freshly scrubbed look of a choirboy on Easter Sunday. The bartender continued to stare at Abner, his soft mouth foolishly agape.

Abner thought of turning around and leaving the place, but he could see the silhouettes of cops against the barroom window above his head. Abner crossed to a place at the bar, said "Rye with water chaser" to the plump and rosy young man who tended it. The bartender gazed at him wonderingly for another second, then turned to fill his order from the back bar. Abner was aware that the men on each side were covertly observing him with sidelong dartings of their eyes.

Suddenly Abner had to choke back laughter. For the first time he had noted the name of this place. He had read it in reverse on the window above his head. "GAY RENDEZ-VOUS." Any but the most naive would enter here forewarned. This was a "gay" joint, a place where effeminate men sought the companionship of their kind. The unheralded appearance of burly, snow-soaked Abner Ellison must have jarred the regular customers. Now that he was conscious of the character of the place Abner observed his surroundings more closely. The walls were hung with photographs of professional strong men, lifting bellbars, holding miniature globes above their heads like Atlas, assuming poses that flexed the muscles of their arms and legs and back to the fullest extremity. There was nothing very remarkable about the customers themselves. If you looked closely, though, you noted little things. Some had manicures that were too glossy, some had collars that gaped too wide, ties too exquisitely knotted, handkerchiefs that spilled too far from the pockets of their jackets. At the far end of the bar, facing the front, was a little man who was more flagrant in advertising what he was. He was middle-aged and his face was wrinkled from dissipation, but spots of rouge glowed on his cheekbones and his marcelled hair had obviously been dyed a shade of brassy gold. The little man had grown bold. He was staring openly at Abner.

As the bartender placed Abner's drink on the bar, the little man addressed him in a shrill voice. "Edgar," he called, "do you see that big, strong man the storm blew in here? Do you know that big, strong man? Do you, Edgar?"

Other customers tittered nervously. The blushing bartender said, "Now, now, Bobby, be nice."

Bobby wasn't going to be nice. "Do you know him, Edgar?" he persisted. "Do you think that big, strong man's a cop? Cops

91

have been coming into our clubs lately, you know. They raided Ethel's Place on Barrow Street just the other night and arrested the bartender. You don't want to go to jail, do you, Edgar, you big, fat thing?"

There was more tittering. Abner gulped his drink. The bartender said, "Now, now, Bobby."

Outside a city ambulance had arrived. They were lifting the old derelict into the ambulance. Cops and prowl cars were still around. Abner gestured for the bartender to refill his glass.

The little man at the end of the bar grew more brazen. He addressed Abner directly. "You, you big strong man!" he cried. "Are you a cop? Or are you just another butch?"

Abner swallowed the second drink. He saw the cops climb into the prowl cars, heard the ambulance clang away. He could feel the drinks. He'd drunk at Ricky's flat and at Gipsy May's place and he'd taken a swig from the bottle in the dark passageway and now he was drinking here. The whisky kindled a smoldering fury inside him, a fury born of frustration. His fear and his helplessness and his desperate wanting to be with Pat combined into a futile anger that made him long to lash back at the little man with rouge on his cheekbones.

His head turned, his dark, angry eyes sought the eyes of the little man.

Abner's deep voice drowned out the chorus of female tittering and giggling. He said, "You want to know who I am? I'm a man they want for murder, friend. My father was a murderer, too."

He turned from the bar and pushed his way through the door. The room was now as dead and heavy with silence as it had been when he entered.

Abner walked fast, the frozen snow crunching under his feet. He reached Sixth Avenue and let the first subway he found swallow him. He boarded a train without thought of its destination. The rumble and clatter of the subway made him think of the lumbering tanks that had plowed through the hedgerows and mutilated forests of France. He had been a soldier then and in the little villages young girls had thrown flowers at him. Now he was an outcast, running, running, and the young girl he loved was a prisoner and horrible hands were reaching out to clutch her and they said that it was all his doing. He sat slumped in the subway, his face hidden by the upturned collar of his coat. He picked up a castoff tabloid and read of the murder and the kidnapping and the clues upon the floor that old Dab Ashton couldn't solve. Then he read another

92

story dealing with a new investigation of police brutality and it was an unpleasant reminder that Sansone had a thousand cops on the prowl, hunting for him, Abner Ellison. They might be waiting at the next subway stop. Or the next.

He glanced up and for the first time he saw the little panel that announced the route of the train that he was riding. "Washington Heights," it read. Ironically he was heading home. Back to the street where he had grown up with a beloved little girl alongside him. Back to the scene of a murder. He saw the tiny cuts that the glass slivers had made upon his hands. "Back to the scene of a murder with bloody hands," he thought.

He got off the subway at a familiar station and hardly realizing where his legs were taking him he walked through familiar streets in the snow and darkness. Twice he paused in sheltered places and lit cigarettes and drank from his bottle. He was drunk now and he knew he was drunk and he didn't care at all. Nothing made any difference now.

At last he found himself outside the high, forbidding walls of the Mad Hatter's castle. Just across the street was the Linton house, the house that once had sheltered him with warmth and love and kindness. No one kept vigil at the house. It was dark and silent, befouled by the awful deed of murder.

He wondered vaguely why he had come here. Then he knew. He had come here because he wanted Pat and in his whisky-fogged mind the desire for Pat had become the only thing that mattered. His thoughts of Pat were all mixed up. She was a little girl with a freckle-spattered elfin face and sticky hands and he was saying to her, "You shouldn't eat so much jelly roll. You'll get a tummy ache." She was an eager, warm young woman whose breasts were pressed against him and she whispered, "Carry me up to my room."

Dab Ashton had said something earlier that evening, something about her being in this crazy castle. Long ago Dab Ashton had told fairy tales about Pat and the Mad Hatter's castle.

"The little princess," Abner murmured. "The little princess in the tower."

Abner Ellison looked down stupidly at his blood-stained hands.

16

THERE WAS a knock on the door.

But it couldn't possibly be a knock.

It was the middle of the night. It was the dead-still middle of a dark and snowy night and no one would climb up to this boarded tower room in a deserted castle at such an hour.

It couldn't be a knock. It sounded like a scratching. It wasn't anything human outside the door. It was rats in the wainscoting. Rats were horrid things and Pat Linton feared them, but the thought of rats came almost as a relief as she sat there beside the stove, huddled in a blanket, with the lamp casting a wan pool of light around her shivering figure.

She heard it again. It didn't sound like the noise that furtive, scurrying rats might make. It sounded like human fingers tapping lightly at the heavy door. Suddenly she knew for sure that there *was* someone outside the door. The hour didn't matter. They might come at any hour. This hour in the dead stillness of the night might be the best hour for them.

If they had come to murder her.

There was another sound, so faint in the thick silence that it was almost inaudible. A sibilant, hissing kind of sound. The sound of someone whispering.

For minutes she was frozen there immovably by cold and terror. But at last she removed her shoes very carefully, laid them down cautiously, soundlessly. She tiptoed to the door, praying no board would creak. She leaned against the door, her ear to the crack, holding her breath.

Someone was there. Someone was breathing heavily. Someone was tapping fingers lightly against the door. Someone was whispering. Most of the words were indistinguishable. A few she could hear.

"Suspect . . . Suspect tower . . . Drunk. Drunk to come . . . Don't want to . . . Don't want to kill. . . . Oh, God. Oh, God . . . Don't want to kill . . . Time. Mustn't remember time . . . Don't want to kill . . ."

She was racked with uncontrollable sobs. She sobbed inside herself. She made no sound.

94

17

As THE KNOCKING on the door continued Dab and Ricky Sperber exchanged glances. Danny roused from his toe-toasting nap and began to bark furiously despite his master's ssh-ing admonitions. And then the telephone rang.

Ricky threw up his hands, said to Dab softly, "You may as well answer the door. They've heard Danny."

Dab called toward the door, "Just a minute! Just a minute, please!"

Dab picked up the phone, Madame Sorel said, "There's someone coming up. A rude one. He .would not wait to be announced. . . ."

Dab said, "Thank you, madame, he's already here."

He went to the door, opened it a crack, looked into the angry, fire-red face of Inspector Sansone. The old man said unpleasantly, "You keep late hours."

"You pay late calls," Dab replied.

"You got a body hidden inside there as well as a dog?" the inspector asked. "Or can I come in?"

Dab opened the door wider. Danny stood barking at the old policeman, a small furry torrent of snarls and yaps.

"Your dog?" Sansone asked Dab.

"Mine," said Ricky Sperber. "His name is Danny and he doesn't seem to like you, sir."

"Who're you?" the inspector asked.

"The dog's master," replied Ricky. "Sperber by name. Unsuccessful writer by occupation."

Dab observed the old man. He obviously had been drinking heavily, although he held his liquor well enough. He reeked of alcohol.

The inspector turned to Dab. "I understand you like snow," he said.

"I've always loved snow," the actor replied, wondering what on earth this could mean.

"Like it so much you go walking in a snowstorm at midnight?" the inspector asked.

There was a sinking sensation in the pit of Dab's stomach.

He made a conscious effort to control his voice. "Don't tell me I'm so important that you have me followed on my midnight strolls," he said. "I'm flattered."

"We wouldn't tail you, mister. You're a law-abiding citizen who co-operates with the police. You told me so yourself, didn't you? A cop from Mercer Street happened to run into you. Cop named Ferguson. Said you were hanging around in the park and he thought you were suspicious until he recognized you as a law-abiding citizen. Said you met a man. He'd connected you up with Linton and Ellison, so he hung around and watched you from behind a tree to see what happened. This man you met had a dog. A cocker." Sansone gestured toward Danny. "Like this dog."

"Same dog," said Sperber innocently. "The friendship of Mr. Ashton and myself has blossomed from that chance meeting in the park and certain mutual interests. Furthermore, Danny likes Mr. Ashton. He is an excellent judge of character, this dog."

Sansone passed over the implied insult. The dog still snarled at him. "Ferguson's an ambitious cop. Wants to be a detective. Thought he might have something. But he just watched you out of the park, didn't follow you. He did go back to Mercer Street, went upstairs to the detective squadroom and told 'em about what he'd seen. The precinct boys didn't think it was important, but they called Homicide just in case. Boys there had instructions to call me at any time if there was a development in the Linton case. They finally caught me at my lodge, where I was attending a smoker. I called your hotel here to check. You weren't home. I kept calling. Finally I grabbed a cab and came down here. Old lady said you'd gone up, so I came up."

"Well, you're here," said Dab. "So have a drink."

The old inspector nodded. "No reason I shouldn't. Not on duty. And I like Bourbon. It's a man's drink."

Sansone accepted the drink, sipped it, said, "Were you two with Abner Ellison tonight?"

Dab phrased his reply carefully. "Mr. Sperber has told you the truth, Inspector. We met tonight for the first time. I was walking in the park. He was walking in the park. He encountered me and asked for a light. He is a devotee of the theater, and he recognized me as an actor he had seen. We got to talking and he invited me to a tavern for a drink. If Abner Ellison is in hiding we would hardly be likely to encounter him in a tavern. We drank together and I invited Mr. Sperber and

96

his delightful dog to my rooms for further conversation and refreshment. You came in. That's the only story there is."

Sansone said to Sperber, "Where do you live?"

Without hesitation, Sperber replied, "The Penton Hotel on University Place. It is almost as old but it is by no means as elegant as this hostelry. It is inexpensive, however, and the management does not object to dogs. By the way, sir, our host has forgotten the common courtesies. I gather you are the police, although we have not been properly introduced. Allow me to say that I can vouchsafe that everything my friend of an evening has told you is true. He spoke of this murder and of his indirect connection with it, so your visit does not surprise me, even though I am a stranger."

. "My name is Sansone," the old man said. "Detective Inspector Sansone. Give me another drink, Mr. Dab, and I'll take my leave. I'll buy your story this time. I'll accept you as a law-abiding citizen. But let me tell you this. If you see Ellison, tell him to come in. I promise nothing. But others may be looking for him and they're tougher than the toughest cops."

The inspector took his second drink in two swallows. He yawned, rose. "Cop-killings keep an old man up too late," he said. "I'll say good night."

Danny growled at the policeman as he left the room.

By mutual consent Sperber and Dab remained silent for several moments after the inspector closed the door. Danny continued his angry muttering. Finally he re-established himself beside the fire. Dab opened the door a crack. The hall was empty.

"Where do you really live?" he asked Sperber. "Where is Abner hiding?"

"In a tenement on Sullivan Street," the chubby little man replied. "It's best I don't give you the number. Then you can say truthfully you don't know where Abner can be found."

"Suppose the inspector has you followed? You'd lead them straight to Abner."

Sperber said, "I don't think I'll be tailed. I think he probably came straight from his smoker in a cab as he said he did. In that case, he's alone and if he tries to follow me he'll be easy to spot. But I'll take no chances. I did live at the Penton when I first got out of stir. A friend of mine still lives there. I'll go from here to the hotel. I know the night clerk. I'll tell him to send anyone who asks for me to my friend's room. I'll wait awhile. My friend stays up all night anyway and likes company. Then I'll leave by the back stairs through a side door only residents know about."

97

"How will I keep in touch with you and Abner?" Dab asked.

"Do you think hotel employees will listen in if I call or that your phone may be tapped?"

Dab shook his head. "Madame Sorel is a Frenchwoman. She believes in the inviolate privacy of the individual. If they tried to tap the phone, she'd have to know and she'd inform me. She has no awe of the police or anyone else."

"I'll call you, then. I'll have to find another place for Abner. The inspector knows my name. It seemed wise to tell him that much truth in case he made inquiries. He might possibly trace my connection with Abner through my employer. And he could easily get my address from the parole board if he started digging."

"You'll need money," Dad said, reaching for his wallet.

"No," said Sperber. "Not now. When it's needed I'll call on you."

"Take care of Abner," said Dab. "Take care of him for me. He's my boy, Sperber. It's strange I never married. I've always wanted a son, I think. And Abner's the only son I ever had."

Ricky Sperber waved a hand toward the cards. "You'll read the message Phil Linton left," he said.

"I'm not too sure," said Dab. "Not any more. This is the first time in my life I've fully realized that I'm growing old. I have no confidence in myself and I'm dreadfully afraid. I've swaggered and preened in the make-believe world of the theater and pampered myself with foolish hobbies that I tried to justify. Chess, I thought, taught mental discipline. Playing with puzzles made the mind agile, resourceful. Now the best friend that I ever had has called upon my small talents to avenge his death, to save two people that I love. And I feel completely helpless. . . . How is it, Sperber, that different people can see such different things in those little cards?" Dab asked.

Sperber shrugged. "Who knows what another really sees?" he asked. "A woman who's lovely to me might seem a hag to you. Are we sure that the color blind aren't the only ones who see true color, that the insane aren't the only ones who look on life in its true perspective? The eyes and the mind are tricky things. Few men see the same things or reason the same way. It requires the eyes and the mind both to read Phil Linton's message. If he was a simple man, it must be a simple message. Attack it that way."

"The simplest solution is the one the police have accepted," Dab said. "It means Abner Ellison is a murderer. Is he, Sperber?"

"Do you think he is?"

Dab said, "No, but I love him. He's my boy. Did he do it, Sperber? Could he have done this thing?"

Sperber rose. "He didn't do it," he said. "He's not guilty. I'm entirely certain of that, sir."

"Thank you, Sperber," Dab said softly.

Sperber put the leash on Danny, who had been rubbing himself against Dab and was reluctant to leave his new-found friend. At the door, the dog looked back at the old actor with moist, sad eyes.

"I'll call," said Sperber.

"Good-bye, my friend," said Dab. "And thanks for all you've done."

Dab went into the bedroom and undressed. He lay down on the bed. He was so tired that his body ached, but he knew he wouldn't sleep. When he closed his eyes, the vision of fingerprint symbols took form beneath the lids.

It was a fixation, his mind returning ever and ever to those forms. A man with a fixation could not think clearly. And more than ever before in his life he needed to think clearly now. He must rest, sleep, awaken refreshed to face the thing again. Cool air came through the open window, but his pajamas were damp with sweat. At last he dozed a little. Not for long. A loud ringing shattered the stillness of the room.

Dab was shaking from the shrill and sudden noise as he fumbled for the lamp switch. He picked up the extension phone beside his bed and answered it.

A muffled voice said, "Are you alone?"

"Quite alone," Dab answered.

"This is Ricky Sperber. Abner wasn't home when I got there. I've looked every place. He simply isn't anywhere. He's disappeared."

18

THE WHINING, sobbing, muttering thing was no longer outside the door of the round room in the tower. How long since it had gone away? Was it hours? Minutes? Pat Linton didn't know. She had lost all sense of time. The lamp and the stove still burned in the room. Pat sat huddled on the floor beside the door, her ear against the crack, listening. Listening for a sound that had long since died away.

She thought of the thing outside the door as being inanimate. It had sobbed and whispered, but her conscious mind could not accept it as being human. Some of the words she had understood. "Drunk . . . Time . . . Kill." Those words had been repeated time and again. It was some crazed and senseless thing, an enormity beyond her experience, that had been crouching there, an evil thing that whispered to itself and muttered to the darkness.

She had sat there listening, waiting. Waiting for the door to open. The thing had gone away. But she knew it would return. She was afraid to move, fearful of sleep. It would be coming back.

The room stank with the acrid odor of kerosene from the stove and lamp. She had no thought of turning off the light or heat. She was wasting fuel, of course, and when all the fuel was gone there would be only cold and darkness.

It might be better if the mad and muttering thing returned when all her fuel was gone.

The door would open soon.

It might be best if the door should open upon darkness.

She had no wish to look upon the naked face of Murder.

19

Dab tried twice to say something into the mouthpiece of the telephone, but no sound at all came from him. He swallowed hard, tried again and managed little more than a croak. His mind seemed completely dead. The news of Abner's disappearance, coming as it did when he was violently roused from fitful sleep, had numbed him. For a moment he was in a state of almost complete shock.

Ricky Sperber said, "Hello. Hello, are you still there?"

Dab found his voice at last. "Yes," he said stupidly. "I'm still here."

"Here's what happened," said Sperber. "I went from your hotel to the Penton, as I said I would. I told the clerk I'd be in my friend's room if anyone asked for me. I went up to

100

my friend's room. I stayed there maybe twenty minutes. No one asked for me. I went down the back stairs and out the side door. No one at all was around on the street, but Danny and I were lucky. We caught a passing cab immediately. I went to my house on Sullivan Street. My apartment was deserted. There was no note, no sign of any struggle. I waited a while, thought Abner might have gone out for cigarettes or something. I remembered how he said he was going to hit the bottle to make him sleep. I looked for the bottle. It was gone. I went back to Gipsy May's place. And here's the bad news.

"A cop had been there right after you and I left. He had been there before when he was off duty with another cop who seems to be a regular habitué of the place. If I'd known Gipsy May had cops for customers I'd have never taken Abner there, of course. But this cop had seen me and he was asking about me. Gipsy May let my name slip out. She says she didn't but Alma Trent says she did, definitely. And Alma herself gave him her address and said I lived right next door. My name's on the mailbox, so he wouldn't have much trouble finding my apartment. The front door is never locked. May says this cop gave his name as Ferguson. That's the same name as the cop Sansone mentioned, the one who met you in the park. May and Alma say he knew your name, anyway. I think he came directly to my flat while I was with you and took Abner in for questioning."

"Oh, God," Dab groaned. "Sperber, what are we going to do? Where would they have Abner? Mercer Street?"

Sperber said, "If they do, they won't admit it. We'd never be able to get to him. They can hold him seventy-two hours without a charge, and Sansone probably has him in the back room of some remote precinct by now, working him over. The thing we have to do is get a lawyer and a writ, if they've really got him. Logical lawyers are Burke and Holmquist, his employers, of course. Burke doesn't take such an active part in the firm any more. I drive for Holmquist. He lives out at Pineport, Long Island, and doesn't use the car much in the winter. Comes in on the train. I live at the house in the summer, but he keeps me on salary and I stay in New York in the winter. I'm kind of an errand boy at his office most of the time."

"Can you call him right away?"

"Not much point," Sperber replied. "No use in waking him in the middle of the night. He couldn't do anything

101

before morning. It takes an hour to get in from Pineport. He usually comes in on the nine o'clock train. I'll call him about eight."

Dab glanced at a little clock beside the bed. "It's barely four," he said. "That's four hours."

"I know," answered Sperber. "Four tough hours. But Abner lived through the Battle of the Bulge and that lasted longer. And there's always a chance the police don't even have him."

"Sansone said the others would be even tougher," Dab said bitterly. "Look, Sperber. Tell Holmquist I've got money and I'll pay him anything, anything he asks."

"He'll go to bat anyway," Sperber said. "He likes Abner."

"I'm going to try to find out if the police do have Abner, meantime," Dab went on. "I'll call Romano. He's not a cop like Sansone. He's a human being. He was Phil's good friend. And he seemed fond of Abner."

"You can try," said Sperber. "But I don't think you'll get much from the cops. Not at this stage. I know how they work. Especially in cases where a cop's been killed."

"I can try," Dab insisted desperately.

"Yes," said Sperber, "you can try. That's all any of us can do. If Abner *should* show up, I'll call back, of course."

Dab hung up the phone. He shivered. He crossed the room and lowered the window. He donned the purple Sulka robe. Once he had been very vain about the robe. Now it seemed to him a foolish conceit to cover his old bones with such rich material.

He went into the living room and paused long enough to light a fire. At this hour the old hotel was frigid.

He called Manhattan West. Lieutenant Romano was not on duty. They were cagey about giving out the lieutenant's home telephone number. To tempt them, Dab indicated that he might have some information about the Linton case. There was a long pause. Then they asked him to hold on. Suddenly he realized that they were going through the mechanical process of tracing the call. He hung up before the process could be completed.

Romano lived in the Bronx. There was no Bronx telephone directory in the suite, only the Manhattan book. Dab called information. Romano's number was listed and he obtained it readily enough. Finally Romano's sleepy voice answered.

Dab said urgently, "I want the truth, Lieutenant. Have the police arrested Abner Ellison?"

Romano said, "What makes you think they have, honey boy?"

Dab said, "Please. Just answer my question."

"If they have, I don't know about it," Romano replied. "I went off duty at six. Maybe if you tell me why you think he's been arrested I could make some inquiries."

"I had a phone call," Dab said vaguely.

"From whom?"

"I—I can't tell you," Dab replied. "I mean, I don't really know. It was just a voice. The voice said the police have Abner and that he needs me, then hung up." It was a poor lie, but it was the best he could produce at the moment.

Romano thought a minute, then he said, "If Sansone's got the kid and wants to keep him on ice, he'll keep him on ice. If my station knows anything, they'll tell me. But they might not know. I'll call them, anyway."

"You might try Mercer Street," Dab said. "I think maybe a cop from Mercer Street put him under arrest."

"Did the unidentified voice tell you that, too, baby doll?" asked Romano. "You're a rotten liar, Mr. Dab. All honest men are bum liars. But I won't ask more questions now. I'll call my own place and I'll call Mercer Street. I'll ring you back in a little while and let you know what gives. But don't let Sansone know I'm doing this for you."

"I won't. I won't do that, Lieutenant," Dab promised.

Dab sat by the fire. There seemed to be no warmth in the flames. He was shivering uncontrollably. He no longer saw the cards upon the mantelpiece. He had forgotten them completely. He was trembling, nauseated, physically ill.

He thought at last he saw himself for what he was. A futile old man. A posturing mimic. A man who had never lived or faced life's problems in any real sense. Instead he had led the lives of characters who existed only on a playwright's paper. He had no wife, no children of his own, and he would never have them now. Like a parasite, he had tried to foist himself upon Phil Linton's family, to bask in the reflected warmth and love and comfort of simple people in a simple house without assuming the problems and responsibilities such human relationships entail. He had thought that helping Abner through college, lavishing little store-bought luxuries on Pat, assuring Phil that his own purse was always open to his friend were enough to win him a place in their affection and esteem. But these things were not enough.

Phil Linton had left him a legacy. He had left him Pat and

103

Abner to protect. He had left him a murder to avenge. Phil Linton had trusted him and he was not worthy of the trust. Pat might well be dead by now. Abner might soon be led to the electric chair. And the murder of a good man remained unsolved.

He continued to excoriate himself.

Phil must have known how limited my talents are, he thought. He didn't ask much of me as he was dying. He used to chide me about the time I waste on chess and puzzles. All he did was ask me· to solve a simple, childish thing. And I can't do that.

Those cards up on the mantelpiece were no melodramatic cryptogram out of a tale by Edgar Allan Poe. They formed a simple message left by· a simple, practical man. Now the cards were mute testimony to the complete inadequacy of old Dab Ashton, the play actor, when he was faced at last with grim reality.

Romano called back at about four-thirty.

"If they've got Abner Ellison, neither Manhattan West nor Mercer Street knows about it," he said. "Or else they aren't telling. I'll be downtown by eight, and I may learn more then. I'll call you, or drop by your hotel."

Ricky Sperber did not call back all during the long night. Dab cursed himself. He hadn't learned the address on Sullivan Street or any phone number where Ricky might be reached. Later Dab stood at the big bay window and watched pale dawn spill over the snow in Washington Square. At some time or other he dressed himself. He had picked a rumpled suit at random from clothes put aside for the presser. The suit had a small check pattern. He wore the first shirt his hand touched in the drawer. It had a pin stripe. The fastidious J. Dabney Ashton never combined checks and stripes. He did not bother to shave. His jowls were unsightly with a gray stubble of beard. The usually proud mustache drooped disconsolately.

Eight o'clock passed and Ricky Sperber did not call. If Holmquist takes the nine o'clock and it takes him an hour to get to town he should be in by ten, Dab thought. It will take him a few minutes from the station to his office. I'll call Holmquist myself a little after ten. He was looking up the number of Burke and Holmquist when the phone rang. The desk announced Lieutenant Romano.

Lieutenant Romano took one look at Dab. When he spoke, his accustomed flippancy was gone. He did not call Dab "Baby doll" or "Honey boy." He said, "You look like a sick

104

man. I'd hardly know you. Your face is gray as dirty snow. You're taking this thing hard, Mr. Dab."

"I'm all right," Dab said. "I didn't get much sleep."

"If it makes you feel any better, I don't think the cops have Abner Ellison," Romano said. "I nosed around and asked as many questions as I could without letting on you'd called. Sansone may be holding out, pulling a fast one, but I don't think so. I saw him a minute. If he had Ellison, he'd be happy. He's not. He's got a bad hangover, in fact."

Dab said nothing.

Romano gazed steadily at the actor for a minute. Then he said, "I think you'd better trust me a little. I'll play along with you as much as I can. I know you were lying about the call, of course. You must have known where Abner Ellison was hiding and you must have known he'd disappeared from there. If Lenny Fassio's got him, he'll be killed. For Abner Ellison's sake, I think you'd better talk. This is too much for a man take on himself. It's murder, Mr. Dab. And kidnapping."

Dab stared at Romano vacantly.

"I don't know anything," he said. "I haven't anything to tell you."

The phone rang. Dab's reactions were slow. Romano reached the phone first, said, "I left this number in case there was a break."

Romano said noncommittal things into the mouthpiece. He hung up the phone. He turned to Dab.

"They've found the car that Abner Ellison reported stolen. Found it in a place called Pineport, out on Long Island."

20

She stirred. She wondered if she were back on the bed or if she were still lying beside the heavy door in the round tower room. She wasn't sure whether she was asleep or awake. There'd been a sense of movement, or she'd dreamed there was. Perhaps she was in an automobile again. She decided she was asleep and dreaming and didn't want to awaken.

She was stifling, but she didn't seem to care. There was an odor, a strong odor. Perhaps they were placing the rag down

105

on her face. Yes, that was it. They were placing the rag down on her face in the automobile and she would sleep. They wanted her to sleep.

She tried to force her eyelids open. They would not quite open. It hurt to try to open them. It would be better just to sleep on and experience the strange sense of motion, like riding in an automobile, that was a part of the dream.

If her eyelids should open, she knew what she would see.

She'd see a white rabbit's foot swinging to and fro in front of her eyes.

21

"THAT WAS Inspector Sansone in person calling me," Romano said. "He's going right out to Pineport. He would like to have me bring you there."

Dab was thinking of the call he hadn't received from Ricky Sperber and the call he wished to make to Holmquist. "I don't want to go," he said, and realized he sounded like a stubborn, petulant child.

"I think maybe you should go," said Romano quietly. "The inspector was very particular I should bring you along. I've got Grierson outside with a Department car. It's quit snowing and the roads shouldn't be too bad."

"Why does he want me?" asked Dab. Then a look of fear came into his eyes. "Did—did they find Abner along with the car?" he asked. "Have they murdered Abner, too, Romano?"

The lieutenant shook his head. "I haven't any reason to believe they found Abner, dead or alive," he told Dab. "The inspector just mentioned finding the car and wanting me to bring you out to Pineport. Why don't you want to go? Are you ill?"

Dab said, "I planned to call and engage Holmquist to represent Abner."

"Look," said Romano, "nobody can represent Ellison until we find him and charge him with something." He looked at Dab searchingly. "Funny you mentioning Holmquist," he said. "Holmquist is a boat enthusiast. He's got a place at Pineport. The town's a big yacht basin. Another prominent yachtsman owns a showplace out there. Lenny Fassio. Bought it through dummies, and now he's in his highly respectable neighbors can't get him out, it seems. Come on, Mr. Dab. Put on your coat. The fresh air will do you good."

Dab rose uncertainly, got an overcoat and hat from a closet. When he put them on, Romano regarded him with a strange look, a look that bordered on pity. "Aren't you going to wear a necktie, Mr. Dab?" he asked.

Dab put his hand to his throat, said, "Oh." He went into the bedroom, returned wearing a loosely adjusted polka-dot cravat. Romano didn't pay much attention to his clothes, except for keeping them cleaned and pressed. His wardrobe consisted mostly of blue suits, white shirts and solid-colored ties. But even he knew that checks, stripes and polka dots didn't blend too harmoniously, and he had always admired the quiet elegance of the old actor's appearance.

Detective Grierson was standing on the sidewalk beside the car, watching a snowball fight between kids in the park. He looks like a cop, thought Dab. All of them except Romano look like cops. Phil Linton didn't look like a cop, either. But the others, Sansone, Grierson, that meddlesome Ferguson, all the rest, they've got the same look, the cop look. It isn't just that they have to conform to certain standards of height and weight. It's something about the set of the jaw, the tightness of the mouth, the narrowness of the eyes. It adds up to a look of suspicion and cynicism.

As Dab climbed into the back seat beside Romano, he wondered if actors were cut to a pattern, too. Could you spot them on the street? Were they all like him, phonies who hid behind grease paint and fright wigs because they couldn't face up to the realities of living?

Romano said to Grierson, "We're going to Pineport, out on the Island. Know the way?"

Grierson started the motor. "Pineport? Sure. Not far from Jones Beach. Place there called the Blue Sunset owned by Pal Palladino, the orchestra leader. Nice place, built on piles, right over the water. Dining room's enclosed by blue glass so the sun off the water won't glare in the customer's eyes. Good seafood. Family and I eat there sometimes summers after a swim. Pretty expensive for a cop, though."

"It's the Blue Sunset we're heading for," Romano informed the driver. "They found Abner Ellison's car in the parking lot of the Blue Sunset. Place is closed in the winter, of course."

Grierson said, "No kidding? They find Ellison, too, maybe? Did Fassio chill him before he could talk?"

107

Dab winced. Romano said, "I don't guess they found Ellison. Inspector Sansone didn't say they had. We're to meet him out there."

Dab had never owned a car because he found the mechanics of driving irksome. But usually he enjoyed a ride in the country in someone else's car. Abner had taken him for rides in the disreputable old jalopy they'd found beside a place called the Blue Sunset. Those had been good rides. Abner always liked to explore the back roads. Sometimes they got completely lost. Abner kept an old army blanket in the car to serve as a lap robe. He wondered if the blanket were in the car now? Was there anything wrapped in the blanket? Was Abner's body wrapped in it? Or Pat's? He shuddered.

"Cold?" asked Romano. "We got a robe."

"I'm not cold," said Dab. It was a long ride, a long hour. The landscape was pleasantly monotonous with snow. Now and then they saw the water of bays and inlets. The water was cold and gray with a frothy crest to the waves. Once, far off, Dab saw a rust-colored tanker belching curly black smoke against the dun curtain of the winter sky. "We'll take a trip to Europe, you and Pat and I," he'd said to Abner when Abner was a little boy. "We'll ride to Europe on a big, slow boat and we'll watch the porpoises diving alongside us and maybe we'll even see a whale. And when we get to Europe, we'll take another boat down a river called the Rhine and we'll see a lot of castles, not like that silly one the Mad Hatter built across the street, but real castles, hundred of years old, where kings and dukes and barons lived."

"And princesses?" piped Pat.

"And princesses," Dab had assured her. "Beautiful princesses like Pat, with soft brown hair and little rings of freckles around their noses."

They had never gone to Europe, though, not the three of them. Dab had gone abroad before the war, when Pat and Abner were still in school, but he had not sailed the Rhine. By that time the Rhine was an unpleasant place that resounded with the *heils* of dedicated bullies and Dab imagined its ancient waters were polluted by the unthinkable refuse of the Nazi concentration camps. And later on Abner had gone to Europe on a different kind of boat, and he had left a finger there.

And now, through some mephistophelean miracle, the finger had returned to point and point like a mocking guidepost to a madhouse.

At last they reached Pineport. Fine homes and pretentious

108

yacht clubs were set well back from the road, hidden behind snow-fuzzed trees and shrubbery as if their owners resented outsiders even glimpsing their bastioned luxury. The shopping center of the town was lined with branches of New York's smartest stores. Even the groceries presented sleekly modernistic façades that reminded Dab of expensive beauty salons on Fifth Avenue.

They drove through the town and out to a slender point of land that jutted well into the water. A pointing finger of land, Dab thought. The Blue Sunset was boarded up, but even so it was a handsome structure that seemed bright and new and inviting. Beside the building was a large expanse of parking lot. Only two cars were in the lot. One was a Police Department car that had brought Inspector Sansone, Captain Haas, the fingerprint man, and other officers to the scene. The other car Dab recognized as Abner's battered Ford.

As soon as Dab stepped out of Romano's car, a dog began to bark frantically. A golden cocker spaniel escaped from an officer who was attempting to hold it in leash, leaped at Dab, whining a frenzied welcome as its tail spun like a top. The dog sniffed to make sure it was not mistaken, then tried to climb Dab's leg.

Inspector Sansone regarded Dab stolidly. "The dog seems to recognize you, Ashton," he said. "Do you recognize the dog?"

Dab said, "It looks like Danny, the little dog Sperber had in my place last night."

The inspector nodded. "It is the dog. I've sent an officer to call the SPCA and check the license number, but that's just routine."

Dab reached down to pat Danny's head. The dog let out a scream of pain. There was a cut and clotted blood on Danny's head.

Inspector Sansone said, "Step over here, Ashton, and look inside Ellison's car. Don't touch anything. Just look."

Dab tried to brace himself but he began to shake. "What —what's inside, Inspector?" he asked weakly.

"Come on, man, take a look," said the inspector roughly.

The ceiling light of the car was turned on. Captain Haas was already busy dusting the steering gear for fingerprints. The inspector pointed. "On the floor in front," he said.

A gold-cased lipstick was on the floor. On it was engraved the initials "P.L." Dab had purchased the lipstick case at Cartier's and had filled it with a rouge that Margot Lane, Pat's favorite actress, had recommended. It had been a birth-

109

day present. Beside the lipstick lay a little memo book, bound in worn leather and stamped in gold. The stamp read "Patricia Linton." She had kept it all this time. Abner had saved his pennies to buy it when he was very young.

Dab's voice was hoarse. "Did you find—did you find her body?" he asked.

"You think she's dead?" asked Sansone. "You think Ellison killed her, too? No, we haven't found her. We only found the car and what's inside it and the dog. The dog was inside the car. Shut in."

A black and white sedan marked "Pineport Police" turned into the parking lot, tooled to a stop a few yards from them. In the front were two uniformed men. In the back was a very old man and a very old woman. The man was bearded, wore a pea jacket and a soiled yachtsman's cap. The old woman was incredibly clad in a mangy brown fur coat and a sunbonnet.

A tall man with a weathered face stepped from the car. He wore a badge that identified him as chief of the Pineport police. He looks like a cop, too, Dab thought. They all look the same.

The tall man got out of the car, went directly to Inspector Sansone. "You Inspector Sansone?" he asked. "I'm Chief Alger, Pineport. You got here fast. Those two in the back of the car reported a strange auto parked here about eight o'clock this morning. At least the woman did. Said she heard it and another car drive up about five-thirty this morning. Wanted to report that and other suspicious happenings, but her husband's stone deaf and he claims she's always hearing things, so he wouldn't let her come down till he saw the car out there in the lot. It took us awhile to check the lists and find out it was a hot car. Even then we didn't connect it up with a homicide and kidnapping squeal till we called you people."

"There was another car," Sansone said. "Tracks in the snow are plain enough. Captain Haas will make moulages, but I doubt they'll tell us much."

"Those two in the back are town characters," he chief went on. "Old Cap Morton and his wife, Louise. Crazy Louise, we call her. They run a bait and tackle place and rent boats in the summer. Live in the same shack all winter. Palladino pays the old man something for keeping an eye on the Blue Sunset when it's closed, but he doesn't leave much in it, anyhow. You can see the Mortons' shack from here, down there by the old boathouse."

110

Alger pointed to a tumbledown structure at the water's edge. Sansone nodded.

"Ordinarily I wouldn't even bother you with the screwy story Louise has got to tell. She's crazy, but harmless. But since this is a cop-killing and a kidnapping, maybe you'd better talk to her." Alger beckoned to the old people in the local police car. The woman came trotting forward eagerly, the bearded old salt at her heels. The woman was hideously ugly. One eye was half-obscured by a obscene droop of the lid.

Good Lord, thought Dab. She belongs with the other hags around the cauldron in Act IV, Scene 1, *Macbeth*.

Crazy Louise began to sputter words at once.

"It was afore sunup this morning, I heerd them cars coming up. I heerd them plain. My old man's deefer'n a marlin spike and he couldn't hear a mainmast drop, but I heerd 'em and . . ."

"Hear as good as you do," the old man interrupted her.

"See him?" shrilled Louise. "He's a-reading my lips. He reads my lips and thinks he's hearing. Deefer'n an anchorchain, he is, the old fool, and I wish he was struck dumb, too."

"Hear as good as you do," the old man insisted. "Only don't hear things which ain't there to be heard. Don't hear no angels singin' or witches wailin'. I'll put you in the County sure if you keep a-hearin' things that ain't there to be heard."

"He's jealous," said the old woman, pointing to her eye. "He wasn't borned with the veil, like I was, so he's a poor believer and wants me in the County because I know what the wind says and I hear the drown-dead sailors shrieking. . . ."

"Just tell your story," the inspector admonished her.

"It was around five-thirty, afore sunup, give or take a minute," Louise declared wisely, " 'cause I got a alarm clock with magic numbers that shine out in the darkness like a angel's eyes. That was the time I heerd the cars come up. This old man was a-snorin' like a pig with its belly full of slops, so I shook him hard and I says, 'Git up, git up,' I says, 'the robbers have a-come to steal all Mr. Palladino's things and he's a payin' you good wages to pertect his place.' "

"Hear as good as you do," the old man declared. "Warn't nothin' to be heerd. You'll go to County, sure, you keep mutterin' about axes."

"Axes?" Sansone said.

The old hag nodded sagely. "Axes," she replied. "Mur-

111

derin' axes. The old fool wouldn't wake. Just made blowfish sounds. So I opened up the door. The moon was down and it was tar-pitch black and I couldn't see 'em then, or nothin' else. But I heerd 'em again. I heerd 'em down on the pier, by the old boathouse. That's when they got the axe."

"What axe?" the inspector asked impatiently.

"Our axe. I looked. It ain't nowhere. Old fool left it out when he was choppin' kindling wood. And the murderin' robbers got it. The ones what come here in the cars."

"How do you know?"

"I heerd 'em say. The water carries sound a long way off. I heerd this one say, 'What you goin' to do with the axe?' And I heerd the answer, too. The horrible answer."

"What was the answer?" the inspector asked.

Louise became coy. She wanted them to plead with her. She skipped the part about the axe, said, "Later on when the sun was up and he was hog-full of breakfast vittles, the old fool come out and looked, and there it was, the car, so finally we walked to town and saw the chief."

Chief Alger shook his head despairingly. "Tell them what you think you heard down on the pier, down by the boathouse," he urged.

She took her time answering, teasing them.

She said, "I heerd about the axe. Then one said, 'Git on inside.' Then the other said, "What're you gonna do to me?' he said. It was horrible."

Louise's husband shook his head. "Daft," he said. "Crazy-daft, she is. This time it's the County, sure."

"Tell us," said the inspector. "What did this man say he was going to do to the other man with the axe?"

Louise relished another delicious moment of tense silence. Finally she spoke, her voice portentous.

"He said 'I'm gonna chop your finger off!' And then I heerd a horrid scream. And then there was a shot."

22

THE FINGER. The pointing finger.

The police officers exchanged significant glances. Dab looked dazed. He stood there with Danny in his arms, stroking the cocker's silky hair.

Crazy Louise was fairly cackling with delight at the effect of her words. Her old husband was furious. "It's the County sure this time!" he flared. "Telling policemen lies about chopped-off fingers, you crazy old woman! They'll put leg-irons on you, mark my words! They'll chain you to a wall, they will!"

Sansone said to Chief Alger. "Did you investigate this? Did you find anything on the pier or in the boathouse to support her story?"

The chief jerked his head, indicating they should move out of hearing of the cackling old woman. Sansone, Romano and the other officers followed Alger. After a moment's hesitation, Dab walked toward the little knot of men, stilly carrying the whimpering dog in his arms.

Alger said, "Like I say, the old girl's nuts. Always running to us with stories about shrieking demons in the night. We checked her story about the car because her old man verified the fact a strange car was parked in the lot. The officer I sent out here took a quick look at the pier and boathouse, just in case. Nothing suspicious. If it hadn't been a homicide and kidnapping squeal, and a cop at that, I wouldn't even have bothered you with her wild yarn."

"A chopped-off finger," Romano said. "It could hardly be coincidence she'd invent a story about a chopped-off finger. I think we'd better take a look."

The chief said, "If somebody chopped a man's finger off, then shot him, he'd hardly leave the body lying around in a spot like this. One little shove and the stiff is under fifty feet of water."

Sansone nodded. "True enough," he said. "But we'll have a look just the same. There might be something down there."

The policemen, followed by Dab, headed for the pier that was bordered by the Morton's shack on one side and the boathouse on the other. Crazy Louise ran after them. Her husband shrieked, "Come back, you crazy woman!" but she pretended not to hear him. The old man, moving at a halting, rheumatic gait, followed his wife, cursing and grumbling.

The wooden pier was slick with ice. A cold wind blew off the water. The frozen surface of the pier itself was too hard to record an impression, but there were the footprints of two men in the softer snow of the ground that led to it. Haas, the identification man, warned them to steer away from the footprints. On the pier, stacked against the boathouse, was a pile of driftwood.

Crazy Louise reached them, panting hard. She pointed

113

a gnarled, trembling finger at the woodpile. When she regained her breath, she said, "There! The old fool left the axe there! And it ain't there now! You see!"

Chief Alger said, "They might have dropped the axe into the water, too, of course."

They went down a rude ladder to the boathouse. The door was closed but there was no lock. The interior was very dark. Grierson played a flashlight into the gloom. Two old fishing scows, caulked and trestled, had been stored there for the winter. Tarpaulins were lashed over them. Captain Haas took Grierson's flashlight, swept it over the floor. He motioned the others back. He knelt down. When he rose, he said, "There's a lot of muck on the floor. Oil spots here beside this trestle that just could be blood. Wood's so damp you can't tell at a glance."

"Grierson," Romano said, "tear off those tarpaulins."

Grierson went to work on the knots and fastenings. From the darkness back of him Dab heard Crazy Louise's screeching voice. "There's a dead man in the boat! There's a dead man without a finger!"

Dab stroked the dog. His hand was trembling violently. *Abner was dead. Abner was lying there beneath a canvas covering in a rotten old fishing boat. Or it might be Pat, brown-haired Patty, the little princess in the tower. One of his kids was in the boat, obscenely dead.*

Grierson was no seaman. He made long work of the knots, grunting as he labored. At last he had loosened the tarpaulin. He pulled it back. Haas flashed his light into the boat, stood on tiptoe, peered inside.

"Nothing here," he said. "Try the other one."

"This one's easier," Grierson said at once. In a matter of seconds he had the boat uncovered. The flashlight flooded into the boat. Grierson gasped, exclaimed profanely.

"This is it, Inspector," he said. "This is it, all right."

They crowded to the boat. Crazy Louise was fairly crowing with unholy delight at the discovery. Dab was sick. Sicker than he had ever been before in all his life. But he moved forward, too. Mechanically, his hand continued to stroke the whimpering dog.

The body of Ricky Sperber lay on the floor of the boat. He had been shot through the stomach. Ridiculously, the beret was still upon his head at a jaunty angle. A bloody axe was in the boat beside the corpse.

The middle finger had been severed from Sperber's right hand.

114

Chief Alger said, "Why, I know this man. He works summers as chauffeur for Mr. Holmquist right here in town. They say he's an ex-con. I think he did a murder rap."

Sansone looked Dab straight in the face. For the first time in his life Dab knew that he was hated. Men must look like that when they're about to kill, he thought. The old inspector continued to stare at Dab, but when he spoke, he spoke to Alger.

"He works for Holmquist, you say? He did a murder rap?"

"That's right," the chief replied. "I think he helped to kill a cop a long time ago."

The inspector continued to look directly at Dab. "So he killed a cop?" he said. "Do you know where he did time, Chief?"

"I heard they had him in the place the cons all call Siberia. Clinton Prison, up at Dannemora."

"Clinton Prison, up at Dannemora," Sansone repeated parrotlike. "They had James Ellison in Clinton Prison, up at Dannemora."

Finally Sansone spoke to Dab. He spoke very softly, but Dab thought he had never heard such menace in a human voice.

"You lied to me, Ashton," the old man said. "You lied to me last night. You've been lying right along. You know where Abner Ellison is hiding, and I'm going to sweat it out of you. You can consider yourself in custody, Ashton. We're going to have a little talk."

The inspector had moved a step or two toward Dab. The dog seemed to sense the menace of the old man, to smell it. He tried to struggle out of Dab's encircling arms, snarled furiously. Dab could think of nothing at all to say. He clutched the writhing dog.

All Dab said was, "Quiet, Danny. Quiet, boy."

The inspector turned to Chief Alger, said, "Chief, this is a local case, of course. It's your baby. But because of the Linton angle, we'd like to sit in."

"Sure," said the chief. "We're not too well equipped for homicide cases, even though Mr. Lenny Fassio did move out here a year or so ago. He's been very quiet since he came here. Just stays at home or sails his boat and doesn't bother anybody. I'll have to call in county help on this, anyway. I'd like your help, too, even if it's kind of unofficial."

"Fine," said the inspector. "If we co-operate, we'll get somewhere. We'll get somewhere pretty quick now, I think. I'd like to make use of your police headquarters, if I may.

115

Do you have a nice back room where Mr. Ashton and I can have a little talk?"

"Sure," said the chief. "We've got a fine back room. Hot and cold running water, even."

The inspector's chauffeur had gone off to find a telephone in order to check Danny's license tag, a task that seemed useless now. Haas and a policeman Dab didn't know remained behind with the local officer who had driven Chief Alger to the scene. Grierson drove Dab, Romano, Sansone and Alger into the town of Pineport. As they left the parking lot of the Blue Sunset, a weird figure danced and cavorted and shrieked at them. It was Crazy Louise, driven even madder by the excitement and her important part in it.

"I told you so!" she screamed. "I told you it was murderin' robbers who come here in the still of night! They'll come again and chop the fingers off my old fool husband with a axe!"

In this rich community, even the police station was a handsome building. It was constructed of white-washed brick on which snow-covered ivy grew in thick festoons.

The back room to which Alger led them was not an unpleasant place at all. It was comfortably furnished and winter sunlight streamed into it from a large window. Alger excused himself. He had reports to make of the murder, the medical examiner to inform.

Dab sat down in a swivel chair. Danny lay in his lap and went to sleep. Sansone, Grierson and Romano formed a circle around him. But there was no blinding light upon his face. Only the winter sun.

Cops, thought Dab. *They all look alike. Even Romano looks like the others now. They've all got the same grim expressions. They're all sadists, all of them. This is the kind of thing they wait for, live for, the kind of thing that gives them their sense of importance, power. Beating a man down. Making him tell them intimate, personal things he doesn't want to tell. Goading him, goading the dignity out of him. Degrading him. They love it. All of them love it. Even Romano loves it.*

Dab rubbed his hand across his chin. *I wish I'd shaved,* he thought. *I must look like some helpless vagrant they've dragged off the streets to bully.*

He caught a glimpse of the hand that was nervously stroking Danny's back. *My fingernails are dirty,* he told himself. *I don't remember a time before when I let my fingernails get dirty. Not since I was a kid.*

116

The old inspector stood directly in front of Dab. His face was apoplectically red. He was furious. He glared at Dab. His fists, the enormous fists, were clenched hard. *He wants to beat me,* Dab thought. *He wants to flail down again and again with those big, hairy hams, break my nose, blacken my eyes, knock the teeth out of my mouth. I can feel how hard he wants to hurt me, make me cringe, cry out.* The inspector didn't say a word. He didn't seem to trust himself to speak.

Detective Grierson was there, off to one side. His rank was very subordinate. He seemed to push himself into the background. He was very tall, heavy-shouldered. He looked from Romano to Sansone and back to Dab. His role was that of an interested spectator, ready to take a part if called upon. He was even smiling a little, enjoying himself.

Romano was first to speak.

Romano spoke calmly. Dab thought there was pity in his voice. *I was wrong about him,* Dab told himself. *He isn't enjoying this. He's a little embarrassed even, having me so completely at his mercy, as if I were naked, chained.*

Romano said, "Mr. Dab, I think you'd better tell us about that phone call you got around four o'clock this morning. That's a good place to start."

Dab tried to collect his befuddled wits. He decided he should tell them the truth. At least a little of the truth. Some things he must hold back.

They stood there waiting. Dab opened his mouth several times, but he did not speak. They did not urge him. They merely waited.

"I—I lied," he began at last. "I lied because I know Abner Ellison isn't guilty. I lied because he's my boy and he trusts me. I would keep on lying for him, but it's no use now. No use."

He paused, fumbled for a handkerchief, wiped sweat from his face. The handkerchief was soiled. Soiled handkerchiefs had always offended him. He looked at the handkerchief for a moment, then he said, "It began earlier than the phone call. I got a letter, a special-delivery letter. It told me to be in Washington Square Park, at a certain place, at midnight. I went there. Ricky Sperber came up to me. I had never seen the man before, but he knew me. He identified himself. He told me he had been in prison with Abner's father, that Abner had arranged a job for him as Holmquist's chauffeur. He told me Abner was safe, that he was hiding him until this thing cleared up. He told me Abner had nothing to do with

117

this awful thing, that he was being framed. Sperber and I left the park. We went to a tavern and had some drinks."

"You went to a speakeasy," Sansone corrected him. "A place called Gipsy's Cosmic Tearoom. A smart cop named Ferguson checked that. He checked something else. He found out where Sperber really lived. He didn't live in the Hotel Penton. He lived on Sullivan Street, in a cold-water flat."

Dab nodded. "He told me that. He told me he lived on Sullivan Street. But he wouldn't give me the number. He thought I shouldn't know."

Sansone said, "This Ferguson will be a detective soon. He found the number on Sullivan Street. He went there last night and knocked on Sperber's door. No one answered. He kept going back all night, every hour or so. Still no one answered. He remembers once when he went to the house, a little before four o'clock, a beat-up old Ford like the one we found out here was parked directly in front of the place. When he went back later, the Ford was no longer there. Ferguson made, a report this morning. When I got it, I remembered Sperber had lied about his address. I sent men down to Sullivan Street and had the apartment opened. No one was there."

"Go on, Mr. Dab," prompted Romano. "Tell us about the call."

"A little before four o'clock, Sperber called me on the phone," Dab said. "He said that Abner had disappeared from the apartment, that he'd searched everywhere and couldn't find him. I thought the cops' had Abner. I called Lieutenant Romano. I told him a little lie, I'm afraid."

"You've told too many lies," the old inspector said. "Two men are murdered. A girl is kidnapped and maybe murdered, too. But you've kept on lying to shield the guilty man. Sperber wouldn't have been murdered if you hadn't lied. Not that a cop-killer's any loss."

Romano said, "What else do you want to tell us?"

Dab looked at Romano searchingly. Were they going to press him about seeing Abner? He didn't want to tell them about seeing Abner. It wouldn't help. He'd told them almost all the truth.

"I have nothing else to tell you," Dab said. "Nothing else at all."

There was a discreet knock on the door.

The inspector called, "Come in."

A large young man dressed in the uniform of the New York

118

police entered, looking apologetic. He held a dog collar, with a license tag attached, in his hand.

"Excuse me, sir," he said to the inspector. "I've been chasing you everywhere. Went back to the Blue Sunset and they said I'd find you here."

The inspector shook his head. "Never mind," he said curtly.

"But, sir," the large young cop protested. "I've got important information. If we'd looked close at the dog license, we'd have known it wasn't issued by the S.P.C.A. The S.P.-C.A. only issues licenses for New York City. This license was issued right here, by the Incorporated Township of Pineport, Long Island. I had to check it at the town clerk's office. That's what took so long."

"We know," said the inspector without interest. "It was issued to a man named Sperber."

"No, sir!" The young cop contradicted the inspector emphatically. "It wasn't issued to a man named Sperber. It was issued to a man named Lenny Fassio!"

23

"ARE YOU SURE of your facts, man?" Inspector Sansone asked the large young cop. "There can't be a mistake about this?"

"No, sir," the young cop declared. "The dog belongs to Lenny Fassio. The clerk even let me bring the original license to show to you." He handed a strip of paper to Sansone.

A grin spread over the old man's red face. It was the most unpleasant grin Dab Ashton had ever seen. "Lenny Fassio!" Sansone exclaimed. "Lenny Fassio tied up to a murder squeal by a metal tag and a piece of paper that's on record. I've waited twenty years or more for this." He nodded to the young cop. "Look outside and see if Chief Alger's still there. If he is, ask him to come here."

The inspector seemed to have forgotten Dab completely. The cop returned with Alger. The chief said, "I was just leaving. Got to get back to the Blue Sunset."

The inspector told the local police chief about the dog's registration. Danny, the cause of all the excitement, slept

119

peacefully on Dab's lap, wheezing and snoring and twitching occasionally when a dream disturbed him.

"I want Fassio brought in," the inspector said to Alger. "Can you bring him in, Chief?"

Alger said, "I can bring him in if he's at his place. We don't see much of him. Out here, he's a model citizen. We only get a glimpse of that big foreign-make car of his occasionally. If I could make a charge against Fassio stick, I'd be the most popular guy in town. Pineport people don't like having a mobster for a neighbor. But during the year or so he's been out here he's given no cause for complaint."

"If he isn't here," the inspector said, "he must be in Manhattan, in that fancy penthouse of his up by Central Park. I'm going to call town and have them hit there, too, at the same time you move. I want Fassio brought in. We've finally got something that warrants holding him for questioning, anyway."

He returned to Romano. "Pick up that phone and call the Holmquist residence," he said. "Holmquist is probably at his office, but if he should be home, tell him we want to talk to him."

Romano found Holmquist at his residence. The lawyer was suffering from a slight cold, he said, and had not gone to his offices that day. Nothing he told Romano was pleasing to Inspector Sansone.

Holmquist said that he was shocked and grieved to learn of Sperber's violent death. Sperber had called the office the previous morning to say that he was ill and would not report for work for a day or two. Holmquist stated that he believed Sperber had observed the conditions of his parole scrupulously and doubted that he had had any guilty association with Lenny Fassio or his mobsters. He admitted that Sperber might have seen Fassio and his hoodlums at the Burke and Holmquist offices when they were there on business. He also said that Sperber might have seen Lenny Fassio at the Holmquist residence in Pineport. The gangster had visited his attorney at the latter's home during the course of the senatorial investigation.

Holmquist denied any knowledge of Sperber's dog or of the license issued to Lenny Fassio. He said that during the summer, when his chauffeur was living on the place in Pineport, Sperber had come to him and asked permission to keep a dog. The lawyer had denied permission to his employee because Mrs. Holmquist was deathly afraid of dogs. It amounted to a kind of phobia with her, he said. He did not know if Sperber

120

had acquired a dog when he moved to the apartment in New York. If he had, Holmquist could not account for the license in Fassio's name.

Holmquist stated flatly that Abner Ellison had not appeared at the office and to his knowledge had been in touch with no one at the office since the murder of Philip Linton.

Then the lawyer dropped a bombshell.

He said that the police would be unable to pick up Lenny Fassio for questioning in New York. Fassio had flown to Hot Springs the day after Linton's murder. Holmquist obligingly supplied Romano with Fassio's address at the Arkansas resort.

Inspector Sansone bridled when he was apprised of all this. "I've got a few more things to ask our Mr. Holmquist," he declared. "I'm going to pay him a call before I leave this town. In my book, criminal lawyers are as rotten as the hoods they defend." He banged his fist down hard on a desk. "And we'll pick up Fassio. We can extradite him, and we will. I'll get on that right away. Also, we'll pick up a few of the muggs he's left around New York. We'll bring in that right-hand man of his, Johnny Barrone."

"If we can find him," put in Romano. "He doesn't stay in any one place very long."

"Find him!" the inspector ordered. "And bring in that flat-faced gunsel with the shoe-button eyes, the one who probably put Mike Stella on the spot when he was ready to sing."

"Bansa," said Romano. "He's even harder to find than Barrone."

"Get into town and start finding 'em," the inspector demanded. "I'll be in myself as soon as I finish up this business out here."

Romano nodded toward Dab. "What about him?" he asked.

"Oh, him," said the inspector. "Take him into town, I guess. Ashton, I don't like liars. You stay in your hotel where we can get in touch when we want you. We'll be talking to you again, probably."

Dab said, "This dog's got a bad scalp cut. He should have a vet look at him."

Sansone chuckled. "I tell you what," he said. "You told me you want to help the police. The dog is evidence. Suppose we put him in your custody. You take him to a vet and charge it to the city."

121

Dab said, "I guess I'm still competent enough to take care of a dog."

With Grierson driving, it took less than an hour to reach the city. Dab asked them to take him to Greenwich Avenue, where he remembered having seen a veterinary hospital. Danny's scalp wound was washed, treated and bandaged. The bandage made Danny look as if he were wearing a jaunty cap. The dog's owner had worn a jaunty cap, a beret, Dab recalled. The dog's owner had more than a scalp wound. Ricky Sperber was dead. *If I weren't a stupid, blundering old man, he might still be alive,* Dab told himself.

Since Danny's collar was being held by the police, Dab bought a new one, with a leash, from the vet. On the way to the hotel he stopped to purchase canned dog food.

When Dab led Danny into the old hotel, Madame Sorel was stalking about the lobby. She had not yet gone on duty behind the desk. She was engaged in a late-afternoon routine she called "Checking the arrangements." When she saw Dab, she exclaimed, "What is it, please, the old one is up to now? A dog wearing a dustcap! Such an absurdity!" Her keen old eyes regarded Dab critically. "You are unwell," she declared. "Definitely. You have the beard on your face. I have known you for many years and never before have I seen you with the beard on your face."

24

ABNER ELLISON was riding a Brooklyn subway now. It was late afternoon and for the past twelve or fourteen hours he had been riding subways most of the time, it seemed. He had ridden subways to the Battery and to the nether reaches of the Bronx and to Queens and to Long Island and he felt sure that he must also have ridden Brooklyn subways before now. During some of the time the subway cars had been almost empty. During other times they had been filled to capacity and beyond with squirming, pushing, faceless people. The subway was a twilight, subterranean world of hurtling movement and crashing sound, a world in which there was no night and no day, a world of pale, amorphous faces that had no separate identity. It seemed to Abner that he had lived in

122

this weird, murky world forever. For all he knew, an atom bomb might have destroyed the other world entirely.

Once he had fallen into a drunken sleep and had awakened to sheer panic. A cop was shaking him by the shoulder. The cop's face was so close to his that he could smell the garlic on his breath and see gold fillings in his teeth. Abner's first impulse had been to fight his way loose, to hurl himself from the speeding subway, but the cop was strong and held him firmly.

"Wake up, buddy," the cop had said in a voice that was not unkind, "you can't be sleeping on the subway."

Abner had begun to laugh hysterically. He couldn't help it. He had thought the cop was about to arrest him for murder and the man with the garlic-fouled breath was concerned with a minor misdemeanor. The cop had even been solicitous. "You've had too much to drink, buddy," he had said. "You sure you're on the right train? You know your way home?"

Later on—or maybe it was earlier—Abner had awakened to see a sailor and a girl, the only other occupants of the car, in a shockingly intimate embrace. There had been a gin bottle on the seat beside them, he remembered. The girl's skirt was pulled up to her hips and black garters accented the plump, pink flesh of her upper leg. She had discovered the staring Abner and wriggled out of her husky lover's arms, her hands fumbling for the buttons of her waist. "Hey, cut it out," she cried. "We got a audience."

The sailor had looked at Abner contemptuously. "So what the hell?" he asked. "It's just a drunken bum."

There was law and order, lust and drunkenness even, in the twilight world of faceless people and shrieking sound.

Abner's bottle had been emptied and thrown away a long while ago. He was no longer drunk but the inside of his mouth was dry and bitter and his nerves were raw as butcher's beef. He had not eaten since the night before and he had no thought of food, although he felt an aching sense of emptiness and weakness. The subway smell, the smell of hot metal and stagnant air and human bodies was stifling Abner now. He could stand no more of it. The screeching train came to a jarring stop. Abner saw a sign that read "Prospect Park." He hurried from the subway. He had to smell clean air even if it meant arrest.

He remembered Prospect Park in Brooklyn. Dab Ashton had brought him here when he was a boy. Old Dab had a lively interest in so many things, among them nature study. They had identified the trees in the park and watched the

123

boats on the lake and wandered through the displays of strange flowers and ferns in the botanical gardens.

On this cold and snowy day the park was a great, white, empty waste. As far as his eyes could see there was not another person moving on the paths. There would be park police, of course, but they would hardly be alerted to apprehend a murder suspect. Abner took a path, following an arrow that read "Botanical Gardens." It would be pleasantly warm in the brick and glass buildings and the fragrance of flowers would clear the subway smell from his nostrils. They would be unlikely to seek a suspected killer in such a floral setting.

The air cleared his head and roused him from his stupor. But it did nothing for his shattered morale. "I've got to go back," he told himself. "I've got to go back and face it. I can't hide in subways the rest of my life and I can't just dodge the thing by drinking whisky."

Then he thought of the enormous risks involved. Because of the clues that Phil Linton had left upon the floor he would risk the electric chair. He did not think of that now. "If I go back, they'll kill her," he told himself. The hideous hands he had been seeing in his dreams would become real hands of flesh and bone and cartilage and they would reach out of the darkness and crush the breath from Pat Linton's slender throat. Abner Ellison was shaking and it was not cold that had brought the spasm.

Just inside the building that housed the botanical specimens a polite attendant greeted Abner. "You're rather late, sir, I'm afraid," he said. "We close in fifteen minutes."

Abner managed a weak smile. "I'll only stay a few minutes," he promised. "Just long enough to warm myself."

"It's a cold day, all right," the attendant said.

Yes, Abner thought. It's a cold, dark day for Abner Ellison. The coldest and darkest he's ever known.

The cloyingly sweet smell of flowers and the spicy, biting tang of ferns did little to dispel Abner's dark depression. The odor of the place reminded him of a funeral. They would be having a funeral for Phil Linton soon and there would be banks of flowers, mostly from police officials. There'll be policeman there, so I can't attend, Abner thought. I wonder if a murder suspect should send flowers to the funeral of a murdered man?

Abner saw only two other persons wandering through the gardens. One was a little old lady with furs at her neck and a Queen Mary hat as flowery as the blossoms in the hothouses.

124

The other was a square-built man who moved around as cautiously as a cat.

Abner stood by a glass case in which orchids were displayed and observed the square-built man. The man looked familiar. He seemed to be observing Abner with interest. As the man drew closer, Abner recognized him. He had seen the square-built man in Holmquist's office. He was one of Lenny Fassio's mobsters, an important lieutenant, Abner thought. He could not think at once of the man's name. It was something like "bananas." Bansa, that was it. Bansa was one of the gangsters who had been questioned when the stoolie, Stella, had disappeared. Bansa was one of those who had stood on his constitutional rights at the Senate investigation of crime. This was a strange place indeed to encounter a man like Bansa.

Abner glanced down at the orchids as Bansa approached him. The blossoms had the tawny, spotted look of leopards. As he stared down at the flowers he could sense that the square-built man was moving toward him with the soft alertness of a cat. A low, barely distinguishable voice spoke into Abner's ear. Bansa said, "Hello, Mr. Ellison. I see you know where to come when the heat is on. I guess you listen to the radio, too."

Abner turned and looked into Bansa's flat, expressionless face. He said, "The radio?"

Bansa spoke out of the side of his mouth, like a convict, hardly moving his lips at all. "Yeah, the radio," he said. "My kid, he's queer for them cops and robbers programs. He was setting listening to one and I was setting drinking a can of beer and all of a sudden they broke off the program to say there'd been another kill and they had the heat on Fassio. So I come over here, just in case the cops come to my house asking questions, see? I always come here when the heat is on. I don't live so far away. Cops ain't smart enough to come looking here."

Abner said, "I didn't hear the radio."

Bansa chuckled. It was a barely audible chuckle. "I guess you got enough heat of your own," he said. "You had the heat since the cop was chilled and the dame was snatched, I guess. I read about it in the papers. It's funny you don't know about this kill, though. They found your car right near the stiff."

"My car, you say?"

"According to the man, it was. And you should've known the stiff. He worked for Holmquist, too. An ex-con name of Sperber."

125

Abner felt suddenly sick. Beads of sweat began to crawl over his body like wet lice.

The little old lady in the Queen Mary hat bustled officiously between Abner and Bansa. She adjusted steel-rimmed spectacles to study the card beside the display of orchids.

"Ah, *Cypripedium!*" she exclaimed. "Isn't that nice?"

"Yeah, lady," Bansa answered. "That's just peachy."

The little old lady looked into Bansa's flat, hard face. She said, "You don't look like a flower fancier. What are you doing here?"

Bansa said, "I just love flowers, lady. I grow 'em in a window box."

"Really? What do you grow?"

Bansa chuckled. "Violets, lady."

The little old lady snorted. "You can't grow violets in a window box," she declared. "I could tell you weren't a flower fancier. People who grow flowers get a certain look." Her spectacled gaze rested on Abner. "Now this young man," she said. "He might grow flowers. He has the look."

She moved off in a huff.

Bansa said, "Okay, flower boy. So there's been another kill and your car was there and the heat's on Fassio. Fassio's at the Springs, so he's clean. Fassio's always clean when the heat is on, but they're bringing him in just the same. I think maybe Johnny the Baron wants to talk to you. Johnny the Baron takes over when the heat's on Fassio."

"Who?"

"Johnny the Baron. His square name's John Barrone."

Abner recalled the man. He had been another of those they'd grilled when Stella disappeared, another who had sat glumly in a senatorial witness chair and refused to answer.

"Does Johnny know about the girl?" asked Abner.

"You asking *me* about the dame?" said Bansa. "I don't know nothing about dames. I'm a family man with a wife and kids."

"Where could I see this Johnny?"

"He should be heading for the Catskills. Johnny always heads for the Catskills when the heat is on. There's a hotel called the Happy Haven. Pretty name, ain't it? It ain't open in the winter except when Fassio or Johnny want it for a conference."

"I can't go that far," Abner said. "Isn't there somebody in New York I can talk to about the girl?"

Bansa moved closer to Abner. He leaned against him. "You can go, flower boy," he said. "That thing you feel against

126

you didn't come out of no popcorn box. It makes a big, loud noise."

The attendant called, "Everybody out, please! We're closing up, folks."

Bansa said, "You see? Even the man there says you gotta go."

Bansa still pressed himself against Abner as they walked out on a path of the deserted park. Abner said, "You don't have to keep a gun on me. I'll go. I want to talk about the girl."

Bansa said, "Now you're acting right sweet, flower boy. But I'll keep the heater on you just in case."

"Do you know about the girl?" Abner asked.

"I know a lot of things," said Bansa. "I know enough not to talk. Maybe Johnny will talk to you if he's in the mood. Johnny's going to like me for bringing you in, flower boy. That ain't bad, having Johnny the Baron like you."

Abner pulled away from Bansa, made a sudden turn into a path that led toward a building marked "Men." Bansa, caught off guard, made a grab for him, clutched Abner's arm. "Hey, wait up!" Bansa said. "My car ain't this way."

Abner continued to walk fast, with Bansa holding to his sleeve, trotting after him. "I've got to use the men's room," Abner said, without breaking his stride.

"Listen," Bansa said. "We can stop on the way. It's a long drive with snow on the road."

Abner kept walking. "It'll only take a minute," he told Bansa.

Bansa let go of Abner's sleeve, but stayed close to him. He began to titter. His tittering sounded remarkably like the forced laughter of the effeminate men in the Greenwich Village bar. "You must be nervous, flower boy," Bansa said. "Maybe guns make you nervous. Oh, well, when you gotta go, you gotta go, I guess. But don't forget I'll be right with you."

Abner opened the door of the low building, walked in ahead of Bansa. There was a small entranceway inside. Swinging doors led to the tiled lavatories. Abner pushed open a swinging door, held it wide for Bansa. As the square-built man started through, Abner slammed the door back hard. The door crashed into Bansa, knocked him off balance, sent him staggering into a wall. Abner charged, head down. Bansa had his gun out now. He couldn't raise it soon enough. Abner's head thudded into Bansa's belly, Abner's left hand clutched the wrist of Bansa's gun hand. The revolver exploded into the

127

floor. Bansa gasped. The acrid smell of cordite blended with the stench of disinfectant. Abner straightened, whirled the limp Bansa around, twisted his arm behind his back. Bansa's right hand still held the gun. Abner exerted pressure and the fingers that gripped the gun slowly relaxed as Bansa groaned. Abner took the gun from Bansa's hand without releasing his hold on the wrist. He dropped the gun into his pocket.

Abner twisted Bansa's arm higher up his back, kneed him in the buttocks, shoved him through the swinging doors into the lavatories. Abner placed his right hand beneath Bansa's curved elbow, pushed. Bansa screamed.

Abner said, "Talk. Talk about the girl."

Bansa said, "Rat, bastard, you'll break my arm."

Abner said, "Yes, I'll break your arm. Talk. Talk about the girl."

Bansa said, "You stinking rat bastard," tried vainly to struggle free.

Abner's left hand pressed Bansa's wrist higher up his back. Bansa was making squealing sounds. Abner lowered his right hand, hit the point of Bansa's bent elbow hard with the palm. The bone snapped with a clearly audible crack. Bansa's scream was high and thin, like taut wire in the wind.

Abner released the broken arm, turned the square-built man around, clutched him by the collar. He shoved Bansa against the wall.

Bansa's face was fishbelly white. Plump sweat bubbles slid slowly down the flat surface of the agonized face. Bansa's bloodless lips mumbled obscenities.

Abner slapped Bansa's face time and again with the back of his hand.

"Talk, Bansa," Abner said. "Talk about the girl."

"Rat bastard," Bansa said.

Abner's fist crashed into Bansa's face. Thick blood dropped from Bansa's nose to the floor. Teeth showed through split lips.

"Talk, Bansa," Abner said. "Talk about the girl."

Bansa's hard eyes glazed over. His smashed mouth moved and murmured.

"The girl," said Bansa. "The girl . . ."

Bansa's body slipped out of Abner's grip. It kept on slipping down against the wall until it rested on the floor. Bansa's dull, dark eyes stared up, unconscious.

For long moments Abner stood looking down at Bansa. Then his body became rigid. There was a sound. The outside

128

door opened and closed. He heard men's voices in the entranceway.

A voice said, "Fine damn weather for a sparrow cop. Nothing in the park today but us park police and the squirrels."

A second voice said, "It's cold all right, but we get relieved in another forty-five minutes. Good thing I brought the bottle, huh?"

The first voice said, "No, not out here. Let's go inside. Hey! You smell something? Like burning paper?"

"I can't smell nothing. I got a cold."

"Smells like somebody'd shot off a firecracker in here. Let's look."

Abner had been dragging Bansa across the tile floor to a row of stalls with swinging doors. He pulled Bansa into one of the stalls, propped him up on the only seat there was. He stuffed the gun back into the pocket of Bansa's coat.

A voice, inside now, said, "Well, here's the bottle. Cheers."

The other voice said, "Hey! Look here! Look down here on the floor."

"Well, I'll be damned. If it ain't catsup, it must be blood."

"Who'd be using catsup in a place like this?"

Abner wiped his hand across Bansa's bloody face. He smeared his own face with blood. He took out a handkerchief and stained it with blood. He pressed the handkerchief to his nose and left the stall.

One of the park policemen held a whisky bottle in his hand. He said, "Hey, what's the matter, bud?"

"Nose bleed," Abner answered. "Cold weather always gives it to me. It's all right now."

Abner went to a bowl, washed off the blood.

The policeman said, "You lost a lot of blood. You all right?"

"I'm all right," Abner answered.

The policeman suddenly realized he was holding the whisky bottle. He seemed embarrassed.

"Maybe you could use a little drink," he said. "But don't say nothing. We ain't supposed to drink on duty, but, man, it's cold out there."

Bitter laughter welled up inside Abner. A policeman was asking him for a favor. He forced the laughter back, said, "Yes, I'd like a drink. I won't say a thing."

The two policemen and Abner drank from the bottle.

"Well, back to the squirrels," said one of the policemen.

Abner left the building with them. "So long and thanks," he said.

129

The park policeman said, "You sure you're all right now? You got far to go?"

"Just to the subway," Abner answered.

Just to the subway, he thought hopelessly.

Back into the void.

Back into the murky world of faceless people.

25

Up in his room, Dab unharnessed Danny. He removed his coat and hat and threw them on a chair. Dab Ashton was a neat man who usually hung his clothes up properly. He sank down on a sofa, exhausted. After several unsuccessful attempts, Danny managed to scramble up on the sofa beside him. The dog licked Dab's face affectionately.

Dab said, "You trust me, don't you, Danny? Don't trust me too much, boy. Terrible things happen to the people who trust me."

He couldn't face shaving, dressing, going down to the restaurant, but he knew he must eat if he were to continue to function at all. He ordered a light dinner sent up and managed to consume a little of it, although he left enough upon the plate to please the waiter, Pierre, who made caustic comments about the shortcomings of the chef as he cleared away the dishes.

Dab opened a can of dog food and fed Danny. He turned on the radio to a news program. Ricky Sperber's murder had been public property for a long while now. It had been tied up to the Linton case through the presence of Ellison's car on the scene. Lenny Fassio was being picked up in Hot Springs and brought back for questioning.

There was a knock on the door. Dab rose to admit Pirtle. Pirtle accepted a drink, sat down. He looked askance at Dab. Dab told Pirtle of the day's violent happenings, of his fear, his futility, his despair. Pirtle said, "Mr. Dab, you can't just sit around and brood about this thing. You're making yourself ill. Seriously ill. Let's play some chess. It will take your mind off this business."

Before Dab could protest, Pirtle got the board, arranged

130

the exquisitely carved little ivory men in battle array upon the coffee table in front of the fireplace. Pirtle built a fire.

When people do things like that for you, thought Dab, it's because they think you're old. Old and not quite bright.

Dab was a long time between moves. He made glaring mistakes. After fifteen minutes, he said, "It's no use, Pirtle. I can't play. I can't think. I'm in a daze."

"It's nearly ten o'clock, anyway," Pirtle told him. "Go to bed. Get some rest, at least."

Dab didn't go to bed when Pirtle left. He sat there by the fire. At a little after ten the phone rang.

A woman's voice said, "Is this J. Dabney Ashton?" The voice was urgent.

"Speaking," Dab replied.

"This is Gipsy May Daroff. You come to my place. Come right away. The bell is inside the door frame, up high on the right. Ring two shorts and two longs. Come right now, you understand?"

"I—I can't," stammered Dab. "I mean, I shouldn't. I . . ."

"Don't argue with me, Dabney Ashton!" exclaimed the woman's voice. "You come over here! You come right now!"

Gipsy May had hung up with a sharp click of the receiver, but Dab stood foolishly talking into the dead phone. "But I can't come! They'll follow me! I'll lead them there. . . ." He realized finally that no one was on the other end of the phone.

Abner needed him. Abner was at the speakeasy. He should never have gone there. The police knew about the speakeasy. Wildly Dab thought of ways of eluding the police. There was a back door to the hotel but it led only to a blind alleyway. The only exit led to Fifth Avenue where he imagined the police were waiting. Danny rose, put his front legs against Dab.

The dog! He'd take the dog for a walk. They wouldn't think it was suspicious if he walked the dog and he might be able to give them the slip. He donned his coat and hat, put the leash on Danny.

Danny and Dab left the hotel. Dab stood for a minute in front of the door, lighting a cigar with a trembling hand, casting covert glances all about him. Where were they? They might be waiting in any of the doorways or hiding inside the drug store across the street. They were there somewhere, watching him.

Trying to appear casual, he led Danny down the avenue, toward the memorial arch in Washington Square. Danny paused once, tugged at the leash. He was relieving himself

131

against the railing of an iron fence. As Dab crossed the open street area of the square, a taxi heading downtown discharged a passenger. Dab grabbed Danny in his arms, began to run toward the cab, calling to the driver. The driver had started up. He was making a U-turn. He headed back uptown, almost ran over the man with the dog in his arms. Dab stopped the cab, climbed in, carrying Danny.

"Turn right!" he ordered. "Head east! Hurry!"

The driver swerved the car around. There was a roaring and screeching as he headed east. "You must be on the lam," the driver said. "Where to?"

"When you get to Broadway, turn uptown, turn north," Dab said. "There's a five-dollar bill if you do what I tell you."

Dab pressed his face to the back window. There were lights, cars. Any one of them might be the pursuing police car. The cab turned up Broadway. At Fourteenth Street, Dab told the driver to turn back west. He kept his face pressed to the glass. The beams of headlights stabbed into his eyes. His old eyes were tired, burning. At Sixth Avenue, the Avenue of the Americas, he told the cabbie to turn downtown again.

"Just like one of them chases in the movies," the driver commented as he screeched around the corner.

Dab stopped the cab just below Third Street, where a wild confusion of streets converged into the avenue. He thrust money at the driver, carried Danny from the cab. The street was slushy. He slipped and slid over it, crossed against the light, dodged traffic, entered the gloomy little dead end called Minetta Street. He pressed himself against a building. No other car stopped in the swirling traffic of the corner. No one walked into Minetta Street. He hurried to a house halfway down the one-block street, a house in the very center of the V-shaped byway. He looked back of him. No one. Across the street a bum was drinking from a bottle in a doorway. The bum might be a cop in disguise. Dab pushed open the door, entered a dim hallway. His hand fumbled above his head for Gipsy May's bell, found it, rang two shorts, two longs. A panel slid back, slammed shut. The door opened just wide enough to admit him.

There was only one occupant of the room besides Gipsy May. Macey Reed, the bearded poet, sat grumbling at the pot-bellied stove. He was very drunk. There was a teacup in his hand.

Gipsy May said, "I'm closed tonight. No one gets in. Macey was waiting in the hallway for me when I came here to open at my usual time, ten o'clock. I had to let him in.

132

He's unconscious anyway. There was someone else waiting, too. He's in the back room now. He had me call you." She stroked Danny. "Poor Danny," she said. "He's been hurt. Poor Danny, they killed his master. I read about Ricky in the paper, heard it on the radio. Are they going to kill the young man in the back room, too? The young man with the nice eyelashes? Don't let them kill him, Dabney Ashton!"

She led him to the curtained doorway. Behind the curtain an old-fashioned folding door was closed. She slid the door open, said, "It doesn't lock. But if they come for him, they'll have to break in. I won't answer the door. There's a window in back, I unlatched it. If you hear them he can climb out that."

Abner Ellison sat at the round table.

Dab put the dog on the floor, took off the leash. He dropped into a chair, exhausted. "Where have you been, boy?" he asked. "I thought they had you. I thought you might be dead. You must go to the police. There's nothing else to do."

"They killed Ricky because of me," said Abner. "They'll kill Pat, too, if I go in. They killed Ricky and cut his finger off so it would point to me."

"Where have you been, boy? Where have you been all these hours?" Dab asked.

Abner told Dab of fleeing from the policeman, of standing in a drunken daze outside the walls of the Mad Hatter's castle, of the nightmare hours among the zombies of the subway's murky caverns.

Then Abner said, "I found out something about myself today. I found out there is violence, murder in me, just as there was in my father. I almost killed a man. I broke the bone in a man's arm and it gave me pleasure to hear it snap. I smashed a man's face and I rejoiced to see the blood. It was in Prospect Park. I wandered there late this afternoon and quite by chance I met one of Fassio's killers, a hood named Bansa. He told me of Ricky's murder. He pulled a gun on me, tried to take me to the mob at some place in the Catskills. I got the gun from him. I broke his arm and when he stood there helpless I smashed his face. I kept thinking he was one of those who knew where Pat was hidden, one of those who might have put his hands on Pat. I went crazy, I guess. I guess the mob wants me now that they're bringing Fassio in. I tried to make Bansa tell me about Pat. I don't think he knew. Hoods can't take much punishment. That's why the cops depend so much upon the third degree. Bansa wouldn't talk. If Fassio and his mob don't know where Pat is hidden, then the only one who knows must be Fassio's payoff man. I know who he is. I've got to get to him and make him talk. But I'm afraid. I'm afraid now that I might kill him before he talks."

Dab said, "You can't risk this alone, boy. I've been out of my mind with worry since you disappeared.

"Ricky called me a little before four o'clock this morning to say you'd disappeared," continued Dab. "Right after that a cop saw a car that resembled yours parked out in front of Ricky's house."

"That explains it, then," said Abner. "They found out somehow I was at Ricky's place. They parked the car they'd stolen there to flush me out, to see what I would do when I saw it. Ricky must have come back to look for me again after he called you. He would have recognized the car. His first thought would be to hide it. He knew Pineport well, knew that point of land is deserted in the winter. He must have found the key in the ignition, driven out there. They were waiting, watching the car. They followed him and murdered him."

"How did they get hold of your car in the first place?" Dab asked. "That afternoon of the day Phil was murdered, I mean."

Abner said, "That wasn't hard. I never thought anyone would steal a wreck like that old car. You know I'm careless, that I'm always losing keys. Well, I kept the ignition key stuck in back of the front cushion. Anyone who ever rode with me knew that. I had the car parked near the office. When I went for it about four o'clock that afternoon, it was gone. So I put in a report."

"Tell me, Abner," Dab said. "Was Ricky Sperber mixed up with Lenny Fassio and his mob? This dog here had a tag, a license. The license was issued to Lenny Fassio."

Abner said, "Ricky mixed himself up with Lenny Fassio on my account. It was an awful risk for him, for a man who was on parole, and I tried to keep him from doing it. He found out that I was cultivating the acquaintance of Fassio's top muggs, the ones who came into the office occasionally. I was trying to find out who was paying off the cops for Fassio. Phil Linton had told me about this detective I'd never seen telling Sansone I was the payoff man. Ricky had known Fassio and some of his men a long time ago. He looked them up. One night, during that Senate investigation, Fassio went to Holmquist's house to talk things over with his lawyer. He left a golden cocker bitch, a pedigreed prize winner, in his car.

134

Ricky got to talking to Fassio's chauffeur about the dog. Ricky was nuts for dogs. When Fassio came out, Ricky introduced himself, reminded him of their acquaintance in the old Prohibition days. He admired the dog. Fassio complained that the dog had whelped only one pup when he bred her and that the pup was a runt he might destroy. Ricky asked for the dog and Fassio promised it to him. But for some reason Mr. Holmquist wouldn't let Ricky keep a dog at the place in Pineport. When Ricky moved into New York, he got the dog from Fassio and brought it along. I guess he just never bothered to get a proper New York City license, kept the old one on Danny's collar."

"Did Ricky find out who was paying off the cops for Fassio?" Dab asked.

Abner nodded. "He and I together found out after a long, long time. We found a mugg who was ready to spill. I told Phil Linton the truth about the payoff the night he was killed. That's why Phil was murdered. That's why Pat was kidnapped. That's why they murdered Ricky."

There was a sudden commotion on the other side of the folding door. Gipsy May screamed, "No! No! You mustn't go in there!" There were sounds of a brief scuffle. Abner jumped up, overturned his chair, made for the window.

The folding door crashed open. A figure swayed in the doorway, the curtain draped around him like a toga.

It was Macey Reed, the bearded poet.

Macey held a sheet of foolscap in his hand. He disentangled himself from the curtain, said to Dab, "A thousand pardons, sir, if I intrude. But I have just completed a poem. This very moment! An unique poem. A form I never tried before. A poor thing, but amusing, I think, and I need an absinthe. It is an acrostic. Perhaps you wish to purchase it."

Macey Reed tossed the sheet of yellow paper in front of Dab. Dab looked down at it, dazed.

Most men are born to sorrow:
Alas, I was born to borrow.
Can you spare a dollar, brother?
Ease the suffering of another?
You'll feel better, come the morrow.

Riches bring you only sadness;
Enormous wealth's the seed of madness.
Ease your burden, share your shekels,
Divide them with this poet who heckles.

135

Dab sat staring stupidly at the paper. Macey Reed said, "Don't you see? The initial letters spell my name! It's quite clever, don't you think, sir?"

Dab said, "An acrostic! An acrostic that spells your name! And your name has nine letters!"

"Is that significant?" asked Macey. "Are you a numerologist, perhaps?"

Dab grabbed the fountain pen that Macey Reed held in his hand. He made a mark on the paper. He thought a minute, his lips moved. He made another mark.

"Please!" protested Macey. "Don't mark up my poem unless you're prepared to purchase it!"

Dab paid no heed to the poet. He muttered to himself, paused to think, made marks on the paper. Yes. He could remember them all, easily enough. Those fingerprinting symbols were burned into his brain. He said aloud, "The seventh's the exceptional arch."

He made a mark. Another mark. He said, "The last one's tricky. It's the shape of that which counts." He made a final mark, looked up at Reed.

Abner and Gipsy May Daroff stared at Dab in amazement. Macey Reed said, "Well, you've spoiled it, scribbling all over it like that. If you don't think it's worth a dollar, you should at least pay me fifty cents so I can buy one absinthe."

Dab reached for his wallet. He had been carrying a large sum of cash with him ever since Abner's trouble started, thinking the boy might need money. He took five ten-dollar bills from the wallet, thrust them at Macey.

"It's a wonderful poem!" he declared, and his voice rang with its old resonance. "It's worth a hundred times fifty cents. Here, go buy yourself all the Pernod in Greenwich Village!"

Macey Reed gazed dumbly at the sheaf of bills in his hand. His mouth fell open. He said, "I can't understand. But then you shouldn't understand good fortune, should you? You should just accept it."

Dab took Macey and Gipsy May by the arm, led them out of the room. He returned and closed the door.

Abner said, "What on earth was that all about?"

"I know the murderer's name!" Dab answered. "It's written on that piece of paper!"

136

26

"I should have known it was simple," Dab said, "because Phil Linton was a simple man. But the simplest explanation of all seemed to be the theory of a nine-fingered man, the one that involved you as the murderer. Yet it was there in front of me all the time, a childish acrostic that I should have seen almost at a glance. Certainly Phil didn't ask too much of my intelligence. School kids make up acrostics using their own names as the initials, or their sweethearts' names. But I had to think in terms of ideographs, involved forms meant to convey an involved idea, instead of thinking in terms of simple letters of the alphabet. And the police thought the cards meant a nine-fingered man instead of a man with nine letters in his name."

"I'm afraid I don't quite get it," Abner said. "Those were fingerprint symbols on the cards."

"They were letters just the same," declared Dab. "I'll check the cards when I go back to the hotel, before I do anything, but there can't be any doubt. I'm sure now. At first, when the name started coming up, letter by letter, I couldn't believe my eyes. The man appeared to have a perfect alibi. But he also had influential friends—and the alibi was never checked too closely. It sounds incredible. But thinking back on it, he was the only one who could have committed all the crimes, really." He pushed the piece of foolscap toward Abner. "His name is written there," he said.

Abner looked at the scrawl briefly, nodded his head. "I knew, of course," he said. "It had to be. But nothing's solved. We haven't rescued Pat. That's all that counts."

Dab said, "Yes, that's all that matters. I am going to bargain with the murderer, offer him a trade. I am going to offer him a chance to escape in exchange for Pat's life. But first you'd better tell me everything, boy."

For fifteen minutes Abner Ellison talked and answered questions. When he had finished, he said to Dab, "You can't try this alone, of course. He'll kill you, too. I'll come with you."

Dab shook his head. "No, boy. That won't do. That would

137

never do. I know you want to, but we've got to think of Pat. The mere sight of you would spoil everything. We can't take a chance."

"But I can hide somewhere, watch you . . ."

"No, no," Dab said. "There's only one way to save her. Just one chance. I've got to take that chance. And don't forget I'll have a policeman with me, the way I've planned it."

Dab glanced at his watch. "It's almost eleven now. If you haven't heard from me by one, come to the hotel. If I'm not there, I'll try to leave some message, some clue to where I'll be. You can call the police then. It may not be too late. But I have to try it alone first—for Pat's sake."

Back in his hotel, Dab stood looking at the cards on the mantel before he even removed his coat or took the leash off Danny. He considered them one by one. He didn't need a pen and paper. He had not been mistaken. The cards spelled the same name.

Dab rubbed his chin. "I wish I'd shaved," he said to Danny. "I'd hate to be found dead with this beard on my face, but there's no time now for shaving."

I could call Romano, Dab thought. I suppose I really should. Then he shook his head. No. I'll call Allan Walters. Allan must be the first to know. He called Walters' home up by the castle. Mrs. Walters' vague, wavery voice answered. She said, "Allan's so distracted by all this, he just can't stay still. He's really ill, I'm afraid. He's gone off somewhere or other. Down to the station on Mercer Street, perhaps."

Dab called the detective squadroom on Mercer and got Walters on the phone. Dab said, "There's been a big break, Allan. I need your help. Can you come over to my hotel? Can you come right now?"

"Have they found Pat, Mr. Dab? Have they found her?"

Dab said, "I think we'll find her now, Allan. Come on over here and I'll tell you everything."

Dab hung up. He went to the door, opened it a crack, left it open. He sat down in an easy chair beside the telephone. His left hand rested on Danny's bandaged head. His right hand touched the phone uncertainly, as if he were debating making another call.

Allan Walters arrived in less than ten minutes. Dab called, "Come in. The door is open." He did not rise from the chair. Allan Walters came into the room and closed the door behind him. The strain of the past two days showed on the young man. Dab was surprised to note that Walters appeared to have been drinking heavily. Allan had always been very careful

138

about his drinking because of the bitter example of his mother.

"Sit down, Allan," Dab said. "Sit here across from me."

When Walters had removed his coat and taken a chair, Dab said. "I've solved the puzzle on the mantelpiece, Allan. I know what Phil Linton meant by those cards. I know the murderer's name."

"Who?" asked Walters.

"The murderer is a cop," Dab answered. "A cop who worked for Lenny Fassio."

Walters nodded. "I thought so," he said. "It's Inspector Sansone, isn't it?"

"Why do you say that, Allan?"

Walters said, "Sansone helped me along a lot from time to time. He was tough, but he seemed to like me and he gave me a boost or two. But I've suspected right along that he was taking graft from Fassio. There were hints during the investigation that he was. I think Lieutenant Linton found out about it, that Sansone suspected the lieutenant told me. That's why he kidnapped Pat. To keep me quiet and to keep Abner quiet, in case Phil had told him, too. We both loved Pat."

Walters waved a hand toward the cards on the mantelpiece. "And then those cards Lieutenant Linton left on the floor pointed out Sansone's name, just as you said they did."

"You read them that way?" Dab asked.

"Of course," said Walters. "If the cards didn't mean that Abner, a nine-fingered man, was guilty, they had to mean Sansone. I didn't go to college like Abner, but I had some elementary French in high school. Enough to know that the French word sans means minus or without. There should have been ten cards on the floor, ten fingerprint symbols to point out ten fingers. But one card was missing. The pattern Phil left was minus one card, or one finger, if you prefer."

"It was minus one, without one. Sans—one."

Dab said, "That's very clever, Allan. That's the way I figured it myself. But I've been very stupid. I'm growing old, I guess. The murderer isn't Sansone. The murderer is a man who has nine letters in his name."

Walters thought a minute, then he said, "Sansone's first name is Edward. There are nine letters in the name Ed Sansone."

"There are nine letters in the name Ab Ellison, too," Dab answered. "There are nine letters in Dab Ashton. There are nine letters in a lot of names. Look at the cards, Allan. You went to the police academy. You know the names of those

139

fingerprint symbols. Those cards form a simple acrostic, an acrostic that spells a man's name, with a space between the first name and the last name. The initial letters of the names of the fingerprint symbols make up the acrostic."

Dab's fingers still played with the telephone.

He said, "The first symbol is an arch, the letter A. The second is a loop, an L. Then there is the space. Next we have a W for the whorl, another A for the accidental, another L for the lateral pocket, a T for the tented arch, an E for the exceptional arch, an R for the radial loop. There is no fingerprint classification symbol beginning with the letter S, so Phil had to choose a symbol for a characteristic that looks like the letter. The ridge fragment is an S lying on its side. He knew that when I got that far, I'd have the name anyway."

Dab looked straight into the young detective's face.

Dab said, "It spells Al Walters."

Walters looked incredulous. He said, "I can't believe you're serious, Mr. Dab. I had no reason for killing Lieutenant Linton, for kidnapping Pat. I was going to marry Pat. Besides I was up in Westchester with Pat at the time Lieutenant Linton was murdered."

"I've just been with Abner," Dab told Walters. "Pat was not going to marry you. She was going to marry Abner Ellison. She made a date with you to tell you that, not to accept your proposal. They hadn't announced their engagement. It was to be announced at a little family dinner. The letter Phil Linton wrote me and didn't mail, the one he set beside the cards on the floor, was an invitation to that dinner."

Walters' hand moved slightly, and Dab took a firmer grip on the phone.

"You were the payoff man for Fassio, of course," Dab continued. "You had been ever since Mike Stella was put on the spot when he was about to sing. You been spreading Fassio's corruption in the Police Department for a long while now. I often wondered how you could afford such good clothes, a Cadillac, on your detective's pay. You saw a chance of taking the heat off yourself and of ruining Abner's chances for winning Pat. You started rumors that the payoff was from a source in the offices of Burke and Holmquist. A cop, a detective, was caught red-handed. He was going to be demoted anyway, so he took money from you to say that Abner Ellison had bribed him for Fassio. Phil Linton didn't believe the story. He told Abner. And Abner fought back. He and Ricky Sperber began to question Fassio's mobsters. One of them talked a little. You found out that he was talking. You

140

knew that they were getting close to you. You learned that Abner was to see Phil two nights ago when you had a date with Pat. So you planned a murder and a kidnapping. You planned to cast suspicion on Abner for the murder, to kidnap Pat to keep him from talking, to make him hide.

"I should have suspected you the minute I saw that note you sent to Abner, because of the time element involved. Abner got that note around midnight and it said that Pat was kidnapped. Your story was that you did not run out of gas, that Pat was not kidnapped until after twelve thirty. What happened is fairly clear now.

"You had ridden with Abner in his old car. You knew he stuck the key behind the cushion. That afternoon you stole the car and put it in some hiding place you had arranged. That night you took Pat to dinner, she refused your offer of marriage as you had known she would. You didn't try to get into a dance place, as you said you did. You didn't stop for hamburgers. But I imagine that you did drive to the old road you described, that you pretended you were out of gas. But you didn't go there after midnight with her. You went there early in the evening, no later than ten o'clock, probably. You left Pat in the car on the pretense of going back for gas. You stole back in the darkness, crept up and overpowered her—hit her on the head or doped her, I imagine. You drove her to a hideaway you had prepared.

"Then you drove back to the street where Linton lived and waited for Abner to come out of Phil's house. Phil came out with him, but you knew Linton would return alone, that he always went to bed before midnight. When Phil returned, you forced the catch of the window on the porch and shot him.

"You drove your car to some place near Abner's hotel. You called his room to make sure he was home. When he answered, you hung up. You gave the note to a vagrant to deliver at the desk. You were sure the note would keep Abner quiet, that he would disappear and that he would be suspected of the murder because he had been with Linton, because Sansone believed he was Fassio's payoff man. It was ironical that Phil lived long enough to put those cards upon the floor and that they should be interpreted as pointing out a nine-fingered man. Unwittingly, he had played right into your hands because I was too stupid to see that the cards formed a simple acrostic that spelled your name.

"You made an anonymous call to the police, reported the murder. You drove back to the road in Westchester. You

141

siphoned the gas from your tank. You walked back to the gas station and wakened the proprietors. You filled a can with gas, poured it into your car, drove to the gas station and reported the kidnapping as if it had just occurred. You called the police. You thought your story of the kidnapping would furnish you an alibi for the time of the murder.

"I don't know how you found out where Abner was hiding, but you did. Some time last night, or early this morning, you took Abner's car and parked it in front of the house where Sperber lived. You had your own car nearby. You waited. Sperber must have come there a little after four, seen the car and driven off in it. You followed him to Pineport and murdered him. The idea of cutting off his finger must have occurred to you when you saw the axe by the pile of wood. It would be another missing finger to keep Abner in the minds of the police. And you're a sadist, Allan. You're insane. I should have known that. I remember when you were kids, Abner used to beat the tar out of you because you made Pat scream by torturing insects and birds and small animals."

Walters' hand was moving slowly up his coat front, as if he were caressing himself.

Dab said, "There's no use in pulling a gun. You can shoot me, but my hand is on the telephone and I'm going to leave it there. The slightest reflex from the shock of the bullet will jar the phone, light a light on the board downstairs. And an old woman with keen eyes is staring at that board, waiting for that light. If it so much as blinks, she'll call the cop Sansone has stationed downstairs to arrest Abner if he should try to come to me. You'll never get out of the hotel if I jar this phone."

Allan Walters said, "There isn't any cop downstairs. You're bluffing."

"There's a cop downstairs," Dab asserted stoutly. "He's been there ever since they brought me back from Pineport. He doesn't know about you. Not yet. They left him there to watch for Abner. But if the light of this phone on the switchboard blinks, Madame Sorel will send him up here."

Walters' hand continued to move slowly toward his breast. He took a gun from the shoulder holster. He held it loosely, carelessly, the barrel toward Dab. He said, "Pick up the phone. Tell the old woman she needn't mind. Tell her everything's all right."

"That wouldn't help you any," Dab declared. "I talked to her. She knows what to do. If I touch this phone, she'll send the cop. What I might say won't matter."

142

Walters raised the gun ever so slightly. His thumb toyed with the safety.

On the floor, Danny stirred restlessly and whimpered at some figment of a dream.

Dab said, "I don't care about you, Allan. I don't care at all if you get away. All I want is Pat. I want Pat alive. I want to trade with you. I want to trade your life for Pat's. It's the only chance you have now. Take me to Pat. Show me she's alive. I'll give you all the time you want for a getaway if you do that. You can even lock me up with Pat if you want to. I'll find some way of getting out in time."

Walters said, "That cop downstairs would follow us. And Abner knows about me."

"The cop won't follow us. He doesn't suspect you. He has no interest in me. He's waiting there for Abner. And Abner will do nothing, nothing at all until he knows that Pat is safe."

Walters thought a moment. Then he said, "Get your coat on, then. I'll take you to Pat. Pat's alive. I never could have killed her."

"It's not that easy, Allan," Dab replied. "Before I take my hand off the telephone, you have to tell me where you've hidden Pat, convince me that she's alive. You've nothing to lose. Once I move my hand, you have the gun and I have nothing."

Allan Walters laughed. His laughter was a startling sound in the still old room. The sleeping dog squirmed and grumbled at the disturbance. Walters said, "You gave me a bad time for a minute when you said your friend saw the castle tower in those cards yesterday. Then I realized Phil Linton couldn't possibly have known that Pat was there and I could tell by the look on Romano's face he thought it was all plain moonshine. I knew what Sansone would think if his drunken old brother-in-law, Groscz, was accused of harboring a kidnapped girl. So I played up to you. It was a good act, wasn't it? You see, I've had Pat in the south tower of the castle right along. It seemed a good place. No one would ever think of her being right across the street from home. That old barn is practically soundproof, and it's boarded up. A while back, when I knew that Abner was getting close to me, I went to see Groscz. Known him for years. He'd do anything to get money for his booze. He's the only one in the castle now. His nephew, who's supposed to live with him, is a horseplayer. Made a big killing last fall and went to Florida for the races. A few weeks back I bribed Groscz to lend me the castle

143

keys one night. They're not kept at the estate offices, as I said they were. Groscz has a full set. I told Groscz I had a girl that was dying to see the inside of the castle. He got a kick out of lending me the keys. He thought I was taking Abner's girl there, and he never did like Abner. I had duplicates made of the keys and returned them to him, said the girl wouldn't go with me after all. Groscz is either in a gin-mill or dead drunk in the caretaker's cottage all the time. He's some watchman. I got in and out any time I wanted to, to prepare things, to see that the burglar alarms didn't work. Of course I didn't go to see Groscz yesterday, when I pretended to. But I knew the best way of keeping you and the cops away from there was to put on an act and make sure Sansone heard about it. And I figured Sansone would suspend me, which I wanted him to do. I had things to take care of."

Walters reached in his pocket. He drew out a key chain with a rabbit's foot attached to it and tossed it across to Dab. There were ordinary keys on it, a house key, a car key, a locker key. There were three other keys that were queerly wrought for intricate locks.

"Those funny-looking ones on the end are the duplicates of the castle keys," Walters said. "The service entrance, the castle door, the tower room keys."

They were peculiar keys, Dab thought. They might well be the keys to a peculiar place like the Mad Hatter's castle. He said, "I don't know whether or not I should believe you, Allan."

Walters shrugged. "It's up to you," he declared. "The cops won't get me, because I'll blow my brains out. I'll kill you first, of course. They'll be a long time finding Pat if that happens. She might even starve to death or take pneumonia before they find her. There's not much food left, and very little fuel. And that tower gets mighty cold."

Dab took his hand from the phone. He rose, said, "I'll take a chance. I'll go with you."

He walked to the chair where he had thrown his coat and hat. He stumbled against the coffee table where the little chessmen were arranged in battle array. Several of the pieces fell to the floor. Dab leaned down to pick them up.

"Never mind that," snapped Walters. "Let's get going."

Dab and Walters donned their coats and hats. Dab took the key with the hotel tag attached to it from the inside of the door. He looked at the sleeping dog. "Good-bye, Danny," he said softly. "Be a good boy, Danny." He left a light for Danny.

144

Dab locked the door, held the key with the tag attached in his right hand. Walters said, "Go in front of me. And don't forget the gun's in my pocket, right up against you."

At the foot of the stairs, in the lobby, Walters grasped Dab's arm, led him to a door at the left. "Isn't this the dining room?" he asked, opening the glass door and switching on a light. The old dining room was deserted. Walters switched off the light, said, "I hear they have good food here. I always thought you might invite me down to have a meal with you and Pat and Abner, but you never did."

Walters still had his hand on Dab's arm. He ushered him straight across the lobby, past the desk where Madame Sorel sat bending over her ledgers. There was a little lounge to the right of the lobby. Walters looked in. One table lamp was burning in the lounge. No one was in the room. Walters whispered to Dab, "There's no cop here. You lied to me. You shouldn't tell lies, Mr. Dab."

Walters urged Dab toward the street door in front of the desk. Dab said, "Just a minute. I want to leave my key." He put the key down in front of Madame Sorel, under the flat of his hand. He stared hard into the old woman's keen, black eyes.

Walters nudged Dab. They left the hotel.

Madame Sorel said to the empty lobby, "Definitely, the old one acts more strangely every day. In twenty-five years he has never before left his key at the desk. He always carries it in his pocket."

She shrugged, picked up the key. Under the tag was a small piece of carved ivory. Madame Sorel picked it up, shook her head. "He stared at me so hard you might have thought I was a naked hussy in the *Folies Bergère*. And why should he leave this little man from a chessboard with his key?"

27

F OR TEN MINUTES after Mr. Dab left to meet a murderer, Abner Ellison sat at the table in Gipsy May's back room. During that time the bell to the speakeasy rang twice, but Gipsy May refused to answer the door. Finally the tension grew too great for Abner. He rose from the table, opened the

145

folding doors and went to the front of the speakeasy. Gipsy May said, "You're safer back there, young man. You can get out the back if somebody starts to break my door down."

The old poet had placed the entire fifty dollars on Gipsy May's small bar. He was standing unsteadily beside the pot-bellied stove that he had belabored and insulted for so many years. He held a glass of Pernod in each hand. "Drink!" he called to Abner. "Tonight everyone drinks at the expense of the greatest lyric poet in the world! Tonight Macey Reed even buys drinks for Fascists!" He jerked the door of the stove open and dashed the contents of one of the glasses into its glowing interior. "Drink, Fascist!" he bellowed.

Abner said to Gipsy May, "I can't stay here, but I don't know how to thank you for what you've done."

"Nonsense," Gipsy May replied. "I've done nothing. I like to help young men who're in trouble. Especially young men with nice eyelashes."

Abner said, "You're kind, but I can't stay. I'm keeping your trade away. Besides, Mr. Dab may need my help."

"Is Dab Ashton in trouble?" Gipsy May asked. "Where'd he go?"

"He's trying to trap a murderer."

Gipsy May nodded calmly. "He'll catch him, then," she asserted. "Dab Ashton is a very efficient man. I've always said so. He's not dreamy and impractical like most poets and painters and actors. I admire practical people, maybe because I'm so impractical myself."

Abner smiled. "He's in danger, though," he said. "I've really got to go. Good-by, and many thanks."

Gipsy May shook her head vigorously. "Don't go!" she urged. "Please don't go out of here, young man! The police may be waiting just outside. Why, they'd shoot you down like a dog."

The word "police" had attracted the drunken attention of Macey Reed, who was refilling his glass from a Pernod bottle. "Police!" he repeated and spat at the floor. "Gestapo! Are they waiting for you, boy? Will they smash your head with their clubs and drag you off to their torture chambers?"

On an impulse, Abner put his arms around Gipsy May, drew her to him, and kissed her on the mouth. Gipsy May gasped. "My!" she exclaimed. "My goodness! That's the first time a young man has kissed me in twenty years! Be careful, dear. Don't let them shoot you. There are too few men with nice eyelashes, you know."

146

She unbolted the door for Abner, glanced out into the hall. "No one's here," she said. "The hallway's empty."

Abner left the speakeasy. The crooked street outside was a place of shadows, a forgotten old-world byway in the most blatantly modern of the New World's cities. Shadows of the narrow, peaked houses sprawled in the dim glow of the street lamps on the snow. Smaller shadows moved fitfully and furtively through the gloom. In this section of the town vagrants and jack-rollers from the Bowery often came to prey upon the well-heeled drunks, the "tourists" from uptown who gulped bad liquor and sought exotic excitements in the Village sucker traps. Abner jumped as one of the shadows lurched suddenly from a doorway and accosted him.

The shadow was a thing of rags and fetid breath and a mumbling mouth. "Please, pal, I don't wanna bother ya, pal, but could I ask ya for nine cents, pal, just nine cents, that's all, pal. I don't want no coffee, pal, but I'm cold and got the shakes and if I get nine cents more, pal, I could get a pint. How 'bout it, pal?"

Abner found a coin and thrust it into the filthy claw that clutched toward him. As he walked away the cackling voice followed him through the darkness, "Thanks, pal, you know how it is, pal. You're a pal, pal."

Abner turned up Minetta Lane and into MacDougal Street and walked rapidly toward Washington Square. Barroom doors flew open and flung the sound of raucous laughter and screeching jukebox music into the night. On the icy street in front of Abner a young girl hurried, teetering on spiked heels. A car cruised to the curb and a leering face was thrust from the window toward the girl. The face said, "Hey, babe! Hey, babe, ya wanna take a ride? Hey, babe ya wanna little lovin'?" The girl on the spiked heels hurried heedlessly along. Behind the shaded windows of apartment houses young people laughed and danced and kissed and copulated, middle-aged people stared at the contrived dramatics of television screens, old people read newspaper reports of violent happenings in a world that moved too fast for them.

Across the park, in an ancient building of faded brick, an old man waited for a murderer and, perhaps, for death.

At Fourth Street Abner took a northeasterly path that cut through the banked snow of the park like a great, black furrow. In the park on this cold night nothing moved but the flickering, lacy shadows that the bare, tangled branches of the trees cast on the snow. Abner left the park when he reached

147

the Washington Arch and the thought came into his mind that this imposing, graceful heap of stone had been designed by a murdered man named Stanford White.

From here Abner could see the bay window of Dab Ashton's corner suite. Light glowed yellow behind the window blind, but Abner knew that murder is not always done in darkness.

For a few moments Abner stood staring at the window. Then he crossed to the west side of Fifth Avenue and took a post beside a drug store. From this point of vantage he could command the windows of Dab's suite and the hotel entrance. He stared fixedly at the entrance. For a while no one at all went in or out of the hotel.

There were passers-by. A young man shielded his girl from the cold with a sheltering arm. An old man tested the pavement in front of him with a cane before he took each faltering step. A man with a top hat and white tie and a woman with a billowy skirt and short fur jacket stood in the gutter and screamed at passing taxis. When people passed near him, Abner pretended to stare into the drug store's lighted window, but his eyes still watched the hotel entrance covertly. In the drug-store window were displayed lotions and perfumes and powders to make women's bodies soft and desirable, and, in ludicrous proximity, were piled elastic trusses for ruptured males.

Traffic flowed by spasmodically, moving with unaccustomed slowness on the snow-slick streets. A Cadillac passed the hotel and parked around the corner soon after Abner took his post. Abner paid no special attention to it. His eyes were riveted upon the hotel door. Abner did not see Allan Walters until he appeared suddenly in the lighted doorway. At the entrance, Walters paused, glanced up and down the street, peered through the glass of the door into the hotel lobby. In Dab Ashton's window the light still glowed, a beacon for a killer.

In the seconds that Walters paused outside the doorway, Abner's hands balled into hard fists, he took three steps forward to the curbing, stood trembling on the edge of the slushy gutter. Just across the street was the man who had murdered Phil Linton, the man who had killed a kindly, pathetic little ex-convict; the man who might murder Dab Ashton if Abner let him walk through the door, the man who held the girl Abner loved a prisoner. Abner wanted to beat and break Walters as he had beaten and broken the mugg named Bansa a few hours before. He longed to gouge his strong thumbs and

148

fingers into Walters' throat until the last breath hissed from his open mouth.

But he knew that he was helpless.

He knew now that Walters was crazed and that all the strength of his arms and hands, all the tortures that his angered mind might devise, could never force the all-important revelation from him. He had to depend upon old Dab for that. He had to count on old Dab's cleverness. That was the last slim hope of rescuing Pat in time.

Allan Walters entered the hotel. Abner Ellison took up his vigil beside the drug store again, his whole body shaking with impotent fury.

Hours passed—or Abner thought they did.

He looked at his watch and saw that it was barely eleven-thirty.

At just about this time, two nights before, Phil Linton had walked down a dark street to meet his murderer. Now old Dab Ashton was face to face with the man who would not hesitate to murder him.

Barely eleven-thirty, Abner thought desperately. *And Mr. Dab said wait till one o'clock. One o'clock will never come. One o'clock is years from now.*

Maybe they'll come out, Abner told himself. *If they come out, I can follow them.*

Suddenly Abner realized that he didn't have a car. His car had been stolen and now the police had it as evidence in a murder. He'd been a fool not to watch the traffic. He had no idea if Walters had arrived by car. Several cars were parked in the immediate vicinity. None near him was a Cadillac. The Cadillac was parked around a corner, out of sight.

Abner glanced around searching for a cruising taxi, as if he had immediate need of it. He saw none. *If they come out,* he thought, *I'll follow them and if they get in a car, I'll get in, too, and make Walters take me to Pat.*

He had no real plan. His tortured mind was not functioning properly. He knew that if Walters and Mr. Dab suddenly appeared across the street, any act of his would be an act of desperation.

Abner stared at the doorway of the hotel, seeking figures that did not appear. He stared at the yellow-glowing window blinds, seeking silhouettes that did not show. The sockets of his eyes ached and burned from staring. He begrudged himself even the brief respite of blinking his lids.

Finally he could stand the tension no longer.'

He walked to the curbing, stepped off into the slushy street,

149

crossed Fifth Avenue. He walked directly to the hotel entrance. At the entrance, he paused, as Walters had done. He peered through the glass pane of the door. He could barely discern old Madame Sorel bending above her ledgers. He could not see Allan Walters and Mr. Dab who were a few feet to her right.

Abner actually pushed the hotel door open an inch. Then he realized the complete. futility of the gesture. Cursing himself, he closed the door and crossed the street again. He glanced at his watch. The hand was crawling slowly upward to midnight. More than an hour more before the time that Mr. Dab had set.

Abner sensed that a figure was moving toward him. He glanced sidewards. A cop was within a dozen feet of him and coming closer. It was a young cop. He walked with the cocky assurance of a man who is proud of his harness and his shield. The cop's face was the same face that Abner had seen beneath the transom of Ricky Sperber's door the night before. Abner ducked hurriedly through the door of the drug store.

A moment after Abner entered the drug store, Patrolman Ferguson turned up Eighth Street, his back toward the hotel. Ferguson was an alert young policeman, but he did not have eyes in the back of his head. He did not see Dab Ashton and Allan Walters exit from the hotel.

Abner could not see them, either, of course? He was in the drug store now, walking rapidly toward the rear, glancing over his shoulder apprehensively. There were only two people beside the clerks in the store. A woman who seemed slightly drunk was drinking coffee at the soda fountain. A man was buying cigarettes from a sleepy clerk. The drug counter was at the extreme rear of the store. Abner walked to the counter. The clerk had red hair and a wispy mustache. He was listening to a news broadcast on a small portable radio he had connected behind the counter.

The clerk said, "Yes, sir?"

Abner opened his mouth to speak, could think of nothing to order. He became conscious of the newscaster's voice.

". . . murder at Pineport, Long Island today. Police say that Lenny Fassio, alleged boss of New York rackets, was picked up at Hot Springs late this evening and will be brought to New York for questioning. Fassio, it is said, has waived extradition. Police are still seeking Abner Ellison, young lawyer in the firm of Burke and Holmquist, Fassio's attorneys, whose car was found on the murder scene. . . ."

The red-headed clerk said, "You seem interested in the

150

murder, sir. Lots of violence these days. Did you wish something?"

With an effort, Abner turned his attention to the clerk.

"Oh, yes. I wanted—give me a small box of aspirin. I—I've got a headache."

"Everybody has their headaches these days, I guess," the clerk replied.

The clerk placed the aspirin on the counter. Abner picked up the small package with his left hand. He put money on the counter with his right hand. Suddenly he was conscious that the clerk was staring at the hand with the missing finger.

Abner turned abruptly and walked rapidly toward the door at the front of the store. The red-haired clerk called, "Hey, you, mister! Wait a minute."

Abner did not turn his head. He continued to walk fast, making for the door. Another clerk came from behind the cigar counter, held up a restraining hand, stood directly in Abner's path. The cigar clerk said, "Just a minute, sir!"

Abner paused. He thought of bowling the cigar clerk over, rushing out the door. But the red-haired clerk had already reached his side. He proffered coins to Abner.

"You forgot your change, sir. My, you must be nervous. You'd better take one of those aspirin tablets."

Abner mumbled something, stuffed the coins into his pocket. He peered through the door. The street seemed deserted.

He walked out into the street. He glanced up at Dab Ashton's windows. Yellow light still glowed behind the shades.

Abner took some small comfort from the glowing light.

He had no way of knowing that the lighted rooms were occupied only by a dog that whined as if it mourned the dead.

28

THE CADILLAC was parked around the corner from the hotel entrance. There were few pedestrians on lower Fifth Avenue at this hour of a winter night. As Walters opened the door of the car, Dab paused, looked back toward the old hotel. It had been his home for many years. He did not really think he would ever see it again. He hoped they would remember to feed the dog.

"Looking for help?" asked Walters. "There doesn't seem to be any. Get in the car."

Walters steered the car with his left hand. His right hand rested over the gun beside him on the cushion. He said, "Don't be nervous, Mr. Dab. I'm a good driver, even with one hand. I won't get you killed in traffic."

On the way uptown Walters said, "You wondered how I found out where Abner Ellison was hiding. It was you who tipped me off, you know. You've been pretty dumb, right along, for a man who's supposed to be so smart. When you called to urge me not to go back to the castle, you said you had an important appointment at midnight. I figured it couldn't be with anyone but Abner, so I watched the hotel from across the street. You're an easy guy to tail. I followed you and the little fellow down to Minetta, waited there. This Sperber came out and looked around. I think he spotted me, so I moved on down the street. After a while Sperber stuck his head out again. Then Abner Ellison came out the door. I tailed him to the house on Sullivan.

"After a while I guessed he was in for the night. I decided to park Abner's car in front of the house. I'd been drinking quite a lot and my mind was kind of fuzzy, but I guess my idea was that if Abner had the car he'd try to drive out of town and that would be something else against him. I left my own car parked down on Sullivan and came uptown on the subway. I had Abner's car in the garage right back of my house. I never drank much before, but I've been hitting the stuff hard all during this business. When I got off the subway, I wanted a drink. There's a place on Broadway where old Groscz spends most of his time. I thought I might rope Groscz a little, just to find out if he had any idea that there was something in the tower. He was in the ginmill, and he was drunk. He didn't suspect anything at all. I bought him a lot more drinks and had some myself. I had to half-carry him to the castle. I put him to bed in the caretaker's cottage.

"Being inside the grounds gave me an idea. I wanted to be close to Pat. Crazy idea, wasn't it? Pat didn't know who kidnapped her. She was chloroformed. She stirred a little bit on the ride to town and I put the rag on her face again but she never saw me. Anyway, I climbed up to the tower and I stood there outside the door. I knew she'd be sound asleep inside, but I stood there and kind of tapped a little against the door, very softly. I talked to Pat, whispered to her, although I knew she

152

couldn't hear. I told her I was drunk. I told her I didn't want to kill her. I told her you suspected she was in the tower but that you couldn't do anything about it. It was crazy, all right, because I knew she couldn't hear and I didn't want her to hear, of course. I kept begging her not to remember the time she was kidnapped. That was the one weak point of my plan, Pat remembering the time she was kidnapped. Everything else she'd tell would be just like my own story. The old road, running out of gas, going back to the station. But if Pat remembered the time, I was sunk. Of course I thought I might say she was confused because of shock and so forth."

It occurred to Dab that Allan wasn't talking to him at all. Allan seemed to be talking to himself, reasoning with himself.

Walters said, "I had a plan, you see. I was going to track down Abner, kill him when he resisted arrest, plant the murder gun on him. Then I was going to dash up to the castle and rescue Pat all by myself. They'd think I was crazy, but they can't break you for solving a murder and a kidnapping. They might even promote me. Not that I need a promotion. Fassio pays me twice what the city does. Anyway, I'd be a hero and I'd marry Pat, if she only didn't remember the time. That was the chance I took, Pat remembering the time. She was snatched more than two hours before the time I said she was. I didn't expect Ellison to stay so long at Linton's house. Linton usually went to bed pretty early. I might have made her think she was mistaken about the time, if there'd been only a little difference."

"You took another chance," said Dab, "in not finishing Linton off instead of leaving him there dying."

"That's another thing," Walter said seriously, as if he could not understand at all. "I meant to shoot him through the heart. I couldn't somehow. I had to shoot him low, so he'd suffer, even though I wasn't going to be there to watch him suffer. Why was that? If he'd had a pencil and paper, I'd have been cooked. Or if you hadn't been so dumb about those cards."

"You're sick, Allan," Dab replied. "Mentally sick. You can be treated. There are places . . ."

Walters said, "No. I don't want any of those places. Anyway, I stayed outside that door a long time, talking to Pat, even though she couldn't hear me. Then I came to my senses and got Abner's car and drove it downtown and parked in front of the house on Sullivan. I planted Pat's lipstick and memo book in the car. I went to my own car and sat down to watch and it was only a little while before a cop went into the house. The

153

cop looked like Ferguson, from my own precinct. He came out. Then the little man with the dog arrived. He saw the car, looked at the license, and he put the dog inside, climbed in himself and drove away. I had to follow. When he parked out there in the lot in Pineport I went up to him and pulled a gun. The dog yapped, so I hit him with the gun barrel to quiet him. I took the little man down by the water and I saw the axe and I thought I might as well cut his finger off to remind the cops of Abner. I cut his finger off in the boathouse before I killed him. It would have been easier to kill him first, but that wasn't the way I wanted to do it."

Walters had driven very carefully all the way uptown, although he had been steering with only one hand. He had observed the lights, the traffic rules conscientiously. He drove into a street one block uptown from the Linton house, the street where he lived with his mother. The Mad Hatter's castle ran the full block from Linton's street to this one. Walters parked at a small gate in the high, forbidding brick walls of the castle. As Dab got out of the car he saw the enormous clock, the Mad Hatter's Tic Toc clock, across the river. It was twenty-seven minutes after midnight. In thirty-three minutes, Abner might go to the hotel, might call the cops. But would one o'clock be too late?

Walters took a flashlight from the glove compartment of the car. He opened the gate with a key that hung on the chain with the rabbit-foot charm that Dab had returned to him. Dab preceded Walters into the courtyard of the castle. He was surprised to note that Walters left the gate ajar.

The courtyard was very dark. The marble statuary that had once decorated the squares of European villages loomed pale as tombstones in the darkness. Walters flashed the light on the flagstones, guided Dab to the door of the caretaker's cottage. No light showed in the building. Walters tapped tentatively on the door, his gun in his hand. There was no answer. Walters said, "Groscz is either out or dead drunk inside. He's lucky."

They crossed the court again and Walters used the largest key to open a door of the castle itself. He flooded the flashlight into the interior of a vast, baronial hall, where furniture was swathed in spectral garments. Walters found an enormous candelabrum with two-foot candles. He lit several of the candles. Ancient suits of armor, dark old paintings, dim tapestries seemed to move out of the gloom as the candles flared. *If this is my last scene*, Dab thought, *I'm playing it against a properly Gothic setting.*

There was a magnificent, sweeping stairway at the end of

154

the hall. Dab nodded toward the stairs. "Let's go up," he said. "Let's go up to Pat."

Walters pulled covers from two high-backed chairs. He said, "Sit down. There's no hurry. Pat will be the last to die."

"No!" cried Dab. "Take me up there. Lock me in. Then get away. You can get to Mexico, to South America, anywhere. There's no need for more murders, Allan. You've got a chance to get away."

"I have to kill her," Walters said quite calmly. "I have to kill her now because of you. I'll have to kill you, too, of course. I think you must have known that all the time. But we'll wait till Abner comes."

"Abner isn't coming here! Abner has no idea that Pat is here, that I am here. . . ."

Walters grinned. It was a cheerful, boyish grin and because of that, it seemed more horrible upon the face of a demented murderer.

"I wondered how you'd leave word for him," said Walters, conversationally. "I'd thought I'd give you a chance to write a note if it was necessary, because this is the best place for killing Abner, and I want him here. You were pretty clumsy when you knocked over the chess pieces, picked up the piece, gave it to the old woman with your key. Remember when I was a kid and you taught me to play chess, Mr. Dab? The piece you left at the desk was a castle, wasn't it?"

29

LIEUTENANT ROMANO glanced at his watch. After midnight. When you were on a case with Sansone, you simply didn't sleep. It wasn't that the old man ordered you directly to stay on duty. He just kept making suggestions of things that should be done, and if you wanted to go home you had to make a point of saying so. Few cops had the temerity to do that with Sansone. He'd kept Haas out at Pineport making moulages and working with the county men until it was determined through ballistics that the slug in Sperber was a forty-five that had been fired from the same gun that killed Linton. Then after the Hot Springs police had been reached by phone, Romano had to make arrangements for flying two detectives down to Arkansas to pick up Lenny Fassio, and privately, Romano thought that questioning Fassio this time would do no more good than it had ever done before. But old Sansone was enthusiastic. The cops had not been able to locate either Johnny Barrone or the gunman, Bansa.

Finally it had seemed that they might break away, that the red-faced old man could find nothing else to check and doublecheck before Fassio was brought in for questioning. And then Romano had foolishly said that tomorrow Haas might check the prints on Pat's lipstick against fingerprint cards that Phil Linton had probably filed up at his house. One of Linton's hobbies had been to fingerprint all his friends and neighbors.

As a result, Romano and Haas and Grierson were now at Linton's house.

Haas found the little green file full of fingerprint-classification cards in the hall closet. Linton had apparently taken the fingerprints of everyone in the neighborhood.

Haas said, "Well, I get one break anyway. These cards are filed alphabetically by the person's name. They aren't filed under the Galton-Henry system of evaluating all ten fingers according to the numerator and denominator. It's hell to find single fingerprints in a file, unless you're using the Battley single-point system that some police departments employ."

Haas examined the classification card that bore Patricia Linton's name. He compared it to the tape-lifted prints from the lipstick. He frowned. He said to Romano, "There's one thing certain. The prints on the lipstick were *not* Patricia Linton's. The lipstick had been wiped clean before these prints on it were made. Person who made them had a nice, oily skin, too. They have no resemblance to the fingerprints on Pat Linton's card."

Romano said, "In that case they may be the murderer's prints."

Haas said, "If they are, the murderer's a woman. Or else he's a child or a man with a hand as small as a midget's."

Romano skimmed through the cards in the file. "There must be a hundred or so cards here," he said, "but only about a dozen appear to be women's prints. Probably Phil fingerprinted the neighbor ladies and Pat's school friends. How about a quick check of the cards with women's names on them?"

Romano selected cards from the file, handed them to Haas. Haas examined each quickly, pushed it aside, went to anoth-

156

er. He hesitated over one card. He put a magnifying glass on it, laid the tape-lifted prints on the card, nodded. "This is it," he said. "The right thumb and right forefinger. Here's the person who made those prints on the lipstick."

Romano looked at the name on the card. "It doesn't seem possible," he said. "Are you sure?"

"I'm sure," Haas replied, packing up the equipment. "They tell me fingerprints don't lie. At least that's the theory we've always worked on."

Romano said, "But these prints on the card were taken from Al Walters' mother! The old lady hardly ever goes out of the house any more. She even has her wine delivered, I understand."

Haas said, "The date on the card shows those prints were made several years ago. Maybe she was more ambulatory in those days."

"Well," said Romano, "she lives right around the corner, on the other side of the castle. It's late, but we'll go over there."

"You'll go over there," Haas replied. "I'm through for the day. I was technically through a long time ago. I'm an identification man. I'm supposed to work only in laboratories or on the scene of a crime." He took something from the small case he was carrying. "Here. I put the lipstick and the memo book on peg boards and marked them for identification. You can take 'em along with you."

Haas handed Romano two glassine envelopes. Inside each was a piece of heavy, perforated cardboard. String inserted through the holes secured the lipstick and the memo book to the peg boards. Romano pocketed the peg boards, said to Grierson, "We may as well drive the car around. It's a steep hill and I'm tired."

Mrs. Walters answered the bell immediately, but she opened the door only a few inches. She wore a soiled wrapper. Her gray hair was disheveled. Her eyes were glassy. Romano introduced himself. He said, "We met a long while back at Phil Linton's house. I know your son. Is he home?"

"I'm sorry," said Mrs. Walters opening the door wider. "He isn't home. He called to say he'd be late."

"We'd like to speak to you," Romano said.

She led them into an untidy parlor. The furniture was dusty, the floor unswept. A pint bottle of cheap wine stood on a table, beside a half-filled glass. The bottle was almost empty.

Mrs. Walters glanced guiltily toward the bottle. "I have

157

to take a little stimulant," she explained. "It's medicinal. I have palpitations."

Romano showed her the peg boards. "Did you ever see these articles before, Mrs. Walters?" he asked.

Mrs. Walters reddened, looked embarrassed.

"Why, yes," she answered. "They're Patricia Linton's. They have her initials, her name on them. She must have given them to Allan to keep for her that night they had a date, that night she disappeared. I found them in the pocket of the suit he was wearing." Her face became more crimson. "I—I was cleaning out the suit so I could send it to the presser."

"What did you do with the lipstick and the memo book after you removed them from the pocket of the suit?" Romano asked.

Mrs. Walters moistened her lips. She said, "Well, I—I think I must have put them back in the pocket. I—I decided not to send the suit to the presser after all."

Romano wondered why such a simple statement could make the woman look so guilty. Then he knew. A cop learns a lot about alcoholics in the line of duty. There was an axiom in the department that a junky would murder to get the stuff. A drunk wouldn't murder, but he would steal. Poor Mrs. Walters had been rifling her son's pockets in the hope of finding loose change that she might spend for wine.

"Do you know where we might find your son?" Romano asked.

"He called from Mercer Street to say that he was going over to see Mr. Dabney Ashton at his hotel, and that I shouldn't wait up for him. He isn't in more trouble, is he, Lieutenant? The inspector had him suspended, you know. The poor boy's so upset, so nervous . . ."

"It's probably nothing at all important, Mrs. Walters," Romano assured her. "We just want to ask a couple of questions. Thank you and pardon us for intruding at this hour."

When they were out on the street, Grierson said, "Well, that explains how her fingerprints got on the lipstick."

"Yeah," Romano answered, "but it doesn't explain how the lipstick and the memo book got in Ellison's car out at Pineport. Drive down to Washington Square. I want to talk to Walters." He saw the big, bright clock on the bluff across the river. "Twenty-five to one," he said. "If you take the highway and open her up, we can get there by one o'clock. There shouldn't be much traffic."

As they roared uphill past the Mad Hatter's castle, Romano said, "There's a big Caddy parked there by the castle gate. You don't think the Mad Hatter could have slipped out from under the Iron Curtain, do you?"

They veered into the downtown entrance of the highway. Grierson said, "Al Walters has got a Caddy like that. Always wondered how a detective could pay the tariff on it. The installment plan's a wonderful thing."

"You don't suppose that's Walters' car, do you?" Romano asked.

"No reason it should be," Grierson replied. "There's plenty of parking space right in front of his house and he's got a garage out back."

The car pointed downtown.

Romano chuckled. "Poor old Dab Ashton," he said. "He was trying so hard to take the heat off Ellison. You know what he did? He tried to persuade me that some architect thought they had Pat Linton locked up in a tower of the Mad Hatter's castle!"

30

ALLAN WALTERS said, "I'll kill Abner first. Then I'll kill you. Poor little Patty will be last."

Good Lord, thought Dab, *he sounds like a housewife casually enumerating her chores for the day.*

Walters took a pint bottle of blended whisky from the pocket of his overcoat. He offered it to Dab. Dab shook his head. Walters drank deeply, said, "I guess it isn't as good as that Bourbon of yours. I don't know much about whisky, but I've drunk a lot of it the past few days."

The wavering candlelight reflected on Walters' eyes. *There's something about his eyes that isn't right,* Dab thought. *It isn't just the candlelight or the drink, he's had. His eyes are crazy. They're wrong. They've always been like that, only I never saw it before.*

"You don't have to kill Pat," Dab said desperately. "There's no reason for killing anybody else. Give me the key to the tower. Give me Pat. That's all I want. You can get in that big car of yours and drive away and they'll never catch you."

Walters said, "I'll drive away. But I have to kill Pat first.

159

I have to kill her because I love her, don't you see? I couldn't leave her for another man. And I have to kill Abner because I hate him. I've always hated him. And I have to kill you because you spoiled it all. I had a plan. I was going to be a hero and marry Pat. I'd have got a Department citation, a medal, maybe. Pat would have loved me if I'd been a hero. Abner was a hero. He got a medal. I'm a couple of years older than Abner. I was a rookie cop and I could be deferred and I didn't go to war, but Abner did. He enlisted. Pat despised me because I didn't go to war."

"Pat didn't despise you," Dab declared. "She was very fond of you, Allan. No one despised you."

"They all despised me," Walters said. He nodded wisely, took a drink. "It was because of my father and my mother. My father deserted us when I was two years old. My mother took to drink. When I was a little kid the other children used to follow me around and tease me. They had a poem about me. They used to yell it at me and write it on the castle walls with chalk. '*Allan's father was a skunk and Allan's mother is a drunk.*'"

Dab felt sick. It's not his fault, he thought. Horrible as it is, it's not his fault. He can't be blamed.

"Run, Allan," Dab urged. "Run now, while you can. If Abner does come here, he'll bring the police."

"I have to wait for Abner," Walters said. "Pat loved Abner. He won't bring the cops. He'll run from the cops. The cops suspect him of a murder. They wouldn't listen to him. They wouldn't come up here after me just because you left the chess piece with that old woman."

The trouble is, thought Dab, what he says is true. Abner won't go to the cops and the cops would not come here if he did. In a little while Abner will be coming through that door, alone, unarmed, and he'll be killed.

"You despised me, too," Walters went on. "I used to admire you when I was a kid. I used to think you were great because you were a famous actor and had your picture in the papers. But you liked Abner and Pat. You never bothered with me. You gave Abner and Pat seats to your matinées, but you never asked me along. Only once. I was eighteen then and Abner was sixteen and Pat was only twelve. It was the first night of some play, I remember, and you'd bought Abner a tuxedo, but I didn't own one. I had to rent a suit and it cost five dollars. Abner's suit fit him fine, but I was skinny then and the suit I rented hung on me like a scarecrow's clothes. That made Pat despise me more. I didn't even see

160

the show. I just sat there knowing everyone was laughing at me."

"I'm sorry, boy," said Dab. "Even if you're going to murder me I'm sorry for you. I never knew."

"Don't be sorry for me!" Walters flared. "I'm boss now. The plan didn't work out, but I'm still boss. I've got the gun. I'm going to run away and keep on running, but I've got the gun and before I go, I'm going to kill you all."

He's not the murderer, Dab thought. I am.

I should have seen what he was like a long, long time ago, but it was Abner and Pat I loved and I never paid him much attention. I never knew the awful hurt he had or what it was doing to him. I could have been kind, understanding.

And I should have seen what Phil meant by those cards the minute Haas showed them to me on the floor. They could have grabbed him then, made him tell where Pat was, Romano, Sansone—one of them—could have made him tell. Even tonight I fumbled it again. When I knew the answer I could have called Romano. But I wanted the center of the stage myself. I wanted to do it all alone. No. No, that wasn't it. I really believed it was the only way, that I could bargain with him. I didn't know that he was mad.

He's not the murderer. I'm the murderer.

In just a little while Pat and Abner will be dead, and I'll be their murderer.

31

For the better part of an hour, Madame Sorel had sat there at the desk staring at the little chess piece. It lay in front of her on a page of the old ledger in which she kept accounts. Definitely an absurdity. An unaccountable thing for the old one to do. She did not like problems which could not be reduced to numerals on the pages of her ledger.

Old Jan, the bar waiter, came up the steps from the basement café bearing a tray with drinks for room service. Madame Sorel called him over to the desk, held up the little ivory piece.

"This thing," she said. "It is from the absurd game on which you waste your time, is it not so?"

Jan nodded. "It's a chess piece," he replied. "It's called a rook."

"Definitely a foolish name," commented Madame Sorel. "A rook is a bird, a raven. This thing has no resemblance to a bird."

Pirtle, who had been playing chess with Jan until the room-service order interrupted the game, came up from the bar. He said, "It's also called a castle. It looks like a piece from Dab Ashton's board. Where did you get it? Don't tell me you've taken up chess, Madame?"

"A rook or a castle, the old one has definitely mislaid his wits," Madame Sorel declared. She told them how Dab had left the chess piece at the desk. "And the way he stared at me! Am I a bug impaled upon a pin that I should be stared at so?"

"That's rather funny," Pirtle said. "There's a castle right across the street from the scene of Lieutenant Linton's murder. Did Mr. Dab leave here alone?"

"He was with the young man who comes here to see him sometimes," Madame Sorel replied. "An agent of police, I think. M'sieu Walters."

"Oh," said Pirtle. "In that case he's safe enough. I've met Detective Walters. A nice young man."

Pirtle went upstairs to his room. Jan left to deliver the drinks on his tray. Madame Sorel sat staring at the chess piece, shaking her head until the dyed red hair fell down in wisps about her eyes.

It was exactly one o'clock when Abner Ellison came through the door. Madame Sorel glared at him.

"Definitely, you must leave!" she declared. "The agents of police are seeking you, I understand. You will bring my hotel into disrepute!"

"It's all right, Madame Sorel," Abner assured her, with his most ingratiating smile. "Mr. Dab is expecting me."

"The old one is not here," Madame Sorel replied stiffly. "He left here more than an hour ago with an agent of police, M'sieu Walters, who perhaps is seeking you. Please leave, young man!"

"Walters!" Abner exclaimed. "Did Mr. Dab leave a message for me? This is most important, Madame Sorel."

The old woman shook her head. "He left only his key. And this absurd thing from a chessboard." She handed the little ivory piece to Abner.

Abner looked at the piece wonderingly. "A castle!" he said. He stared into Madame Sorel's face.

162

Madame Sorel said irritably. "Please not to stare at me! I am no specimen that I should be stared at so!"

Abner continued to speak, but he did not seem to address the old woman at all. He said, "It could only be the castle right across the street from the house! It's the Mad Hatter's castle! Pat's up there, and Walters has taken Mr. Dab up there to kill him!"

He turned to the hotel proprietress urgently. "How long ago did he leave here? Did you say it's been an hour?"

The old woman did not look at Abner. Her eyes were upon the hotel door. "More than an hour," she answered.

"Oh, God!" cried Abner. "They may both be dead by now! I've got to go there. I've got to go there right away!"

He started to turn toward the door. A heavy hand fell on his shoulder. A voice said, "You're not going anywhere, honey boy, except with us."

Lieutenant Romano and Detective Grierson had just come into the lobby. "Frisk him, Grierson," Romano ordered.

"Allan Walters is the murderer!" Abner exclaimed. "Mr. Dab solved the puzzle a little while ago. It was some kind of acrostic and it spelled Walters' name. Mr. Dab was going to see Walters alone, try to save Pat's life. That's all he cared about, saving Pat. Walters has got Pat in the Mad Hatter's castle! He's got Mr. Dab there, too, now. He's had him there for more than an hour. Mr. Dab left this chess piece to show me where he was. It's called a castle!"

Abner handed the piece of ivory to Romano. Romano said, "I don't play chess, but it does look kind of like a castle." He turned to the old woman. Madame Sorel told him the story of Dab's strange behavior. "Unaccountable!" she declared. "Indeed absurd!"

Grierson finished examining Abner for a gun. He said, "He isn't heeled, Lieutenant."

"For God's sake!" Abner cried as Romano stood looking at the chess piece. "They'll be killed. Aren't you going to call the cops, send a prowl car there?"

"Walters," said the lieutenant. "It's funny his name should come up. No, Ellison, I'm not calling any prowl car. I'm not sending out a Signal Thirty-two. I've stuck my neck out far enough in this and I'm not sticking it out any farther. You're wanted for murder and Walters is a cop. I'm not sending a prowl car after Walters because you tell me to. This little chess piece was probably dropped by accident with his key."

"Walters is the murderer!" protested Abner. "He's killed

163

two men already, and he's got Pat and Mr. Dab up there in the castle. . . ."

"Easy," Romano said. "Take it easy, honey boy."

"There was the lipstick," Grierson reminded the lieutenant. "And there was that Caddy parked there by the gate, remember?"

"That's what I'm thinking of," said Romano. "But I'm not sending out a Signal Thirty-two. Old Dab hasn't played fair with me. I don't know what he might be up to. But we'll go up there and take a look ourselves. With the siren open and the blinker on, we ought to make it in twenty minutes." He turned to Abner. "Ellison," he said, "you're under arrest. But there's nothing to do with you right now except take you along with us."

"You want the cuffs on him?" Grierson asked Romano.

"No," Romano answered. "I don't want the cuffs. He's young and strong but I'm the one who's got the gun."

As the three men left the hotel, Madame Sorel raised her eyes to the crystal chandelier that hung from the ceiling of the lobby.

"Such an absurd commotion over a little piece of ivory!" she said aloud. "In France these matters are arranged with more decorum."

32

"HERE HE COMES!" said Allan Walters. "He's out there in the courtyard now."

He rose deliberately and snuffed the tall candles one by one. He shielded his flash, pointed it downward toward the floor. He nudged Dab with the gun. "This way," he said, with no emotion in his voice. "Over to the stairs."

Moving like an automaton, the gun nudging his back, Dab walked toward the stairway. He walked through the darkness, a little pool of light swimming around his feet. Twice he stumbled into furniture. They reached the stairs.

"Up," said Walters. "We'll wait up on the landing."

Dab mounted the wide stairs, the gun pressing against his back. Walters halted him on the landing. For a second the beam of the flash careened upward, picked out a bulky, stolid

164

figure. Dab thought a man was standing there. It was a suit of medieval armor.

Walters took up a position by the railing on the landing, directly opposite the great door to the court. He shoved Dab over to his left. Walters' left hand held the flashlight. His right hand held the gun. Walters switched off the flashlight, but the hand that held it pressed hard against Dab's side. Walters had left the castle door ajar. Dab could hear feet moving over the flagstones of the court.

Walters said softly, "When the door opens I'll blind him with the light. Then I'll shoot. I'll shoot low. He'll live a little while."

The sounds of movement had ceased. The big door creaked as it came open. Dab lunged at Allan Walters and at the same time he screamed, "Abner! Watch out! He's got a gun!"

Walters was quick. The flashlight crashed down on Dab's head. The flame-streak of the gun ripped through the darkness. The sound of the shot reverberated, trembled in the vaulted hall. Dab felt blood on his head as he fell, tumbled down a step or two. Something clattered down after him. It was the flashlight. Dab clutched the flashlight. Blood was running down his face.

Beams of light streaked into the darkness, probing. Walters fired at them. He fired again. The lights failed to find the crouching figure, but there was a shot from the door. It was wild. It crashed into the suit of armor on the landing. The suit of armor rang like a great bell.

Dab pointed the flashlight toward the landing, toward the crouching figure. His hand was shaking. He grasped his right wrist with his left hand, steadied it. He pressed the button of the flashlight. A pale, mad face floated in the glaring beam. A hand flew to the blinded eyes of the face. Other beams of light found the face. There was another deafening crash, another flame-streak through the dark. The pale face crimsoned, wavered. The face swayed out of the light into the darkness. The light beams flooded up the stairs. Feet were running. Abner was there beside Dab, saying, "You're hurt. There's blood . . ."

"I'm all right," gasped Dab. "Get Pat. She's in the tower. The south tower. Get the keys off Walters."

Grierson turned Walters' body over. He said, "Dead. You got him right between the eyes, Lieutenant."

"I could hardly miss with that spotlight on him," Romano said.

They found the keys that hung from a chain with a good-

165

luck charm. They mounted the stairs. One flight. Another. And then a narrow flight as steep as a ladder. The first key didn't fit the tower room door. The second opened it. Three flashlights played their beams into the round room of the tower. There was a stifling odor.

Patricia Linton lay just inside the door, on the floor, partly covered by a blanket. She didn't stir.

"Oh, God, she's dead. He's killed her," Abner said. He bent down beside her, raised her head.

"The stove," said Romano, pointing. "She was overcome by fumes. Get her out. Get her air."

Patricia Linton's eyelids fluttered open as Abner lifted her. She looked into his face. "Abner!" she said, like a child who makes a pleasing discovery. "Abner, I'm so sleepy."

"Yes, it's Abner, darling. You're going to be all right."

The flashlight played about the room, paused at the carton of groceries, the empty cans and jars.

Patricia Linton wrinkled her nose, puckered her forehead, like a little girl who has something important to explain.

"I didn't touch the pork and beans," she said. "But I ate up all the jelly roll."

166

www.ingramcontent.com/pod-product-compliance
Lightning Source LLC
Chambersburg PA
CBHW020643180626
46816CB00003B/1096